S0-CAI-218

A WYATT
BOOK for

W

— ST. —
MARTIN'S
PRESS

Also by Alan Steinberg

POETRY
EPSTEIN ON REFLECTION

DRAMA
THE ROAD TO CORINTH

CRY OF THE LEOPARD

ALAN STEINBERG

A Wyatt Book *for*
St. Martin's Press ❦ New York

FIC
STEINBERG
A

CRY OF THE LEOPARD. Copyright © 1997 by Alan L. Steinberg. All rights reserved. Printed in the United States of America. No part of this book may be used or reproduced in any manner whatsoever without written permission except in the case of brief quotations embodied in critical articles or reviews. For information, address A Wyatt Book for St. Martin's Press, 175 Fifth Avenue, New York, N.Y. 10010.

Design by Maureen Troy

Library of Congress Cataloging-in-Publication Data

Steinberg, Alan L.
    Cry of the leopard / Alan L. Steinberg. — 1st ed.
        p.   cm.
    "A Wyatt book for St. Martin's Press."
    ISBN 0-312-15507-7
    I. Title.
PS3569.T375467C78   1997
813'.54—dc21   97-11293
                                                    CIP

First edition: August 1997

10 9 8 7 6 5 4 3 2 1

To
Jacqui and Ariana
Neil and Randy
and especially
Ruth Beebe Hill

CONTENTS

To the Reader

I am the Leopard Man. I
have had other names, of
course, but it serves no purpose to tell them. I am the
Leopard Man. Now and for-
ever. So many stories have
been told about me that it
becomes difficult to separate
truth from fiction. Still, for
those who were kind I must
set the record straight. If I
lapse into dream or vision,
forgive me. It is by such
weakness that we make this
world more beautiful.

CRY OF THE LEOPARD

Out of the Woods

THE DOGS DROVE ME OUT. I TRIED CHASING THEM.
I tried hiding from them. I tried killing them. But still
they came, like lemmings, wandering down from the farms,
catching my scent on the wind, nosing it down to where I
lay waiting in the dark woods. I got sick of burying them,
sick of eating them. I even got sick of thinking about them.

It was a sorry game. I see that now. They'd been too long
at their master's heels. There was no more wolf in them. So
they'd bark and twitch their noses but the beast was gone,
lost in the ages. They thought it was play, like chasing squir-
rels. They gave themselves away with yelps and snarls, even
the big ones, the mean ones. They forgot that hunting is a
silent, deadly business. I began to hate them.

But maybe it was more than dogs. Maybe I got tired of
being alone. The Ancients had a saying: You gain everything
in solitude but character. Maybe it was that. Maybe it was the
leopard's life more than the dogs. It's a high price you pay for
being that alone.

When you give yourself to the leopard the world becomes
a gray, seamless thing. You taste each molecule, see each blade

of grass shiver. But the world itself is an endless gray of fear and hunger. Deep down, the leopard's heart is a place out of time. Nothing stretches ahead or behind. There is only now. Now forever. You have not come to it. You cannot go from it. It is. You are. There is nothing more.

I was master of the woods. Master of the night. Only my hunger was real. So perhaps it was the dogs after all. Because in hating them I became a man. In hating them I had to break out of that timeless time. I had to remember there was something before. And something after.

Then it was I would make my way to the edge of the woods on the darkest nights and look out at the distant lights of the farmhouses, sniffing the air for the smell of smoke and the sweet scent of man. And after a time my heart began to ache. Human dreams filled my sleep.

I would be standing on the top of a steep hill at twilight, the black sky scraping away the last red of the sun. Down below I could see two figures. One, an old woman with a bent back and a stick to help her walk. The other, a girl nearing womanhood. She was wearing a red dress and carrying a large gourd of water balanced on one shoulder.

"Hurry," I would shout down to her. "You must hurry."

The girl would pause and look up and smile, and so fall further behind the old woman. I would yell again, and again she would look up and smile and fall still further behind. The old woman would reach the top of the hill. She would hold out her stick for me to pull her up. But each time I would pull too hard and the woman would come crashing into me, knocking me down. I would scramble to my feet as fast as I could and run to the ledge and look down. And each time my heart would freeze, for the path was always empty.

By then the old woman would be standing beside me. Slowly she would point with her stick to the side of the path. The gourd would be lying there, something dark seeping out of it into the black earth. Beside it, a torn square of cloth the same red color as the young girl's dress. I would start down the trail, but always the old woman would seize my arm.

"She has been taken," she would say. "She is no more."

The old woman would turn back and make her way along a path that led from the embankment. I would sit and weep. The girl had been something to me, of that I was certain. The night would grow opaque, even for

2

me, without moonlight or starlight, and still I would cry. It seemed as if I were crying not only for the girl, but for a whole world of vanished beauty.

Between the dogs in the daylight and the dreams at night, the woods became a torment. So one soft and silent night, with the sharpened edge of a stone, I cut my hair and nails, stole clothes from a farmer's line, and set out for the world of men.

I had not been on that journey long when I found a poster nailed to a tree. The poster read:

SEE THEM ALL!
THE EIGHT HUMAN WONDERS OF THE WORLD!

And it listed them in order:

THE SNAKE GODDESS

THE MONKEY MEN

THE ELEPHANT LADY

THE SIAMESE SWEETHEARTS

THE RUBBER MAN

THE STORK MAN

GOLIATH

And the last one of all, the one that sent shivers through my newborn soul:

THE LION MAN

And under his name, in jagged, blood-red letters:

SEE HIM IF YOU DARE!

I tore the poster from the tree. The date was from long ago, the place far away. But I knew I had to go. I did a little dance, then, beneath the tree. And I roared: a roar both of joy and hunger.

I began to lope down the road. The rain had begun to fall, cold, gray rain that spilled from a blackened sky. Cars swept past me as I ran, circling wide. Once or twice they slowed. But when the misted light illumined me, off they'd go, leaving me to the long black road and the rain.

I could have covered my face, I suppose. Or lowered my head and kept my collar high. But no more. The world would have to take me as I was. I'd learned that much in the woods.

So I hurried down the road, poster in my pocket, rain on my back, and after a while a farmer came by, driving an old truck with a great mangy dog in the back. The hair on my neck stood up. Dogs again, I thought. My nails had been pared, but my teeth were still sharp.

The truck slowed and the dog gave me a long look, its teeth bared. It seemed ready to spring, so I got low and began to growl. But the dog lowered its lip and started wagging its tail, and the farmer stopped and motioned for me to get inside. By then the dog was smiling. So I climbed in front, next to the farmer, while the dog leaned in the side window and licked my face.

"He don't take to just anyone," the farmer said, glancing at me. "In fact, he's damn particular." He nodded his head and smiled. "That's how come I stopped. Ol' Beelzebub in back there give ya the OK. Don't matter to him how a body looks."

We rode in silence for a while. The hate for dogs was out of me, I guess, and the old dog knew. The fields looked soft and still in the rain, and the air smelled washed and clean. Then the farmer spoke.

"Now, I ain't one to pry," he said, "but you ain't one of them freak show folks, are you?"

And that was how it came to me, right then and there, riding in that old truck with the mangy dog licking my face. Just like Simon said: Destiny dropping down like a bit of silver rain.

"I'm thinking about joining up," I said, and reached into my pocket and took out the poster.

The farmer looked at it a moment, then slapped his knee.

"By God, that's the one," he said. "Yessirree." And he broke out in a grin from ear to ear.

"You've seen it, then?" I said, feeling the blood run.

4

"Seen it? You bet we seen it," the farmer said. "Ain't that right, Beezle?" he shouted. And the dog barked agreement.

And what had it been like? I asked him.

He frowned a moment before answering. I had the feeling he was trying to find the right words not to offend me.

"Well, in a way it wasn't so much," he said at length. "I mean, you know, a freak is a freak. And after a while it don't seem like much."

He glanced over at me, then, with an apologetic sort of look on his face.

"Especially when you been raising cows and sheep," he added quickly. "Cause some of them come out looking strange, all right, with no front legs and two tails and things like that."

Then he brightened.

"But that there Snake Goddess, now she was something. Yessirree," he said, grinning and winking both.

He looked around, as if he were afraid someone might overhear him.

"The Mrs. give me hell," he said, his voice lower, confidential. "Damn near broke my head with a broom. But it sure was worth it," he added. "Ain't that right, Beezle?" he called out to the dog in back.

Did she really look like a snake? I asked him.

"Well, she may have, but that wasn't the part I was looking at." He frowned. "What I was looking at was all woman. You better believe it."

It seemed the Snake Goddess had come out wearing a real low-cut dress and sort of danced around the stage. What had really caught the farmer's eye, so to speak, was the size of the woman's breasts.

"She'd make one helluva milker," was how he put it, shaking his head from side to side.

After the dance she did something with the snakes.

"Real snakes." The farmer whistled through his teeth. "You could see 'em flicking out their tongues and everything. Just curled themselves round this here Snake Goddess, damned if they didn't. And then you know what? You know what them buggers did?"

I told him I didn't.

"They crawled right up her neck and down them great big titties. Yessirree. Right on down 'em like they was bobbing for apples. You should've heard the hollering then, seeing them snakes take the plunge."

I asked him about the Lion Man.

"Oh, him?" the farmer said without much enthusiasm. "He was all right, I guess." He paused a moment, then turned to me. "If you don't mind my saying, you kind of look more like a lion than he does." Then he brightened again. "But that there Snake Goddess, now she looked good enough for the both of them, if you know what I mean." His grin widened and he slapped his knee. Out back, Beezle barked a loud, deep bark.

"You know," the farmer said, suddenly serious, "I never did see them snakes come back out. The Mrs. poked her nose in right then and I had to light out in a hurry. To keep the peace." He looked over at me and smiled. "Now, it ain't quite Christian to say it, but I got me a good idea just where them fool snakes was going."

And with that he burst out laughing.

"Yessirree," he said once more, softly, but what he was acknowledging I didn't know.

After that, we drove a ways in silence. Then the farmer pulled the truck over to the side of the road, on the gravel.

"That's my road over there," he said, pointing to a narrow dirt lane that branched off from the main highway. "I'd ask you to stay," he said, a little apologetically, "but I'm afraid the Mrs. would have a fit. Think you was one of them freak-show boys."

And saying that, he reached down under the seat and pulled out a small bag.

"Got some mighty fine baked chicken here," he said, holding up the sack. "The Mrs. packed it for lunch but I got too busy to eat. You're welcome to it."

I took the bag and thanked him. I'd smelled the chicken right away, of course, but I'd been too excited to think about it. I got down from the truck. The rain had thinned to a light mist.

"Well, I wish you luck," the farmer said. "And so does Beelzebub."

Once again the big dog barked and wagged his tail. I reached up and petted him. Just before the farmer pulled away, he leaned across the seat.

"You give that Lion Man hell," he called out to me. Then he started the truck and headed down that winding dirt road, the old dog pressed against the rear gate, calling out to me in a long mournful wail. It felt good, standing in the warm soft rain, knowing I was on the right road; knowing that no matter how long or far it goes, no matter how many times it curls or dips or bends, it's my road. Mine alone.

2
The Freak Show

I CAME TO THE FAIR AT LAST, THE TENTS SET OUT IN an open field at the edge of a small town. I had climbed a long hill and from the top I saw, shimmering in the afternoon sun, the bright canvases billowing in the wind. You might have thought you were in a desert and had come upon a caravan drawn up for the night.

A hundred smells drifted up to me. Flowers and food. Leather and wood and canvas. And mingled with them all, rich and musky and deep—the scent of animals: sweat and fur and hides. My nose twitched and my brain stirred.

I think I let out a yell and began racing down the hill. I leaped in the air, and a passing car had to swerve around me. But the field was still a long way off and after a while my wind gave out. As I slowed, the place took on a different configuration, grew darker, the canvas ochre instead of white, and blue-black shadows heaped on the meadow grass.

Clouds drifted over the hill, dulling the light. I wandered into a scraggly wood that ringed the fairgrounds and let myself rest. The descent had drained me. Now that I had arrived, I felt less certain.

I let the day set, quiet and orderly, while I rested and watched. Lights appeared in the sky and in the meadow. The wind picked up. The air cooled. Shadows thickened. I felt all my senses come alive, each pore opening wide, each cell turning into the world's vibration. I knew the feeling well. It was the hour of the leopard. But this time, instead of a twisting, churning hunger in my belly, I sensed a hunger in my soul.

I knew it was time to go. I came to the Fair like a moth to light. People were everywhere. I had not realized the place was so alive. All the tents were lighted. Music and the sound of voices filled the air.

In the darkness everything had changed. The lights glistened, as if the stars had shrunk and fallen, then been strung on wires across the meadow. Music blared and voices sang above the whir of motors. I was dazed and blinded; I wandered where I must, drawn by fate or dragging it after me. Past a hundred scents, past throngs of half-moon faces I came, intoxicated by the swirling smells of life.

And there I found it, spread out across the night, ringed with light and rising up from the ground: a prehistoric beast, dark and vast, for all the crimson and amber that splashed around it. There it was, squatting in the smoking field.

THE EIGHT HUMAN WONDERS OF THE WORLD SEE THEM IF YOU DARE!!!

Standing on a wooden box, below the flaming letters, was a man in black. He stood there, lean and still, only his eyes moving, searching the faces of those who drifted by. I drew my collar up around my face, drifted further into the shadows. And then he reached out with his hand and spoke, his voice deep and resonant and compelling.

"Step right up, ladies and gentlemen," he called out. "See the Eight Human Wonders of the World."

As he spoke, a young girl came from out of the tent that towered behind him. She carried a wooden easel which she struggled to open and place on the ground. The man scowled as she fumbled with the latch that held the legs together. He clenched his fist and for an instant I thought he might strike her. I felt the hairs on my back bristle.

But it all passed and nothing happened. The girl managed to open the easel and on it, in painted glory, was a beautiful woman with glistening bare shoulders and a torso covered by a cascade of long, luxurious black hair. From her waist down, however, she was a snake, green and shiny and lined in black. All around her were painted bushes and vines.

The man pointed to the poster and smiled.

"See the Eight Human Wonders of the World," he said again, but his voice had changed. Now his tone was full of mocking. "See the Snake Goddess," he said. "Half woman, half reptile. And all desirable." He let his eyes move across the faces of the people who had stopped to watch. I leaned back in the shadows.

The young girl emerged again, carrying another easel. Before she could open it, the man spoke, his voice now full of compassion.

"See them all. Each one a genuine human oddity. A freak of nature. Each one guaranteed to stand your hair on end. To make you reconsider your notion of what is human." He paused, let his eyes sweep the crowd. "To make you thankful you are you." He smiled, in no hurry now. He had them. You could read it in his eyes.

"You'll tremble at the power of creation. How the Lord works in His own mysterious way. Your heart will pound and your blood will run cold in your veins."

He nodded and the girl opened the easel. This time the painted poster showed the body of a woman beneath a tight red dress. On her shoulders, however, were two necks and two separate heads: one painted with brown hair and one painted with red. The heads were turned toward each other. Across the top were written the words: "Lila and Lola. The Siamese Sweethearts."

"Right inside this tent," the man in black began, his voice now soft and inviting, "right before your very eyes you'll see a woman with two heads. Think about it," he said, gazing at the crowd. "Two brains sharing the same body. Two women with two separate lives. Think of it. Think of what that means."

The crowd had grown quiet, silent almost, as if indeed they were thinking of it, of what it would be to live that way, to be so close to another person forever. Two destinies fused into one.

11

The girl returned with another poster. This time when she opened the easel my heart froze. There, the picture of the Lion Man. I knew it even before I saw the blood-red letters, saw the face and the fangs.

"Right inside this tent," the man said, his voice becoming loud and fierce, "straight from the deepest and darkest jungle where no civilized man has gone, we have for you the one and the only Lion Man. More lion than man. Raised by murderous lions, man-eating lions, in the heart of the jungle."

He stood erect, drawing himself up to full height, looking over the crowd, above their heads, as if addressing the whole world of men.

"Come in," he cried. "See him if you dare."

At that moment from inside the darkened tent there issued forth a piercing roar, a sound that rose above the noise of the Fair. The crowd stirred, shuffled nervously in place, the roar hurled at them like a tormented cry from an ancient dream. Some drew near; others drifted away, anxious to move on. I was left alone, in the shadows, the roar echoing inside my brain, rattling all the memories and fragments of a distant place and time. The man in black descended from his box, his selling done, the roar making any further comment unnecessary.

And then he saw me. Our eyes fixed on each other. He became as motionless as I, one foot still on the platform, the other on the ground. I could see the dark intensity of his eyes, the pupils as black and opaque as the suit he wore.

He did not speak. He did not move. But I could see his eyes take me in, measure me. It was a look of pure absorption, until it seemed the night itself grew darker. Beyond that, nothing. No other movement. No other sound.

He finished his descent, stood with both feet on the ground, facing me.

"You must come," he said simply, and he reached into his vest pocket and held something out to me. I took the small piece of white paper on which were written the words: "Admit One."

He turned his back and moved inside the tent, and I was left standing alone. I wish I could remember what I thought then, standing there, letting the thinning crowd shuffle past me. But I cannot. Not with any certainty. Perhaps I was thinking nothing at all. Perhaps I was only thinking of the lion's roar. If I could remember maybe I would know something more about destiny, about whether it is a destination or a journey, a going or a coming home. But I only know that I found myself inside the tent, in the amber gloom, smelling the musty decay of canvas.

"Sit close," someone said. "Sit very close."

The light inside grew even more dim and yellow, and the air had a thicker, staler smell. Rows of rickety wooden chairs formed a ragged half-circle around a small wooden stage.

Most of the chairs were full with the shapes of people. Off to the side I could see an empty chair. I slipped into the seat and hunched down, comforted by the gloom. It was a sadness I felt, but for whom? For those of us gathered in the dimness? Or those about to perform? Or was it myself I mourned?

The drums began to roll, and the man in black came gliding onto the stage waving a white wand.

"Ladies and gentlemen," he cried, his voice echoing in the gloom, as if the canvas walls had become dense like granite. "Welcome to the greatest spectacle of all: The Eight Human Wonders of the World."

He smiled, and his teeth glowed in the dim light. He moved to the edge of the stage.

"Illusion is what gives life meaning," he said, and he was looking right at me when he said it.

Next he took his cane and tapped the floor and a small white dove flitted through the air and landed on his shoulder. Then he threw the cane in the air and the bird vanished; in its stead silken handkerchiefs rained down. One landed on the man beside me, a farmer dressed in overalls.

The man in black leaned down.

"Keep it," he said. "A gift from the Snake Goddess."

"Goddamn." The farmer, laughing, glanced at the people seated nearby.

The memories of what happened next have never fused into a whole. They have remained separate and distinct, like sudden glimpses of a landscape lit by lightning. I will do my best. I remember a roar from behind the stage somewhere—deep, guttural, raging. Then a voice cried out.

"Unchain the Lion Man. Unchain the Lion Man."

And there was the rattling of chains and the snapping of a whip.

"The Lion Man is fierce tonight," the man in black said. "He's not been fed and he's crazy with hunger. Move back from the stage," he cried. "Move back, please."

"Bring on the girls," someone cried. "Bring on the Snake Lady."

But instead a fat woman emerged. She was dressed in a pink leotard with a little pink tail curled in back. I remember loud waltz music, and she began to twirl herself around the stage, the jowls on her face turning as pink as her tutu. Each part of her body seemed to spill into the other, a sea of flesh, a great lava flow of fat.

Then she was gone and in her place I saw hairy little men with long, thin tails, who bounded across the stage peeling bananas. They hung by an arm from trees that looked like crosses and ate the bananas.

"Unchain the Lion Man. Unchain the Beast," voices cried. The light grew dimmer, the roars more persistent.

"Bring on the girls. We want the women!"

"Back from the stage," the man in black cried. "Back from the stage."

And then the whole place grew still, and into that quiet two women walked, so close together, those two, each carrying a small guitar. No one spoke. Even the roaring ceased. They were dressed in white with lace, and they looked exactly alike except that one had blond hair and the other dark. I remember their round, smooth faces, their large eyes, their mouths shaped like hearts. They moved gracefully, as one, youth and innocence still in their faces. Their arms around each other. Bowing. Smiling.

They sang a song. I still remember that song; it echoes in my brain.

I am Lila. I am Lola.
And we'd like to sing a song for you.
Not a solo. Not a duet.
For we're more than one,
but less than two.

I am Lola. I am Lila.
And we'd like to sing and dance for you.

While I'm sleeping, I am thinking
of all the many ways
we can please you.

It was amazing. Each one took a turn singing a line. They laughed together, all in good cheer. Their voices blended well.

Then something happened. The mood turned sour. Mean.

"You ain't joined at all," someone cried.

"Yeah. It's just a fake."

And each outburst was accompanied by snickers, and whistles, and
laughter.

The women stood patiently waiting for the crowd to still. Then they
came to the edge of the stage, very close, and turned around. One of them
did something to the dress and it fell from their shoulders. You could see
where they were joined together by a lump of flesh along their ribs. Then
they pulled the dress around them and turned back to the audience.

"I go to sleep very early," said one.

"And I go to sleep very late," said the other.

I guess it was all part of the show.

After a while, the man in black returned. And the Lion Man roared.
More misshapen forms flitted across the stage.

"Get ready, men. Get ready," the man in black yelled. "Because here she
is exactly as she was long ago, in the Garden of Eden." He came to the
front of the stage. "Now you'll know why Adam sinned."

Drumming began and out she came. The Snake Goddess. She wore a
long, black silken dress with a slit up one side. And white flesh spilled out
everywhere, strained against the cloth.

She came almost to the edge of the stage. I could see that on her bare
white arms she wore rings, like arm bands. Rings made out of snakeskins.
Another one, really a hoop, circled her waist. Slowly, the Snake Goddess
began to thrust her pelvis in and out. In and out. That seemed to shatter
the stillness that had settled over the audience.

"Shake that thing. Baby, shake that thing," some of the men shouted.

She moved to the very edge of the stage. She leaned over and wiggled some more. She slid her hands up the sides of her dress, up higher, to the top, where she pressed them against her breasts, making them rise above the black silk, like white waves breaking over black rock. And as she did that, one of the men near me reached out and tried to grab her leg. But she managed to step away. She gave him a furious bump or two, then looked at him with a mocking grin.

"Just look, sonny," she said. "Just look."

The drumming grew more insistent. The Snake Goddess increased her gyrations, grinding her hips back and forth, back and forth, so that the slit down the side of her dress would part and we could see her black lace panties. The men around me were shouting and stamping their feet.

Suddenly, the drumming stopped, then began again in steady heartbeat rhythms. The Snake Goddess stood erect, a thin smile forming on her lips. She began to sway slowly, her eyes almost closed, trancelike. As if by magic, or incantation, the snake-belt encircling her waist began to uncurl. No one said anything or moved. All of us were staring at the thing around her waist. We could see a head form, the pink dart of the tongue, the glimmer of an eye. It had been alive all along.

The snake began to crawl up the front of the woman's dress while she leaned from side to side, in rhythm with the drum. Slowly, inch by inch, the snake slid over the silk and onto the soft white flesh of her breast. Here it paused, looking back at us, letting its forked tongue taste the air. Then the snake moved on up around her neck, its head disappearing into the thick spread of her bleached blond hair.

The drum beat slowly, like the pulsing of a vein, while the woman moaned low and soft as she swayed. The body of the snake slithered over the woman's dress and the head appeared around the other side of the woman's neck. It paused again, looking out at us and testing the air. In a moment, the creature began its slow descent back down over the Snake Goddess's other breast, down to her waist. There it stopped, stiff and alert, darting its tongue in and out.

The Snake Goddess kept to her swaying. Then, as if coming out of a trance, she stilled herself. Her half-closed eyes opened wide. In total silence, she reached down and grabbed the snake behind its head, holding it tightly, pulling it from around her waist so that eventually it came free.

She held the reptile up in front of us, held it high in the air. The snake's tail nearly touched the floor. Then she reached down with her free hand and scooped up the tail which she held out to us. She shook it back and forth. It made a loud, rattling noise. She smiled. No one moved.

Slowly she let the tail down, the snake hanging like a banded rope, limp and inert. She gave us all a fierce, triumphant smile. With a last bump and grind, she whirled around and walked offstage.

For a moment a vast silence, and then a single screaming cheer issued from the audience. And thunderous applause. One of the men sitting nearby half-turned to me.

"Ain't that the cat's ass?" he said, shaking his head back and forth.

The man in black appeared on stage again.

"Ladies and gentlemen," he said. "We've come to the great conclusion of our fabulous show. Straight from the deepest jungle, one of the truly great Human Wonders of the World, the one you've all been waiting for, the wild, untamed, uncivilized—please move back from the stage—the one and only . . . Lion Man."

All the time he was speaking, he was looking down at me, as if he were trying to gauge the impact of each word, as if there were a meter somewhere and he was watching the needle jump.

There came another bellowing roar from backstage and then a hair-raising human scream. From the left three Monkey Men appeared, dragging a heavy iron chain over their shoulders. A fourth Monkey Man, brandishing a long, curling whip followed.

The light seemed to dim considerably. I found myself leaning forward, sniffing the air, catching the smell of human sweat. And something else. Something almost animal.

Straining and heaving, as if pulling a tremendous weight, the Monkey Men hauled something out on the stage. It was hard to see exactly what in the murky light. But I could make out the general shape of the thing—humanlike, but covered in an animal's tawny hide. The hair on the creature was thin and matted, not thick and sleek like mine.

Whatever it was, the thing remained crouched, its face turned from the audience. Every so often it would emit a low, growling sound, and make a lunge at one of the Monkey Men. But it was slow and each time the Monkey Man would get away. As if in punishment, the one holding the whip would snap it at the hairy shape.

While all of this was going on, a curious thing was happening inside me. I felt a great stirring of my blood, a surge of energy. I could feel the hairs begin to stiffen all up and down my back. My fists began to clench, and even as they did, I could feel a low growling begin in my throat, move way down, into my chest.

No matter how many times the thing lunged, the Monkey Men were able to bound away. Finally, it gave up trying; not even when the whip began to raise welts on its arms and legs did it try to get them.

The Monkey Men hauled the creature even closer to the front of the stage, but it only settled down again, in a heap, face turned away and covered by its hairy arms. The crowd began to get restless.

"What's going on here?" some of them shouted. A few started to boo.

Now the creature seemed to rouse itself, to make a frantic effort to get back to the comfort of the backstage area. But the Monkey Men leaned hard on the chain and jerked the body to a halt. In doing so, however, one of the Monkey Men was caught off balance and stumbled to the floor. No sooner had he fallen, than the thing gave a leap and landed directly on him.

A terrific scream—a cry of terror and pain—shook the audience, and then the downed Monkey Man began crawling away, moaning, dragging a leg after him. It seemed to be covered with blood and, as he slid across the stage, he left a trail of red behind.

At that moment, the creature turned to face the audience. Hair covered most of the features. But unlike my hair, which was black and dense, his seemed nearly blond and fine, like silken threads. The hair didn't so much hide his features as drape them. You could see his face underneath. You could see that the skin was pale and loose, all wrinkled and sallow. Whether he was old I could not tell, but he looked like someone who had been starving or was ill. The skin seemed to hang from his bones, the way the skin of very old people hangs, as if the muscle that used to hold it has rotted away.

And for all the roaring and growling, the moaning of the stricken

Monkey Man, the blood on the stage, it seemed shoddy and pathetic. And the Lion Man, as if he knew, just lay unmoving. It was as if that last effort of launching himself at the Monkey Man had exhausted him.

"Goddammit," someone near me shouted. "That sonofabitch is old enough to be my grandmother."

"Look at the faggot," another one cried out.

The Monkey Men tried yanking on the chain. The bitten one grabbed the whip and started beating the Lion Man in earnest.

"Move, I tell you," he yelled. "Move."

But the Lion Man only hunched down further.

"Goddamn sonofabitch."

"Hit the bastard! Hit the freak!" some started screaming.

Then someone in back started chanting. "We want our money back. We want our money back." Others joined in.

The man in black came running onstage. He picked up the chain and tried yanking the Lion Man to his feet. But it was no use. He just lay there, hunched over, like a dead weight.

"Hit him. Hit the bastard," the crowd kept shouting.

"We want our money back. We want our money back."

A bottle was thrown on stage. It just missed the man in black.

"Now, hold on a minute," he shouted, but one could hardly hear him.

"We want our money back. We want our money back."

I was watching the Lion Man. He was trying to crawl away, slink off the stage. But the man in black still held the chain.

"You stay here, goddammit," I heard him say beneath clenched teeth.

"We want our money back. We want our money back."

"Goddamn fake. Goddamn sonofabitch fake."

And then somebody threw a candied apple. I saw it go by, a gleaming red blur in the amber light. It hit the Lion Man in the back of the head. He whirled around. For a single instant everything became still. The Lion Man glared at us. He seemed ready to leap from the stage.

And then it passed, that sudden whirling creature-anger. He just sank back down on the stage, like a balloon letting out air. A man next to me half-climbed on the stage and grabbed the chain from the man in black, yanking so hard he toppled the Lion Man over backward.

19

"Where are you going, you sonofabitch?" he yelled.

"Kill the bastard," someone in back cried.

I looked around. Most of the crowd had gone, but a knot of burly men ringed the edge of the stage. They were waiting for the Lion Man to be offered to them.

The Lion Man made a desperate attempt to wrap his arms around the legs of the man in black, to keep himself from being dragged into that screaming mob. But the man in black kicked free. As he did, he looked over at me. I could see a grim smile on his face.

"Help me," the Lion Man said, looking up at the man in black. I realized that those were the first words he had spoken. His voice was strangely ordinary.

Without even thinking about it I leaped up on the stage. Maybe if I had thought about it I would never have made that leap. Who can say? I grabbed the chain where it held the Lion Man by the ankle. I was going to try and break it, but even as I felt the cold metal in my hands, something else happened. I didn't think about it either. I just lifted my head and roared. Roared as loud and as long as I could. I don't know why at all.

Suddenly, I bared my teeth. And then I yanked the chain. The man who was holding it was so surprised he didn't even let go, but held on as he crashed into the stage.

At that point I bent down and ran my teeth into the man's hand, the one holding the chain, just behind the knuckle. The teeth went in, of course. They always do. The blood ran, and the man, screaming, let go.

The Lion Man lifted his head to look at me. It seemed for a moment that time had stopped, snagged itself on something. Then it whirled on again. He got up from the ground and started shuffling off the stage, dragging the chain after him.

Somebody standing near the bitten man got the idea of picking up a chair and throwing it. I watched him swing it over his head. Just as he began to bring it forward I hurled myself at him, flying downward, headfirst, like a plummeting hawk. I got him in the arm with my teeth, pretty deep I guess, for it felt like I'd hit bone. The chair clattered to the ground and he fell over backward. I jerked my head and got my teeth back out before he hit the ground.

20

It was as if everyone was in slow motion but me. I was able to roll over and get to my feet before anybody could move. By the time they could, I was back up on the stage, bent low, growling and ready to spring again. All spinal cord work, if you know what I mean. No thinking involved. I stood crouched, tense, my lips drawn back and my teeth bared, growling like a beast. And there wasn't anything I could do about it.

The Lion Man had got away. Only the man in black was left onstage. He was off to one side, safe from the crowd. He was staring at me. Behind him I could see some of the others from the freak show, the ones I didn't tell you about, like the Rubber Man and the Giant. They were all looking on.

"Jesus," the man groaned from the foot of the stage. "I been stabbed."

There was some mumbling and murmuring, some threats and curses. But the fight had gone out of the crowd, and after a while they left.

It ended like that, like the quiet passing of a storm. The stage was bare except for me and the man in black. And the candied apple. The rest of the freaks looked on from the wings. Outside, the lights had been turned off and darkness had settled in.

The man in black reached down and picked up the apple. He held it out to me. Without even thinking, I took the apple and bit into it. It tasted good, and I ate it in three or four bites, seeds and all. I was that hungry.

One by one, those standing in the wings exited by the back door into the quiet night. The man in black motioned to me.

"Come," he said.

And like an obedient dog, I followed.

They were waiting for me, out there in the field, under the moon and stars. They were gathered into a circle. In the center, on his haunches, sat the Lion Man. The man in black stood beside him. I waited outside the circle.

"It's time," said the man in black, to the Lion Man and to all of them and to me. I tried to see their faces, but their heads were bowed. Not even the Lion Man stirred.

"All those who want him to stay, raise your hand," the man in black said. I knew right away what was happening. I think you do, too.

A few shuffled their feet. Someone cleared his throat. But only one hand was raised. It was the dark-haired Siamese Sweetheart.

21

"Then it's done," the man in black said.

One of the Monkey Men rose and came through the circle toward me. He was carrying the whip. He held the thing out to me. I stood looking at it. I did not move. I could not look away.

Perhaps if the Lion Man had not stood up we might have remained like that forever, like two stones set in a field. But he did, wearily, sighing, mingling fate and will. Everyone turned to look.

He began to shuffle away. The circle broke for him, and he limped off between the Fat Lady and the Rubber Man, drifting across the field like the shadow of a man in moonlight. No one spoke. No one moved as we watched him fade.

I found myself running after him, chasing his shadow down. The whip, somehow, was still in my hand. He seemed to have gone a long way. When I came up alongside him, he had reached the road. It was the road I had followed from the woods.

He stopped, turned, looked at me. A car came by, slowed, then circled wide and sped off into the night.

"Your turn will come," was all he said, then he began shuffling off down the road. I stood watching till the darkness swallowed him. I never saw him again. No one ever spoke his name. But I think of him often. His face fills my dreams, along with Simon and Obaman and all the rest.

The posters were changed. They read:

THE LEOPARD MAN.
SEE HIM IF YOU DARE!

My body hair grew long again. And so, too, my teeth and nails. And in my ears, and in my heart, I heard the cry: "Unchain the Leopard Man."

As the poet said, this is no country for old men.

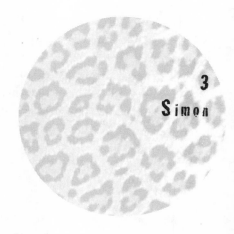

3

Simon

BEFORE I CONTINUE WITH MY LIFE AS THE LEOPARD Man, I should tell you how it all began, how I came to be in the woods. It's no easy matter. What is the beginning or the end of anything? But I think I should tell you about Simon, the landlord's son. He was killed in France in the war with Hitler. He was an infantryman, and one night during an ambush he was shot in the head. And ever afterward I would dream of him, the landlord's son, the young soldier, my only friend.

He was a good boy. And kind. He believed that God had written down the fates of all the men who would ever live and had cast them on the wind. When each person was born, a single destiny would fall on him like a drop of rain.

"And does a person know?" I asked.

"He knows," Simon told me, "because everything else seems like a dream."

And what did it feel like, Simon, that night walking down the narrow road? How does the fate of a dead man feel?

For a long time, I thought it must have been an accident; that he must have been shot by his own men, by mistake. He was still so young, so alert. And I had taught him about the night, about the darkness. We would drift into the evening's shadows and I would make him see that darkness is but a dream we believe in. We are not sightless in the womb. It's only the light of our birth that blinds us.

So I thought it must have been an accident, for that ambush happened at night and Germans have always been uneasy in the dark. But now I think Simon was right. Perhaps God had not forgotten to write down the fate of a young man who was to be shot while walking down a road in France.

It is a quiet evening, a sudden lull in the fighting. Simon is off to one side watching the others and, as always, listening. The men are talking about stealing away to the village, not telling the Sergeant. There is a certain house there, with women. The women are pretty, country women. They like Americans. And besides, it is war. They have to live. So there will be a hardness about them that comes from survival, but they will not yet be heartless. One will still be soft and gentle beneath the tiredness. She will smile. Her voice will be friendly. This is the one for Simon. I am certain of it.

It is decided. The men will go. Simon will go with them. It is time, they say. Life is too uncertain. The men are all older than Simon. They regard him as a younger brother. They see that he is different, not just younger but different. They see that where they pass quickly, he lingers to observe. Sometimes they are impatient with him. This is war, they tell him. But deep down they do not mind. Deep down they sense that he does what he must do. They respect his curiosity and his gentleness. They are only sorry that this is war and that there is no time for gentleness. Some of them know, on those rare occasions when they let themselves think beyond the moment, that Simon will not survive the war. The certainty of this knowing troubles them, but there is nothing to be done about it. It will happen no matter what they do. Perhaps, in a way, they, too, believe in Simon's destinies.

The village is quiet. In the house the women are busy with the small chores of living. They wash. They cook. They clean and sew. It is a quiet night. If the soldiers come it will be after dark. If they do not, it will be another night. They hope it is not the Germans.

They have left the upstairs curtains open. It is a signal to let the soldiers know there are no Germans. Soon there is a soft knock on the door: three times, quickly. It is the Americans. Good. The women are pleased. The Americans talk loud to hide their fear, but they are not unkind. They pay more than is necessary. This, the women understand. It is a little like payment on account, something for the future. It is because they are afraid and lonely. And so the women will lie a little closer to the men, as if they really wished to be there. And they will try to be tender when it is time for the men to go. These are only small gestures, but what else is there to balance the terror of war?

So the soldiers enter. There are smiles and laughter. The men have brought gifts: chocolates, cheese, a bottle or two of wine. Simon has brought the most impressive gift of all: a pair of stockings. The men arrange it so that it is the pretty woman with the tired but gentle face who accepts the present from Simon. She sees the quiet intelligence in his eyes. She understands that she will be the first. In a way that is good, she thinks. She is tired and he will be easy to please. The stockings are nice. She thanks him. She speaks the words first in French and then in English. He smiles and lowers his head. It is a good smile, free and easy. Simon has fine, white teeth. His eyes seem to give out more light than they take in. She will try and be good to him. She will let him see how a man and a woman can be together, how simple and natural it is, like the fitting together of two pieces in a puzzle. She is comfortable with her own body. It is an old friend, a little tired now, a little worn, but still a good woman's body—soft and round and warm. It must be lonely to be a boy so far from home, with guns and death.

They talk for a while. She has learned enough English to speak with soldiers. After all, what can one say? They dance, because the others are dancing. Simon is inexperienced in this, too, but he is graceful. She shows him the steps; he learns quickly. She leans into him, pressing herself against him. He is tense at first, but she is persistent. The wine is good. The music from the old record player, though scratched, is comforting. It fills up the silence. She lets her thighs press against his. He does not pull away. She lets her hair brush against his cheek. She has washed it only this morning, with the soap the Germans bring. She knows it is soft and smells clean. She can feel him breathing more deeply.

Some of the others have gone to the bedrooms. The dancing has been good for them. It has made them both warm and relaxed. She takes his hand in hers, lightly, leads him up to the door of her room. He tenses for only a moment, then follows. Inside, a lamp has been turned very low. The room is small but comfortable. Next to a half-open window is the bed. The woman does not speak. Instead she takes Simon's hand and places it on the top button of her blouse. Her own hands begin to reach for his belt. Simon's fingers do not move. They cling to the button. His heart beats so loud in his ears, he is afraid they will hear it in the next room. He is afraid, even, that the Germans will hear it in their foxholes. She puts her hand on top of his, letting the warmth of her fingers seep into his.

It is much later. The night has turned cool and very dark. The men are walking along the sides of the narrow road, away from the village. They move quickly, carefully, alert but confident. The camp lies ahead. The road is familiar. It has been quiet a long time. Behind them is Simon, as always. He pauses every so often to look behind, as if back at the house. It's as if he can still see the dim light in the woman's room, as if he can still see her silhouetted against the curtained window. Some of the men had heard him cry out in release. In a way, they envied him.

Out of habit, the men turn and wait for Simon. Some of them are re-membering their own youth, their own first time.

Suddenly, a hiss and whine. The darkness becomes illuminated. They see Simon standing in the middle of the road, alone, bathed in light as if he were a statue. There is a burst of gunfire. Figures rise up in the dark. Spurts of red enflame the night. Instinctively, the men dive for cover. The last clear image anyone can recall is of Simon slowly sinking to his knees in a ring of light, his face turned back down the road.

This is always my dream of Simon. I would see him leave the shadows, lean toward a single patch of light. I would try to warn him, tell him to keep to the dark. But always he would step into the light as I reached for him. Always, a burst of gunfire and Simon whirling around with a look of bewilderment on his face.

"You should have taught me about the light," he would say.

Then he would stiffen. I would try to drag him away, for it was terrible to see him like that, the light shining through the holes in his skull. But it was as if he were driven like a stake into the ground and I could never move him. So I would awaken, dripping with sweat, my hands clutching the bedpost. There would be nothing to do but get dressed and walk the streets. And try and remember or try and forget.

4
Obaman

ON A NIGHT LATE IN SUMMER I HAD DREAMED OF Simon again, and had taken to the streets like a man without the hope of forgiveness. The air had the damp taste of autumn, more things beginning to rot than to bloom. Heavy clouds lowered themselves beneath the moon, and the sidewalks were slick with black rain. I had been walking for hours when, suddenly, from behind a darkened street lamp a voice called out to me, low and deep. "I am Obaman."

Then a man emerged. He was tall, black, dressed in strange clothes. His hair was braided into two long spirals which hung down behind each ear. Golden rings encircled his neck and ankles. His chest was bare but draped over one shoulder was a silken red cloth embroidered with golden thread. He wore only a breechcloth below and leather sandals.

"I have been waiting for you," he said.

"You know me?" was all I could think to say.

He smiled, white teeth glistening in his black face.

"You are the Leopard Man," he said simply.

I had not heard that name before. It was the first time, you understand. The very first time.

"You must be mistaken," I said. I was not afraid or anything, though I knew I was near the great black ghetto.

"There is no mistake," Obaman said calmly, taking a step toward me. He said it with such quiet conviction, such certainty, that it seemed foolish to contradict him.

"What is it you want of me?" I asked.

"I would have you come to my house," he answered, standing straight and tall. Then he turned and began walking down the street, the rings on his neck and ankles jingling in the muted air.

I followed him as if he were someone leading me out of bondage. Soon other black men emerged from the shadows, all wearing suits and ties, like undertakers. We walked that way down the rain-wet streets: Obaman at the head, the ones in suits and ties on either side, and I last.

We walked toward the heart of the ghetto, past rows of decaying brownstone houses; past vacant lots strewn with garbage; past stores shuttered and barred. Silently, except for the jingling of the rings, we glided down the alleys until we came to a large brownstone house that stood by itself at the end of a narrow street. Behind it loomed a cemetery, some of the larger tombstones visible in the hazy light.

The building's stones were dark brown and smelled dank, like stones at a river's edge. A steep, narrow staircase rose from the street to a small porch. Obaman at once ascended, followed by the men in suits each of whom took his place on a separate step, arms folded against his chest. Reaching the top, Obaman turned back to me and waited. I stood at the bottom looking up.

"Have no fear," Obaman called down to me.

"I am not afraid," I answered truthfully.

"Then come." He held his hand to me.

I climbed the stairs slowly, and as I did each man bowed his head to me. I came to where Obaman was standing.

"We thank you," he said gently. Then with his fist he pounded three times on the massive door. It opened and we walked inside.

The hallway, dimly lighted, was filled with a sweet intoxicating mist. Hung on each wall I could see wooden masks carved into fierce animal faces. Some were oval with hollow eyes. Some were half-circles with long, flat wooden teeth. Some were painted in bright colors; others sprouted cloth and fibers.

Obaman reached up and took a mask from the wall. It was carved in the shape of a large jungle cat. Two holes cut in the wood represented the animal's eyes, and four more where the fangs would protrude. Obaman held the mask out to me.

"As a favor, would you put it on?" he said.

I held the mask in my hand. It was heavy. The carved face stared at me with its great hollow eyes. I felt almost hypnotized, holding it in that dark, smoke-filled hall. I lifted it to my face. It fit perfectly, my eyes exactly in the places that had been carved for them. And my own teeth, so oversized and curved and pointed, fit exactly into the holes by the mouth. It seemed like a second skin.

Through the eyeholes I could see Obaman staring at me. The look on his face, halfway between joy and terror.

"So be it," he whispered. "So be it."

The other black men who had been waiting patiently behind us fell to their knees. They began a low, incessant chanting.

Leopard Man. Leopard Man.
Heart of a panther.
Brain of a man.

I followed Obaman down the hallway to a large, square room. In the center, dug right into the oaken floor, was a great fire-pit in which live coals were burning. Suspended over the pit on a wooden pole was the body of a whole pig, head and all. Two old black women with grizzled hair squatted on either side methodically turning the pig over and over. They did not look up when we entered.

Around the fire-pit were stones the same dark color as the building itself. I looked up. High overhead I could see an open skylight out of which thin smoke spiraled into the night sky.

Woven weeds covered the walls of the room, and fastened to this covering on three sides were the skins of wild animals—zebra and antelope, cheetah and lion. The fourth wall, the one furthest from me, was bare save for the skin of a huge black leopard, its yellow eyes staring at whoever entered the room. In the smoke and firelight the eyes seemed to narrow and shift the way a cat's eyes move. The enormous jaw was slightly open, huge fangs curving out of the dimness in a white and glittering arc.

"Wait here," Obaman said close behind me. He put his hand briefly on my shoulder before disappearing down that same long hallway by which we had entered. I watched the old women tending the pig. Something seemed very familiar: the dark, the mist, the smell of roasting flesh.

Just then one of the animal skins on the wall was pushed aside and some women entered. They were tall and dressed in white silk robes that clung to their bodies, revealing the outline of firm, dark flesh underneath. On their heads they carried round wooden bowls filled with a steaming liquid whose smell seemed vaguely familiar. Silently, but for the swishing sound of their robes, the women seated themselves against the walls of the room, the bowls placed beside them. They sat, heads bowed, and I doubt if any of them knew I was in the shadows, the leopard mask still covering my face.

A number of black men dressed in suits and ties entered from the same opening in the wall. Some I recognized from the walk in the streets. But here they wore no shoes, and brass rings with small bells fastened to their feet jingled as they entered. They sat in rows before the women, their heads bowed as well.

And then the drumming began: low, insistent, repetitive. The great black leopard skin was pushed aside and Obaman entered. Behind him, the drummers, the large drums held at their sides by leather straps that circled their necks. And following these drummers, another small group of women in whose midst I saw the most beautiful woman I had ever seen. As she entered all the men and women lowered their eyes even further and looked away, as if prohibited from looking at her. But standing in the shadows of the hallway, wearing my leopard mask, I could not tear my eyes away.

She was naked from the waist up; a long red, silklike skirt covered the rest of her body. Her skin was black as ebony, and yet it seemed alive with color and texture. Like a sunset forever gathering and reflecting light. She was tall and lithe, yet softly curved. She seemed a woman in all her beauty but with a girl's open grace. The hair on her head had been shaved off completely, but that only heightened her beauty. For there was nothing to detract from the perfection of her features.

A crosslike figure had been painted in white from where her hairline would have been to the tip of her nose, then from the top of one ear to the other, circling her eyes above and below the eyelids. Two white rings of ivory pierced the middle of each earlobe; two small pearls adorned the corner of each nostril.

Her naked breasts, full and round, swayed slightly with each step. Yet she seemed unaware of her nakedness. She glided over to Obaman who alone stood watching her. She was nearly his height. Obaman motioned for the other women to form a tight circle around the girl, as if to shield or perhaps guard her. I could see that some of the seated men were beginning to shift in their places, darting furtive glances in her direction. But they appeared cautious, frightened almost, and made certain Obaman did not observe their movements.

Then the hair on my neck and back began to bristle. Four black men walked into the room, also entering from beneath the leopard skin. They had the same breechcloth as Obaman, but over their heads and flowing down their backs they wore the skins of four spotted leopards. Each of their fingers ended in a long, sharpened steel claw. I sensed an involuntary shudder from the crowd. These four moved behind the circle of women guarding the girl, arms folded across their bare chests, steel claws gleaming in the firelight. They stared at me through the eyeholes of their leopard hoods.

Obaman lifted his hand and the drumming ceased.

"He has come," Obaman suddenly shouted out into the silence, his voice deep and resonant. "The Leopard Man. Here, to this bitter cold place, to this land of stone hearts." He paused, letting his arm sweep over the heads of the seated people, everyone staring at him. "As I have told you. As I have promised."

No one made a sound. No one stirred. I could hear the collective beating of their hearts. Obaman let the silence linger before he began again.

"Those who have come from the land of our fathers have spoken of such a man. A child of the white man. A child of the leopard. They have spoken of his mothers: one pale and slender like a summer flower, the other sleek and black and powerful.

"This man with the skin of a white man but the heart of a leopard, they have told how the mark is upon him." Obaman paused again, nodding slightly to two of the leopard-skin men who then moved toward me. One of them put his steel claw on my arm. It was cold and sharp and pressed into the skin. I felt a growl beginning to rise in my throat. The smell of the leopard skins filled my nostrils.

"Come," said the leopard-skin man, staring at me with bright, resentful eyes. He led me into the center of the room, to where Obaman was standing.

"Child of the white man. Child of the leopard," Obaman cried as he tore the mask from my face. "Look on him and believe!"

All eyes were on me, boring into my skin, boring down through the muscle and bone into the very heart of me. There was an audible gasp as the mask fell away.

And why not? Why wouldn't they cry out? From where they sat in the firelight, would not my face framed by the matted black hair seem like the face of an animal? Would not my eyes, in that firelit light, seem to glow a smoky yellow? Had not others circled round me, pointing fingers, calling me beast? I had looked at mirrors long enough to know that in a certain light my teeth could look like fangs. And sometimes, feeling rage or bitterness or despair, had I not closed my eyes and let myself roar long and loud, sensing myself in the heart of some steaming jungle? And in my dreams, how many times had I felt myself pressed to the back of some powerful creature, feeling the ripple of its muscles beneath my loins, feeling its wild, ferocious heart pound louder than my own?

And then Obaman shouted, "Have we not waited long enough?"

And all the men and women answered, as in a chant, "We have waited."

And Obaman said, "Have we not suffered long enough?"

And they answered, "We have suffered."

And Obaman said, "Is it not time that we become free?"

And they chanted, "It is time."

Obaman nodded and the drumming began again. The women rose from their places in the back and came among the men, offering them the steaming bowls. Each man took a deep swallow. When everyone had drunk, Obaman took a bowl and getting down on one knee he held it before me.

"Teach us about freedom," Obaman said. "Teach us about courage. For you are the Leopard Man."

I took the bowl and drank. The drink was good, strong and sweet, tasting of milk and honey, and though I don't know how I knew, blood.

Then Obaman took the bowl from me and walked to the circle of women who stepped aside, heads bowed, revealing once more the beautiful girl in their midst. Once again all the men and women lowered their heads and looked away. I did not know where to look.

"Drink, my woman," Obaman said, loudly enough for everyone to hear. "Drink and grow strong." He handed the bowl to the woman who, for a single instant, looked past Obaman to me. I saw the bright gleam of intelligence in her dark round eyes, and something else, something like sadness. Then she lifted the bowl and drank.

At that moment, a movement and a cry from the side, near one of the walls. Looking in that direction I could see a man being dragged from the room by two of the men in leopard skins. Their steel claws had ripped his suit and slashed his skin.

"I didn't look at her. I didn't," the man wailed as he was being dragged out of the room. "Help me," he cried, but no one said anything or moved.

I looked at Obaman. His face was impassive, as if he had not heard. Only the girl showed any human feeling. Her shoulders sagged and her head lowered. I wondered whether she was about to cry. But if she did I could not know; the circle of women closed around her.

I started in the direction of the departed leopard men but Obaman reached out and put his hand on my shoulder. His fingers were hard and strong.

"He has been taken," Obaman said.

I didn't know what to say or do. The two remaining leopard-skin men were staring at me, their bodies tense. My own heart beat wildly. The drums pounded. My head throbbed. I felt a wild hunger welling up inside me.

Obaman took his hand from my shoulder and gestured toward the roasting pig. I knew what he wanted me to do. I knew it without his having

35

to tell me. The saliva came foaming out of my mouth. I lifted my head to the open skylight, let out the deepest roar I could, feeling the vibrations in every bone in my body. Even the leopard men were startled.

Then I ran to the pig and hurling myself at it sank my teeth deep into its throat. Soon everyone was tearing at the pig, ripping off great chunks of steaming meat.

It tasted good. I could never remember anything tasting so good. Obaman stood beside me, smiling. He did not touch the pig. A faraway look filled his eyes, as if he were seeing something from a long time in the past or future.

"Soon," he said. "Soon." But to whom he said this or what he meant, I did not know.

5

Obaman's Sermon

I WANTED TO TELL SIMON, BUT SIMON WAS GONE. HE had taken his walk down his destined road. Instead, I dreamed as never before. Something powerful would bear me away, rising up under me like the earth itself. In great leaping bounds we would move deep into shadowed places, out of which I would catch glimpses of women robed in white billowing gowns as we swept past.

Then the journey would end. In a flash. And I would be left standing in a field of green grass while before me, hanging in the hazy air like a gaudy chandelier, was a blue house. The paint was peeling. The rafters sagged.

And then suddenly I would be inside, by the foot of a spiraling staircase, the way movies cut from one scene to another in a second's time. An old black man would be sitting on a wooden chair tilted against the railing. He would turn to me and smile, red tongue and white teeth bright and opaque.

"Sure is a hot one, ain't it, boss?" he would say, shaking his head slowly. Then he'd get to his feet and begin to climb the stairs, stirring the dense air. "I'll tell her you're here," he would call out to me.

"Who?" I would ask.

He would laugh a careless laugh.

"The lady with the golden hair, boss. The lady with all the golden hair."

He would disappear, that old black man. Perhaps there was a room at the top of the stairs and he had slipped inside. I would walk over to the chair. I would sit in it, lean back as he had. The heat was stifling. There would be a noise. I would turn. Someone would be standing where I had been standing. It was a large man. He had on a white shirt. The shirt was open. His chest was full of hair.

"Sure is a hot one, ain't it, boss?" I would say, in my own voice, in my own trembling voice.

And then I would awaken, still hearing the echo of my words, but whether in my head or in my room I could not say. I would be drained and weak and wet with sweat. The cool air blowing in my one small window felt good against my burning skin. Birds would call out to each other above the city's noise. Sunlight would drain the last of the darkness from my walls, and the voices of my dreams would grow still.

On that next Sunday after the ceremony at Obaman's, I was to meet him at the zoo, early, before it opened to the public.

"I know a keeper," Obaman had told me.

We sat on a stone bench, in the sun.

"Have you been here before?" Obaman asked, glancing around.

"Not inside," I told him, which seemed strange. Many times at night I would walk past, listening to the animals, perhaps pausing to lean hard against the gate, breathing in that damp mixture of mist and animal and man.

On a still night I could hear the soft scuff of an animal's paws, the low growls of the predators, the nervous stamping of the prey. But then I would grow anxious, imagining that I was eavesdropping on something I had no business hearing. I would hurry away, letting the zoo sounds be drowned out by the sound of the city's restless slumber. In the daylight there were, of course, too many people, too many staring eyes.

"Our footsteps flow in our lives' direction," Obaman said when I explained all that to him. Then he smiled his wonderfully bright smile and took in a deep breath of the morning air. He was a brilliant man, Obaman—perhaps too brilliant. And his life, one filled with mystery and beauty and a terrible sadness.

What I knew then was that Obaman had another name, his "day-name," as he called it. But very few people called him by that name. In the daylight he was "Doc," because of the Ph.D. he had earned. At night, among his people, he was Obaman. He taught in one of the city colleges, and had written several important works on African culture, including one on the cult of the Leopard Men. I'm sure that many of the people who knew him only as a teacher and a scholar would have been amazed to know of his other life in the ghetto. But I will not say his "real" name now. Let his reputation rest with the books he wrote.

While we sat there in the warming sun, Obaman told me this story. He told it seriously and with a smile.

"My people tell a tale," he said, not saying who "his" people were, "about the making of the world. They say a great serpent laid an egg. And after a long time the egg was hatched and the world was born. And where the egg had been facing the sun, that part became a Promised Land, a land of milk and honey. But the side underneath, the side in darkness, became a wasteland filled with ice and wind.

"And when people sprang from the land, they, too, were the same. The Man from the sunlit part, he was strong with skin as black as the earth he sprang from. And the Man from the dark side, the cold side, he had skin that was pale and white and thin."

Obaman smiled broadly, stretching his long, lean body, delighting in the sun's warmth.

"Well?" he asked, "what do you think of my story so far?"

"That Promised Land wouldn't be Africa, would it?" I said pleasantly. Obaman nodded.

"Will you hear the rest?" he asked.

The sun felt good on my bones, the dreams of the night far away. It was a good day, Sunday, my day of rest. And not yet any people around to point and stare. I nodded for Obaman to continue and let myself stretch.

"This white man," Obaman began, "the man with the skin the color of snow, he could not get warm. And who could blame him, living like that in a land of winter. So he took to killing all the animals he could find there, so that he could use *their* skins for warmth. But the animals grew wary of him, and so this white man took to roaming far and wide, to see what lay beyond the snow and ice.

"And he became good at roaming and at killing, this white man, this snow man. He could build ships to sail the seas. He could build weapons that made it easy to kill. And he could build great cities in which to store his plunder. But the terrible thing was his heart remained cold. Still, he could not get warm.

"And so at last he came to the Promised land, to the land of milk and honey, to the land of the men with the gleaming black skin. And when the white man saw him, he knew at last he was wrong. For here was the true Man, the man who could run naked under the sun and stay warm. And he knew in his heart, this white man, that no matter how many skins he wore, he could never be like this Man who lived free under the nourishing sun."

Obaman paused, lifting his face to the sky.

"Is that the end of your story?" I asked.

Again Obaman smiled.

"There are several endings," he said, suddenly sitting up straight and looking right at me. "But the one I like best goes like this. All the black men join together and all as one they go and lie down on the white man's land. And the heat from all that blackness melts the snow and ice and turns the land into a vast sea full of newborn life."

"And the white man?" I asked. "The man with the skin like snow?"

"They say he was lost in the flood," Obaman answered, getting up and starting to move away.

I came up beside him.

"The sun is very far away," I said, feeling its small heat on my shoulders. "And all men have cold places in their hearts."

Obaman turned to look at me.

"Isn't that the truth?" He smiled that bright infectious smile.

We continued walking through the nearly deserted zoo, listening to the animals and keepers getting ready for another day. Soon we came to the carnivore section, the roars filling our ears.

We went to the building that housed the great cats. There were lions, cheetahs, servals, caracals, and a host of others. All of them were in square, concrete cages with thick iron bars. Inside each cage were raised wooden platforms for the animals to lie on, stumps of trees for them to sharpen their claws on, and troughs of water to drink from. Almost all of the animals paced back and forth, back and forth, scraping along the bars, their coats worn from the constant friction. Obaman stood before the last cage in the row. I came up beside him. I closed my eyes and drank in the smells. I felt a strange, fierce stirring in my blood. The darkness, the sounds of restless movement, the low, hoarse growling—everything seemed familiar, as if it were a waking dream.

"Hey, look at him, will ya?" I heard a voice shout. "He got a face like a lion."

When I opened my eyes, I could see a small boy with blue eyes and a shock of blond hair looking straight up at me and pointing. The boy's mother, a short, stocky woman in a dark sweater, came hurrying over. Her face was bright red with embarrassment. She grabbed the boy's arm and yanked him so hard that he stumbled against the railing that kept visitors from coming too close to the cages. At that moment, a blood-curdling roar and a rattling of the bars startled all of us. Obaman and I whirled around, instinctively throwing our arms up. The woman screamed and the boy let out a strangled whimper.

A giant black leopard had hurled itself out of the shadows against the bars in an attempt to get at the boy. We could see its contorted face, those massive paws struggling to push through the iron bars, those yellow eyes opened wide. If the leopard could have gotten out, I'm certain it would have leaped straight for the boy's throat.

The woman recovered long enough to drag off the terrified boy. Her face had turned from crimson to ashen white. The boy was trembling, sobbing, hiding his head in his mother's skirt.

"I'm sorry." It seemed to me that I was at fault, the boy coming close only because of me.

Several people, including one of the guards who had been alerted by the woman's piercing scream, had come over and were staring at us.

"What's going on here?" the guard said to the woman. "This guy bothering you?" He pointed at me.

The woman had calmed down some, but the boy still pressed tight against her, whimpering. She shook her head.

Obaman looked from the woman to the leopard to me.

"And the Beast which I saw," he suddenly cried out, "was like unto a leopard." Everyone gaped at him. "Who is like unto the Beast? Who is able to make war with him?" he shouted, his voice echoing through the carnivore building. The leopard, moving back from the bars, settled itself on the concrete floor. Its eyes were now fixed intently on Obaman's face, seeming to listen. The tip of its long tail made sweeping arcs on the floor.

"And all that dwell upon the earth shall worship him," Obaman said, stretching out his arm to point at me. The people turned in my direction. The leopard, its head raised, now turned its eyes to me.

"Hey, what's going on here?" the guard said after a terribly strained silence. He looked first at Obaman, then at me. No one spoke. "Well, step back there," he said, trying to assert some authority.

The woman turned to go, but at that moment the leopard lifted its head and let out a long, rasping roar. The woman paled again and the boy commenced sobbing anew. Obaman raised his fist high in the air, then turned and walked outside, laughing loudly all the way. Feeling strangely exuberant, I hurried after him.

"Leave it to the Bible," he said, as I came up beside him. And he laughed even harder.

6
The Zoo

THAT MORNING AT THE ZOO WAS LIKE A LIBERATION for me. Afterward, whenever the dreams would drive me from sleep, I would dress quickly and make my way there. I would go by the most deserted streets, playing little games with the shadows. Often as I passed beneath a bedroom window, I would let out a low, rasping growl, leaping lightly away, letting the sound seep its way into a sleeper's dream.

I would climb the iron gate surrounding the zoo and pause on the other side, letting the animal smell fill my nostrils. So sweet and pure that smell, so intoxicating. It was as if the zoo were the living heart of the city: beating, beating, unendingly beating—the raw and secret source of our life. I thought of Noah on his ark, the steaming, sweating multitudes, each pressed to each; all the living gathered in one throbbing place, hunter and prey, male and female, slow and swift—all waiting for release, for the sight and sound and feel of wind and grass and earth.

At night everything utterly changed. Gone were the vendors, the milling throngs of pallid people, the children careless in their youth, young lovers stealing kisses beneath the boughs. What remained was not so different from what the earth had been before Man, before we tamed it with our fires and our swords. Not even the iron bars could change that.

And the animals knew. Locked in their cages they knew. Night was for the hunters. I could hear them padding back and forth in their cells—not the mindless to and fro of the daylight hours but the purposeful stride of hunters aware of their prey.

I could hear them pause, hear them scent the air for the trace of blood. And the hunted knew. Even in their enclosures I could hear them nervously scrape the ground, rippling their flanks, twitching their ears, restlessly waiting.

I say this having been there: there is a terrible knowledge in the dark. It cuts to the bone. I don't care inside how many rooms, behind how many doors, we feel it. Civilization has not driven it from our blood, from back where the spinal cord meets our brain. We learn, when the sun goes down, whether, in terms of the night, we feel ourselves either hunters or prey. If prey, we bolt our doors, or light our lights, or quicken our pace, or swerve around shadows, which always seem crouched and ready to spring. Even the daylight brave feel it, feel the restive, hungry spirit of the night. There is no shame in it. It is not something you learn, not something you choose.

Others, with the hunter's heart, grow fierce in the night. Their eyes fill with moonlight. Shadows become caves they shelter in. Darkness is like a cloak they wear. This is not about courage at all. Some of the most timid of us love the night, grow bold or predatory in it. Some of the worst among us—rapers, robbers, killers—do their hunting in the night. It is nothing chosen, nothing earned. Some do not go easily past the circles of light. Some do. That is all you can say with certainty.

That first night at the zoo was as if I had come home. Guards, yes, but only a few. They made slow and certain rounds, but even that was no matter. I could smell them long before they came. I would drift into the shadows. Sometimes they would pass no more than a few feet away. Sometimes I would watch them from the branch of a tree, watch as they carelessly strolled below me. Sometimes I had to fight to keep from hurling myself at them, so smug and safe they seemed. Like Simon before I had taught him, they were trained to believe in darkness. They thought they could not see and they did not.

I never left without visiting the carnivore building. The doors, those massive steel doors, were locked. But it did not matter. I would go around to the back, to the outside cages. The cats inside would stir, make low throaty growls. I kept the scent of man. The light breeze would carry it to them, under the steel doors. But they would sense something more, something in the way I used the night. The stirring would lessen, the growls become greetings. I think they knew.

Always I would go to the far cage, the cage of the leopard. There I would stand, pressed against the bars, hardly breathing. The leopard, I knew, was listening. And so we stood in lonely silence, like two sentries at our posts. The leopard knew. I could hear it brush against the steel door that confined it. I could hear it purring.

There are tribes of natives in this world, on all the continents, who believe we are brothers to the beasts, who believe our spirits drift in and out of bodies until at last our souls are free. This I know: there is leopard in my soul.

So I would stand quietly in the dark, listening to the leopard glide. There were times when it seemed I could see the leopard, as if it had passed through the steel door and into the night. There were times when it seemed so close that I could reach out and stroke the rippling muscles of its back. But night and sleeplessness can play tricks on one's eyes. It is only fair that I tell you that.

And I felt the leopard's sadness, its loneliness, its pride. Something not broken, never to be broken. The leopard would wait, fierce, resentful, watchful, ready. If ever the gate should fail to close, in that single moment the leopard would know what to do. And if that never happened, the leopard would die waiting and unbroken. Its was the true heart of darkness.

"It is good, you have not forgotten," a voice said to me one night as I stood outside the leopard's cage. I was startled. I whirled around. Not often could someone surprise me in the dark.

The man moved out of the shadows to stand beside me. He was an old man; his black skin seemed to hang from his bones. His hair was white, and he wore a long black coat that fell below his knees. At the top of it, where his throat was, I could see what looked like a piece of leather on which something white and smooth was hanging. The old man saw me looking and opened the top button of his coat. On a thin strip of leather hung two white fangs.

"Do you recognize them?" he asked in a hoarse whisper.

"They're from a carnivore," I said.

"They're yours," the old man said, taking the necklace from off his neck and handing it to me.

I held the necklace in my hand, feeling the smooth hardness of the two white teeth. Suddenly, the leopard let out a terrible roar. The old man had gone, melted into the darkness. Afraid the guard might come, I ran from the zoo back to my room. I watched the morning stir itself into the night holding that necklace in my trembling hand.

And what pictures filled my head: rivers strung with beads of light; towering cliffs that splayed the sky; plains of dry and rattling grass that flowed to humpbacked ochre hills; gloomy thickets of wet woven leaves. And something else, something just beyond the edge of sight; something dark and gleaming; something alive and alert. I tried to summon it, to will it into my dreams or memories or visions. But whatever it was, it would not join the shapes that swirled past my inner eye as I sat there by the window.

I tried to think what Simon would have said about what had happened—that first night with Obaman, the zoo, and now the old man and the necklace in my hand. They all seemed like markers along a road. But where that road went, or what it would lead me to, I could not say.

Once in a great while, I would meet other people at the zoo, late at night. They were very seldom ordinary. I remember a woman. I was standing outside the leopard's cage on a cold night filled with sporadic rain. She came out of the mist and stood a few feet away from me. I turned my face to the side and raised my collar so as not to frighten her. She looked very thin, gaunt almost, huddled in the rain. We stood that way for several minutes.

"You think I'm a librarian," she said suddenly. "Don't you?"

I said nothing. I had been thinking no such thing.

46

"Oh, it's all right," she said, turning to me. "I don't blame you. Everyone says I'm the perfect librarian because I'm skinny and pale and wear these thick glasses. But I don't mind. Really. I'm used to it."

I couldn't resist turning toward her. If she was frightened of my appearance she didn't let it show. She looked as if she saw faces like mine every day.

"Did you have an accident?" she asked simply.

"At birth," I said.

"Oh," was her only comment. After that she was silent. The rain had stopped, but the wetness lingered in the air. I could see little wisps of breath seeping from her nose and mouth.

"I am, you know," she said at length, breaking the stillness.

"I didn't know," I mumbled, trying to think of what it was she was admitting to. As I thought about it, she did look as if she would be at home in some library, shuffling in and out of the long rows of numbered books.

"That's why I don't mind, you see. I work for the Public Library. The Plaza branch. Do you know where that is?"

I told her that I didn't.

"Well, you should," she said, as if scolding a child. "It's really very nice. And it has the biggest collection of animal books in the city. Do you know why?" she asked.

I said I didn't.

"Because I order them. That's why," she said. "I like animals. Do you?"

I told her that I did.

"I suppose that's why you're here," she said, then went on without waiting for an answer. "I like all kinds except the ones that kill."

I didn't say anything right away. I was trying to decide how many animals you'd have left if you took away the ones that killed for one reason or another. I didn't think there'd be many.

"That's why I like zoos, you see," she went on very earnestly, staring at me through her thick, rain-spotted glasses. "This way we have a chance to civilize them."

I told her I thought that was an interesting idea, one I hadn't heard before.

"That's why I come here," she said, meaning, I guess, the carnivore section. "I want to try to understand them, why they're so cruel." She moved a little closer to me. "Do you know why?"

"I think they have to survive," I remember telling her.

She didn't say anything right away, but stood there looking at me, a thoughtful frown on her pale, oval, librarian's face. She was shivering slightly.

"That's why I'm a vegetarian, you know," she said finally.

It made sense, I told her, given her views about killing.

Once again we settled into silence. The rain had begun again; little smatterings of drops cratered the dust at our feet.

"I used to eat meat," she said suddenly. "But then I was raped."

"Raped?" I blurted out, surprised by both the word and the association.

"Yes," she said matter-of-factly. "One time when I was coming home from work. A man dragged me into an alley. After that I stopped eating meat."

"Did he hurt you?" was all I could think to say.

She didn't say anything for a long moment.

"Yes," she said finally. "He hurt me very much." She paused again, shivering, as if remembering. "But some good came out of it."

"Good?" I asked, wondering what good could come out of such an awful thing.

"I told you," she said, a little impatiently. "Now I don't eat meat."

"Aren't you afraid to be out alone . . . like this?" I said, motioning to the darkness around us. "At night? After what happened?"

"It happened twice more," she said softly. "But it doesn't matter."

I stared at her in disbelief.

"It doesn't matter?" I said.

"No. You see, they can't hurt me anymore."

"I don't understand," I said, thinking of all the headlines I would read in the papers.

She smiled a wan little smile.

"It doesn't hurt here," she said, touching her fingers to her heart. "Not anymore."

48

I didn't know what else to say. She seemed so certain about it all.

"That's why zoos are good," she said again. "We have to teach all the animals not to hurt each other. "That's why I come here. I want them to know."

I offered to walk her home.

"That's very kind of you," she said. "But I only live nearby."

She turned to go, paused, called back to me.

"Which one is your favorite?" she asked.

"The leopard," I answered.

She was silent a long time.

"Mine's the mourning dove," she said and was gone.

I watched her go, listening to her footsteps fade into the night. I thought about going after her, about making certain she got home safely. But in the end I let her go. It seemed she, too, was following her own road. But I think about her when the nights are long and cold and dark, and I hear the leopard's roar.

There were others, but none I remember so well. One was a young man, a divinity student, who would come late at night and practice talking to the animals, like St. Francis. He was afraid to do it in the daylight, he told me. People would think he was crazy. Or worse, they would come to doubt that God had the power to make such things happen. After all, what if it were only that he was not worthy of such a gift. He seldom came to the carnivore section.

"What could I possibly say to them?" he told me.

And there was the man who came because it made him more virile.

"A half-hour here," he told me jauntily, "and I can go home and do it like a rabbit."

What was it that caused such an effect? I asked him.

"Beats me," the man said. He was in his forties, I guess, a little bald, a little potbellied. "Maybe it's them damn chemicals they got in their blood or something," he finally ventured, "floating in the air." He moved a little closer to me, spoke in a confidential whisper. "Back where they come from, see," he said, nodding at the cages, "they got harems, like these here animals. You better believe it." He preferred to smell water buffaloes, he told me. "Big suckers, them guys," he said. "Got peckers that hang down to the ground. But lots of times they keep 'em inside, see, and I can't get a good whiff of them."

I asked him if his wife knew, because I could see he had a wedding band on his finger.

"Nah. She thinks I'm just going for a walk," he said. "You know, to get some air." Then he winked at me. "But she don't care as long as I come back ready to go."

One time the guard had caught him.

"Jesus," he said. "There I am with my pants down checking things out, to see if the smells are working, you know. And up comes this guard, see, shining his light. I had to do some fast talking, all right. Guy thought I was queer. Had to give him ten bucks to keep him from taking me in."

He, too, asked me what my favorite animal was.

"The leopard," I told him.

"Yeah, I don't blame you, buddy," he said. "If you don't mind my saying, you look a little like one yourself."

I told him I didn't mind.

"I bet they can do it all night, huh?" he said, nodding his head at me and grinning. Then he said he had to go. "I'm just a working stiff," he said, laughing out loud. But before he moved off he did a strange thing. He came right up beside me and took in a long, deep breath.

"What the hell," he said, shrugging his shoulders. Then he turned and moved off, apparently eager to get home.

Once in a while I'd meet up with a thief or worse. But I wasn't afraid of them. Rather it was the other way around. They'd get close, take a good look at me and head off in the opposite direction. One man even dropped the knife he was holding. I took it home. I have it still. I use it to pare my nails.

7

On Being Jewish

I SUPPOSE I SHOULD TELL YOU SOMETHING ABOUT MY life back when I lived above the hardware store, just before the War, before Simon was killed, before Obaman called out to me.

Everything is still clear. Level with the street was the hardware store. Small, with a long, narrow aisle that ran through the middle like a stripe down a skunk's back. Beneath was a cellar filled with merchandise, and a stairwell that led to a small yard surrounded by a high wooden fence. The earth in the yard was claylike; nothing grew well. Above the store was the apartment where the owner lived, and his son, Simon, my friend. And above that, in one large room with a small bathroom, I lived. Alongside my room, a staircase led to the roof.

I worked in the hardware store, mostly for the room and board. The owner's name was Abraham Smyth, with a *y*. That was not his real name, of course. He had it changed after he was driven out of Russia by the Communists.

"Don't ask me what it was before," he told me once. "It was a famous Jewish name." He was afraid the Communists would send an agent to murder him. "They could, you know," he told me often. "Look what happened to Trotsky, poor man."

He was a small man with thin hair, a large, curving nose, and ears that curled outward. His wife had died from cancer some years earlier.

"From America," he told me. "The moment when we had to leave everything and run away like thieves, that's when she started to die."

Simon thought otherwise. "He made her work in the house," Simon said, meaning his father. "He made her work in the store. And everything she did was wrong. I think in the end she believed him."

She was a gentle woman, Simon explained to me. And I believed him. For he himself was gentle and kind, and I could see that it did not come from his father. Simon told me that he thought diseases like cancer grow as much in the spirit as in the flesh.

"Life is good if you don't weaken," were the last words his mother spoke to him. Then she closed her eyes and died.

I know Simon thought about her often, but he never spoke to me of her again. I understood. Some live in our hearts so deep we cannot bear to speak of them. So to guard against their loss or corruption, we put a moat of silence around them.

Sometimes when I thought about Simon and his mother, imagining the sorrow and love in her eyes as she left him to the world and to his coldhearted father, I began to consider my own parents. Sometimes I would drift on a current of thought. Sometimes I would try to will myself an image or a dream. Always, I would feel caught somewhere between memory and desire.

How would a woman feel who had given birth to me? I tried to imagine. All the joy and the pain and the expectation—and then the reality. This face the mirror returns to me. The teeth. The hair. The eyes. What would a woman feel when she saw me in that first faint light of exhaustion and release? The maternal instinct thrust against the horror of the beast.

I tried to see: in the darkness of my room, in the darkness of my dreams. Pale white faces would sometimes float before me. And sometimes dark faces with ivory teeth and glowing eyes. I wanted so much for one face to smile at me, like Simon's mother must have smiled at him. I wanted someone to reach for me, touch me, hold me close. But I could not make the image hold. And the faces, black and white both, would be lost to forgetfulness or reality, and I would be left with an emptiness no less real than the one I imagined for Simon.

Simon's father was not a man to grieve. He was a man given to action. He had changed his name to Smyth so that no one should guess he was Jewish.

"At first I spelled it regular, with an *i*," he said, "but then I got an inspiration. Every Tom, Dick, and Harry calls himself a Smith. Maybe people will think something's not kosher." He winked at me. "So that's when I put in the *y*, so no one should have a suspicion."

For all his attempts at personal disguise, though, he was determined to raise both Simon and me as Orthodox Jews.

"Everyone has to belong to a tribe," he informed me. "Even you."

When I told him that I had been raised a Catholic, he laughed sarcastically.

"How can you respect people who don't believe a pope can make a mistake?" he said. "Even God said he was sorry for making Saul king."

But to tell you the truth, I liked the idea of being a Jew. They were a people used to wandering, used to looking in from the outside.

"But if anyone asks you," Mr. Smyth told me, "don't say. With a face like yours, it's maybe better no one knows. Jews got enough trouble already with noses."

Nevertheless, every night but Friday, I attended Hebrew lessons. I would walk to a small building behind the synagogue. It had been a storage shed once, then converted into a living space for old, retired rabbis. Bunks, on which the men could sleep, lined either side of the main room.

"Who gets which bed?" I asked Simon once.

"It's decided by condition," he told me.

"Condition?"

"Yes," he said. "The sicker you are the closer you get to the bathroom."

"Who judges the degree of illness?" I wanted to know.

"It's mostly done by argument," Simon answered. "But sometimes it comes to actual blows."

"What happens then?"

"The loser wins. It's a matter of logic. The winner must be healthier."

In the middle of the room was a long, narrow table, with wooden benches on either side. Every so often on the table there was a kerosene lamp and a small pile of books. These were the teaching stations for the rabbis. A student would enter, walk to his particular station, and wait for his particular teacher.

"How are these places determined?" I asked Simon.

"By the same principle. The ablest sit furthest away."

Unfortunately, my own station was the one at the head of the table.

"It's nothing," Mr. Smyth explained to me. "He's a little dopey sometimes, that's all. But he specializes in non-Jews." Then he added: "Besides, he don't see too well, and with a face like yours I wouldn't want he should get another stroke."

For a while, there was even talk of my circumcision.

"You should be kosher all the way," Mr. Smyth told me.

I told him that I was already circumcised. That I had been, apparently, even before the Catholic Home.

"Yes, but was it kosher?" he asked. "Maybe it was done by a butcher? Or a witch doctor. Who can say?"

But nothing ever came of it, because soon the war arrived and business boomed. Then Simon was killed and Mr. Smyth could hardly stand to have me around.

"It's nothing personal," he would tell me bitterly. "But with a face like yours, you should have been killed instead."

I understood his bitterness. That the army had refused me and had taken Simon seemed unforgivable.

"It's nothing personal," Mr. Smyth said, "but they're not running a beauty contest, are they?"

That I gladly would have exchanged my life for Simon's, my death for his, I did not tell Mr. Smyth. It would only have made the pain more bitter.

My days were spent, as they had been even before Simon's death, working in the back of the hardware store.

"It's nothing personal," Mr. Smyth told me in the beginning, "but I wouldn't want you should scare the customers." He made a special door for me, so the customers wouldn't have to see my face. It was like those doors you see on barns, where the door is divided in two—top and bottom. Only it was the bottom part that remained open. That way I could take in and hand out merchandise without my face being seen.

It was strange at first to see everything halfway like that. But then I got used to it, and could tell almost immediately by the shoes and walk who had come into the store. I played a game. I would try to imagine what the person would look like from the walk, from what they said. Later, I would ask Simon to tell me. He would be surprised by how often I was correct. I did not tell him I also used the sense of smell in my reconstructions.

There is a story about a man, a customer, that I want to tell you. I remember it very clearly. I think it is important. I was in the back room, as usual, fixing a venetian blind. The door opened, the cowbells rang, and a man walked in. I recognized the walk immediately. He was a small man with a sad, slow walk, as if the world was pressing down on him. He would buy only a few small items and would never bargain. Because of that he earned the contempt of Mr. Smyth.

"Only a fool takes what's offered," he would call back to me after the man had shuffled out.

This time the man walked even more slowly to the counter, the burden of the world on his back perhaps grown even more heavy.

"Please, Mr. Smyth," the man said in a soft, resigned voice, "I'm needing a toaster."

I could hear Mr. Smyth take in a deep breath. The request had surprised him. A toaster, you see, was a major purchase.

"You want should be an electric?" he said. We still sold some of the old-fashioned kind, the kind that sat on top of the stove burner.

I could see the man's feet begin a nervous shuffle.

"Electric, yes," he said. "But please, it should be a small one. Not so expensive."

As soon as he said that I knew the man was doomed. For Mr. Smyth, the words "not too expensive" were taboo, curse words. Invariably, they would bring on his scorn and a lecture.

"You want an electric toaster, but it shouldn't be too expensive?" he said mockingly. "Maybe you want to lift the world without getting a rupture?" There was a pause. I knew what was coming. I had heard it often. "First, you should know I'm not here to steal your money. Second, I'm not here to sell junk. You come to me, you should know I don't sell garbage."

To make a long story a bit shorter, the man agreed, almost against his will, to purchase an expensive toaster. I was the one to get it down from the shelf and hand it under the door to Mr. Smyth. It came in a big carton and was fairly heavy.

I could see the man's feet shuffling again. I could smell perspiration begin to seep from him.

"Mr. Smyth, excuse me, please, but it looks like a big toaster. I'm needing only a small one."

Again, I knew what was coming.

"You're like an old gossip," Mr. Smyth told him, his words dripping with sarcasm. "You see a large man, can you tell me how big his brain is?"

The feet were still. It was too much effort even to shuffle. The man was beaten, broken. He bought the toaster, groaning as he carried it out, either from the weight of it or the weight of the world.

After the door had closed and the cow bells quieted, Mr. Smyth called back to me.

"That's what it's like to be a fool," he said, his voice contemptuous.

An hour later the man returned. His footsteps sounded different, almost determined. I got down from my ladder and hid myself behind the open bottom of the door and peeked out. The man walked to the counter. Under one arm I could see that he was carrying the toaster. In the other hand was a small paper bag. Mr. Smyth pretended not to notice him and went on reading his paper. The man put the toaster on the counter and waited. Mr. Smyth continued to read. After a long time the man cleared his throat.

"Mr. Smyth," he said in that same soft voice, "you'll excuse me, but I think the toaster is a defective."

Mr. Smyth did not answer. He continued to read the paper as if, somehow, it contained all the secrets of the universe. Then, slowly, he turned to the man, as if seeing him for the first time.

"So," he said. "You're back." Then he turned the page and continued to read.

But the man would not be put off.

"When the toast is finished," he said, his head bent as if in sorrow, "it flies out from the machine."

I could tell that Mr. Smyth was turning in my direction.

"Can you believe?" he cried out. "Of course the toast comes out. Why do you think they call it an automatic toaster?" he said to me, to the man, to the world.

"You don't understand," the man said, becoming in his own quiet way genuinely agitated. "It doesn't just come out. It leaps from the machine. It comes out like an eagle into the air. Sometimes it goes on the sink. Sometimes on the floor. There's no telling."

Mr. Smyth waited a good long moment, as if to erase from the world every vibration of the man's voice.

"Everything you have should pop up like that toaster," he said, and I could feel the man cringe. But still, he did not give way. He asked for his money back. When that was denied on the grounds that it had been a policy for years that no refunds be given, the poor man asked for a simple exchange.

"What exchange?" Mr. Smyth shouted, again in my direction. "The toaster is a perfect toaster. What exchange? I can't do it, even if I could. It's against the Board of Health."

"Please," the man pleaded. "It's a defective." He held up the small paper bag. "Here, I got some bread. Let me show you." He reached into the paper bag and took out two slices of bread.

"Can you believe?" Mr. Smyth shouted to me again, clapping his hand to his forehead so loudly it sounded like a slap. "Does this look like a bakery? Besides, it's a strain on the electric. Edison is rich enough."

The man held the bread out before him. His arms did not waver. It was as if they had turned to stone. Perhaps sensing the transformation, the stonelike determination of the man, Mr. Smyth let out a deep breath.

"I got here a real lunatic," he called back to me. But he did plug in the toaster. The man put in the pieces of bread, his arms being flesh after all, and pushed the spring down with a grunt. The toaster began ticking away loudly, like a giant alarm clock. It seemed to take forever. I could smell the toast beginning to brown. Suddenly the clicking ceased, and with a noise like the snapping of an enormous rattrap, the lever shot to the top. The two pieces of toast went hurtling through the air. They flew toward the ceiling, brushed it, then came tumbling back down, end-over-end, till they landed with a thud on the counter.

"You see," the man said, with the faintest hint of triumph in his voice.

"Must be the adjustable," Mr. Smyth said, trying to sound matter-of-fact. But I could tell that he had been startled. He lifted the toaster off the table and adjusted a dial on the bottom of the machine.

"There, it's done," he said proudly. This time he was the one who put in the toast and pushed the lever down. I stayed on the floor, watching. Once again the lever snapped and the toast came flying out, looking this time like two small bats soaring into the air. On the way down, one hit Mr. Smyth on his shoulder.

The small man did not say anything. The look on his face said it all. It was a look of quiet satisfaction. The man had been vindicated.

But Mr. Smyth was not ready to grant him his victory.

"Look," he said. "I got a solution. When the toast is in the toaster, you go get yourself a chair, and you sit by the toaster. And as you sit, you put your hand over the toaster like this. That way, you can catch the toast when it comes out. It's simple, no?"

"But Mr. Smyth . . ." the man began, before he was interrupted.

"What? You afraid of a little work? It wouldn't kill you, believe me. Your wife should be able to spring up like this. Be thankful, if you know what I mean."

The man didn't say anything for a long time. He looked at Mr. Smyth, as if some message were written across his face. Then he put his toaster under his arm and began shuffling toward the door, slowly, wearily. The world had proved too much for him again. Then he stopped and turned around. It was very quiet in the store and in the street.

"God will punish you," the man said, only that and nothing more. Then he turned and walked out. The cowbells settled into silence. Mr. Smyth did not move or anything. It was as if the words were still hanging in the air. The absolute way in which the words were pronounced had made them seem terrible. I myself shivered from the certainty of them.

"A real fool, that one," Mr. Smyth called out at last, but there was a strained, hollow sound to his voice. Then he came into the room where I was and opened the cartons of toasters. One by one, for the rest of the afternoon, he tested each spring.

It was very strange, but on the day the letter came telling of Simon's death, I thought of that incident. Could the world be like that? Could such a curse carry weight? Would God listen to such a thing? After all, it was only a toaster.

Simon himself had an explanation for such things.

"Evil," he told me once, "grows from the smallest deeds."

Perhaps Simon was right. Perhaps the old man and his toaster had to be accounted for. I wonder if Mr. Smyth ever thought of that day and what the man had said.

Yet, in his own way, Mr. Smyth had been good to me. He alone had the courage to take me from the Catholic Home, to bring me to his house, as it were, to introduce me to Simon. And he taught me many things: things of the world, practical things. In the Home, because I had to spend so much time alone, away from the other boys, I had read everything I could, everything I could get my hands on. And so, perhaps without my realizing it, I had come to believe in a world with beginnings and endings.

But Mr. Smyth required me to live in the world around me, even if it was only half a world, a world turned upside down. Still, it was one to balance against my dreams and books. He taught me to work with my hands, to fix things, to measure a day by what you had done, by how you had changed the shape of the world. In a way, he was like the teacher of realism, because earlier only my dreams seemed real.

But working in the hardware store, or walking along the street at night, or wandering in the zoo kept me from falling into the deep well of myself where I might have drowned.

And, too, it was that life in the hardware store that gave me that special quality that Obaman said made me the "true" Leopard Man.

"Fate has taken you," he said to me once, "with your leopard heart and put you in the middle of the white man's world. In the very center."

He meant, I suppose, that by working in the store with all the different products and tools I would learn, firsthand, about the driving force of white civilization, about technology. And in a way, he was right. I did learn how to fix many things—how things worked, how they went wrong.

I seemed to have an aptitude for it, for working in the material world. My secret was to treat every machine, every piece of matter, as if it were a living thing, a creature with a life of its own. The trick, then, was to coax it back to life, to nourish it and make it strong. Old radios became wounded birds whose throats were constricted. Broken tables were like animals with broken legs. There were times I could almost feel the agony of it, the pain of it. It was this skill, as much as my face, I suppose, that convinced them all I was indeed the prophesied Leopard Man.

And for that, for all the terrible joy and sadness it brought me, I am indebted to Simon's father. I don't think he ever knew how much I owed him, and for that I am truly sorry. It might have eased for him the pain of Simon's death.

8

On Being Catholic

B EFORE I WAS JEWISH I WAS CATHOLIC, AND SO I think I should tell you about my early life in the Home. It began like all human life—an awakening from a dream. I opened my eyes and there she was, all in black and white, leaning heavenward and crossing herself with long, lean fingers. Her name was Sister Agnes. Though I asked her many times about that time, that awakening, she only spoke to me of it once—on the evening of my departure. It was up in my attic room, at night, late. She sat on the wooden chair beside my bed. She smelled of soap, as always. She fingered her rosary as she spoke. Her voice was soft and sad. I will try to tell it as I remember, as she said it then, so long ago, as it must have been.

She knew she was being tested the moment she saw me. For an instant, for the space of a single heartbeat, her legs felt weak, as if they might give way. But she recovered—she always recovered—and took a deep breath, and lifted her wimpled face to God.

"Lord," she said, simply, "Thy heel is heavy on my neck."

Then she looked down at me again, all swathed in filthy

white, lying on the black wool blanket of the narrow, attic bed. She crossed herself before she dared reach down to draw the soiled cloth aside.

"Jesus, Mary, and Joseph," she said.

And who could blame her? For I was filthy, and smelled of feces and urine, and I was covered with hair—thick, dark, matted hair. So who could blame her if she stood there a long time, silent, lonely, weary. Hers had been a hard life. No one could deny it. She herself would not deny it. But she struggled not to complain, not to give in to the weariness. She was being tested, she knew. Right from the beginning, she was being tested. There could be no other explanation.

It was a hard life. She had been firstborn. Her parents were Irish and poor, dirt-poor, first-generation immigrants to America. They lived in the city, in the worst of the tenements. But her father had a dream. He would raise up sons. And when he had enough of them, they would buy a farm in the country and live there forever—all of them, generation after generation, till one day they would become their own city, their own state, their own nation. And it was to be her job, as the firstborn female, to care for them all, to see that they grew tall and strong.

And so the children came, one by one, year after year. Both boys and girls. Brothers *and* sisters. Sisters to help her, to ease her burden. But the sisters did not live. Not one female survived but her. They buried five like that, five little sisters. Only once did she ask. They had buried another one. Her mother would not go to the church, not this time, nor to the graveyard. Instead, she sat for days by the window, saying nothing, eating nothing, staring out at the thick, gray sky. She had waited until they had all gone out—the men, her father and brothers. Then she walked over to her mother sitting by the window.

"Mama," she said, "has God put a curse on us?"

Her mother did not say anything for a long time, nor did she turn from the window. She thought that perhaps she had not even heard her.

"Never love anything more than the Lord," her mother said to her in a whisper, breaking that long, mournful silence. Just that. Nothing more. Ever.

They never bought the farm. They never left the city. Her mother died, still silent, still grieving. One by one the boys grew older and moved away. And then one day her father said to her, "Become a nun. It's what your mother wanted." He was drunk, as usual, but it did not matter to her whether it was a lie or not. She had come to recognize the truth of her life before then: God was testing her. She would not let Him down.

She became Sister Agnes. And without willing it or resisting it, she found herself in the Catholic Home for Unwanted Boys. It did not surprise her. It was what she had always done, look after boys until they were grown into men and went away. She did not will it or resist it, either, when it was to her that they brought the most *difficult* cases, the children no one wanted— the deformed or the brutal or the retarded. She straightened her back, took a deep breath and said, "So be it, Lord," and went on with her life.

For this reason, it did not occur to her to complain or wonder why it had been on *her* round of the dormitory beds that I had been found, lying on top of an empty bed, in the attic where no child had been for ages. It was all part of God's plan, part of God's testing, and she would bear it as she had borne all of her other trials.

"I only pray that I shall not weaken before my task is done," she whispered as she looked down at me that first time, and though I could not understand the words, I remember her voice was soft and gentle and it made me smile.

Instinctively, her hand flew to the silver crucifix at her neck, the one left to her by her mother. She had seen my fangs, small as they were.

"It's the Devil's own," she remembered thinking.

But this was a woman who had been tested by God from the beginning, who had buried five sisters and a mother, who had walked out on a drunken father and had become a nun and taken the name Agnes. She would not bend. She would not break. Not if she could help it. So, she took the silver crucifix from around her neck and crossed herself with it, kissed it, and with a steady hand, pressed it to my forehead.

"Give me a sign, my Lord," she called out to the heavens.

But there was no hiss of burning flesh, she said. No shriek or wail. I merely looked up at her, blinking every so often, and smiling my white-fanged smile.

"You may not be Satan's," Sister Agnes told me often, "but one of your parents was an animal, you can be sure of that."

And so it was Sister Agnes took up her cross again. I can almost feel its coolness on my skin.

They tried to find out about me, of course. But nothing came of it, though the police were called in along with all the appropriate agencies, and the parish priests with their secret knowledge of the confessionals. But it was the time of the Depression, and children were being abandoned everywhere. Stories sprang up almost immediately. I had been born to a Negro man and a white woman, or a white man and a Negro woman, for the Home was close to the great, teeming black ghetto, and I was abandoned for shame. Or one of the women had had relations with an animal; or one of the women had been cursed. Or I had been born deformed, or I had been abandoned and raised by dogs, or cats, or worse. The stories were endless.

Sister Agnes heard them all, but I don't think she believed any of them. To her, it did not matter. It was another test from God—her most difficult one yet. Even then, she told me, she knew it would bring her to the edge of her own humanity, to the place where Christian love and charity meet face to face with revulsion and despair.

It was finally accepted, mostly through prayer and measurement, that I was either three or four, stunted in my growth by lack of physical, social, and, especially, spiritual stimulation; and despite my obvious deformities, otherwise mostly human.

It was decided, as well, that I would be raised as much as possible like the others, in the hopes that eventually someone would come forward and claim me.

"Our Lord works in mysterious ways," Sister Agnes often told me, "but none more mysterious than you."

Even the Reverend Mother was bewildered. The record for the Home had been seven years. That was the longest they had kept any boy before something had happened to relieve them of their burden—that is, before a boy came of legal age, or had been sent to the reformatory, or, praise the Lord, had been placed with a family, however questionable the circumstances. In my case, however, there was another option.

"Maybe our Lord will come for you Himself," the Reverend Mother told me. "Pray for it."

I think the Reverend Mother was sorry for Sister Agnes. I don't imagine in all her long years of service she had seen a more beleaguered soul. She told me once she thought of her as Job, that the Lord must have wagered on her as with him. There were times when she must have wanted to intercede, to ease Sister Agnes's burden, to shelter her from the terrible storm. But I think she was afraid. I think she must have remembered what God said to the three comforters who sought to presume for Him.

"We must trust in God," she said to me more than once, "for there's nothing else left to believe in."

I think at first they had hope. I guess I made remarkable progress. I ate everything in sight and grew quickly. I seemed to be especially agile. It was like all the energy in my body had been bottled up and was now let go. I grew long and lean and my hair grew wonderfully thick and black and would glow with a nearly iridescent light. My teeth remained a pure ivory-white and kept their perfect fanglike curl. My senses were alert. It was as if I could see past and hear past and smell past all the other boys.

They hated me, of course. They made my life miserable. They called me Beast, and Animal, and Devil, and a hundred other names. I think they could have tried to kill me if I hadn't been so good at sensing them and getting away. But, it wasn't really their fault. I see that now. They themselves were only orphaned children faced with a terrible deformity. They were only taking the pain they must have felt and turning it to me. I understand that now.

Their torment made me strong. I learned to speak, though the fangs made it difficult for all the sounds to come out right. I learned to read, nearly devouring the books, so hungry was I for the sound of a human voice that did not mock. I would stay up in my attic room long into the night, reading books by the moon's silver light. It was as if I was being nourished as much by words as meat or grain.

They tried to *place* me, of course. In the beginning there was even a kind of optimism about it, a sense that my deformities were so great they might even work *for* me rather than against me; might even call up a greater sympathy in a potential host. Then, Sister Agnes would come swishing down the attic corridor in her habit, a grim smile on her face.

"Look, you," she would say to me as I stood at attention beside my narrow bed. "We have a live one this time."

Then we would begin the long walk down to the "viewing" room, past the dormitories where the boys would line up to jeer and taunt me.

"Beast. Animal. Monster," they would shout, until an icy stare from Sister Agnes would silence them.

And all the time Sister Agnes would be instructing me.

"Don't smile. Don't let them see your teeth at all. Don't stand in the light. Button your shirt. Don't let them see the hair. . . ."

But, of course, no amount of posing or dimming the light would work for long. No matter how much they kept me in shadows, or bandages, or scarves, sooner or later they would see and gasp and cringe or scream and that would be that. Then there would be the long walk back, the terrible long walk back, past the gauntlet of jeering boys whom Sister Agnes no longer had the heart to silence.

It was after several of these "disappointments," as the Reverend Mother called them, that they decided to do something about my "peculiarities." They began with my teeth. I was taken to a dentist who assured them it was going to be a simple job of filing. It took him a week of steady grinding, but he got the teeth so that they would pretty well fit inside my mouth. But before they could find a suitable "prospect," the teeth started growing back, even longer and more pointed than before. After another round or two, the dentist gave up. After all, I had only been a "charity case."

It was the same thing with the hair. Sister Agnes had, in desperation, made the mistake of shaving me. She had lathered up my whole body, from head to toe, and set about it with a straightedge razor. She shaved off every single hair on my body, every single one. But in a day or two the stubble started to show, and in a few weeks it had all come back, blacker and thicker and more matted than before. And that was more than even Sister Agnes could handle.

But such was her dedication that after a while she found another dentist, a "specialist in deformities," who assured her that the only thing to do, "scientifically and absolutely," was to have the teeth pulled.

"You get at the roots, see, like a tree," he said to Sister Agnes as he peered into my mouth. "And that's the end of that."

It took him quite a while to get them out, though. At first, he thought he could do it by hand, with a pair of pliers. He asked Sister Agnes if she had ever read a book called *McTeague*. There was a dentist in it, he said, who could pull teeth out with just his fingers.

"I'd like to arm wrestle him," he said to me, making a fist and holding out his arm. "Just feel that," he said.

He began with a small set of pliers, and when that wouldn't work, he got larger ones. By the end of the day, he was using ones the size of a plumber's wrench. But the teeth wouldn't budge. And that got him mad. He'd go into the next room and give himself a whiff of oxygen. Then, he'd let out a yell and come storming into the room, grab the pliers, brace himself against the chair and heave. But it was no use.

By then the laughing gas he'd given me had nearly worn off, and the pain was so intense I closed my eyes and imagined I was somewhere else, somewhere far away. I began to dream that I was out in a great wilderness. As I looked around the frozen waste, there was a sudden deafening noise and the ice-floor began breaking up. Instinctively, I leaped for one of the pillars of ice that rose up in great spires into the sky. But my fingers, even with my long nails, slipped on the smooth, slick ice, no matter how hard I tried digging into it. Finally, to keep from sliding into the great black chasm opening beneath me, I jerked my head back and drove my teeth, like enamel pylons, deep into the pillared ice. As I did, a terrible scream filled my ears, shattering my reverie.

I opened my eyes. Beneath me, I could see a man writhing on the ground. Streaks of red ran in parallel lines down his snow-white coat. He seemed to be dangling in the air, as if anchored to some place from which he was desperately trying to free himself.

I blinked my eyes once or twice and everything became distinct again. I was not on some frozen tundra but sitting in the dentist's chair, bent forward, a great weight pulling me down. The hand that was clamped to my mouth was the dentist's hand, and below that was the man himself, hanging by an arm, twisting back and forth, half on the floor, half on the chair. His face was white and distorted. I tried to shake my head and open my mouth and free the dentist, but he was snagged on one of my fangs and wouldn't come loose.

Luckily, there was a medical doctor down the hall. Even with Sister Agnes helping me, it took all my strength to drag the dentist there. Through all this, she had remained calm, serene almost, as if the horror of the situation had lifted her to another plane of endurance—like workers in a leper colony. The other patients fled, of course, when I got him there, so we didn't have to wait. The doctor himself was calm, though, and soon he and his nurse had put the dentist to sleep with some ether, right there on the floor, and cut enough flesh away to get my tooth out.

I felt sorry for the dentist, because the tooth seemed to have severed some important nerve in the hand, the part that had to do with gripping. So his dream of someday pulling teeth with his fingers, like the dentist in *McTeague,* would never be realized. He must have figured his disappointment into the bill he sent to the Home, for between it and the doctor's surgery bill, the amount nearly exhausted the whole year's medical budget. It was this, more than the event itself, I think, that finally broke Sister Agnes.

"You beast," she screamed at me, waving the bills in my face. "You buck-toothed abomination, you. Do you see what you've done?"

When I did not answer, could not answer, she beat me with the leather belt she carried to keep the boys in line. It was as if all the disappointments of her life were written on those papers crushed in her hand. The other boys just stood there, letting the blows rain down on me. I think they, too, were sad and took little comfort in the welts and blood.

Then all at once her fury ended. Her whole body seemed to wilt and shrivel. She took a deep breath to steady herself, but her legs buckled, and she fell onto the bed where she half-lay, half-sat, struggling for air.

I had never seen Sister Agnes so weak, so defeated. And it was all my fault, I knew. I had made her like that. I had brought her down. All I could do was reach out and take the belt from her trembling fingers and begin to hit myself with it. Punish myself. Not only for what I had done to make Sister Agnes so angry with me, but to punish myself for the way she was now, so old and tired and broken. I would make up for all of it, for all the shame and suffering I had brought them.

But even as I began to whip myself, Sister Agnes took a deep breath and slowly lifted herself from the bed. She did not look at me as she did, did not look at me as she brushed past me and through the thin circle of boys surrounding me. She did not look back as she passed out of the attic room and down the stairs that led to the dormitories. And whether she had even seen me whipping myself or understood why, I cannot know.

The years passed. I grew hairier and more alone. Like Sister Agnes I tried my best not to complain, taking the jeers and the blows, both, without anything more than an occasional snarl or baring of my teeth. The boys were at me, of course, but who could blame them. The seven years came and went. Sister Agnes grew older and the sense of defeat was always on her face, no matter how much she tried to hide it.

And then one day Legs came, and the torment transformed itself from loneliness into flesh and blood.

Legs was a head taller than the other boys—mostly from the waist down. He was stronger, too, and that made him a natural leader. What gave him his special power was the ability to focus his hatred, to take all the angers and resentments and pain of the unwanted boys and give it a target. And of course the target was me. Before he came I had been merely a freak, an oddity, a kind of victim. But he made them see that I was the enemy, that I was getting all the attention that should rightfully be theirs, that I was bringing shame to them, that I was turning the Reverend Mother and Sister Agnes against all of them, that I was a monster who would someday devour them.

After Legs came, I had to be on guard all the time. They moved past mocking and jeering. They took to ambushing me, to trying to sneak into my room at night to tie me up and do who knows what. They stole my clothes. They stole my books. They told lies about me. They blamed me for everything. They made my life miserable.

And yet, in a strange way, they gave my life a kind of excitement and meaning. I had to be on guard. I had to sharpen all my senses. No telling when or where they'd try to strike. A nap became an adventure. A trip to the bathroom became a journey into enemy land. Their cries of "Beast" and "Animal" called up the leopard soul in me. And it almost ended in disaster.

It was when I was in training to be a Jew, after Mr. Smyth had come and expressed an interest in a "Jewish-inclined" boy. The Reverend Mother called me to her office, and Sister Agnes had come to get me.

"The Reverend Mother has bought a bullwhip," she told me, "and if you do anything wrong she'll peel your skin from your bones. Do you understand?"

I understood. Though the Reverend Mother was a little bitty thing, she was tough as nails. Once I saw her reach up and grab Legs, who was maybe a foot taller, and drag him by the ears the whole length of the dormitory. I could imagine what she would be like with a bullwhip.

This time, when I came into the office behind Sister Agnes, the Reverend Mother was standing at the window behind her desk, looking out. The whip was in her hand.

"How would you like to become a Jew?" she said, without turning around.

"A Jew?" I said, trying out the word more than anything else.

The Reverend Mother whirled around.

"That's what I said, didn't I?" The whip was coiled in her hand.

"Well, that's nice," I said. "Though I'm happy to be Catholic," I added, not wanting to seem ungrateful.

"What makes you think you're Catholic?" the Reverend Mother said, bringing the whip down forcefully on the desk.

"I've been learning the catechisms," I said, glancing over at Sister Agnes, trying to read her expression.

"What else?" the Reverend Mother shouted.

"I go to Mass and Confession," I said, finding it hard to concentrate. Instead, I kept staring at the whip. In her hands it seemed like a living thing, like a snake, waiting to strike.

"Not anymore," the Reverend Mother said. "Not anymore."

She moved from behind the desk to stand before me. I made certain I kept my head lowered and to one side; sometimes if I didn't, she would grab me by the fangs and jerk me around like a puppet on a string.

"You circumcised?" she said to me, out of the blue.

"He is," Sister Agnes answered for me.

"We do it?" the Reverend Mother asked.

"No, he came that way," Sister Agnes replied.

"Good. Then from now on you're going to be a Jew. Understood?" The hand holding the whip had begun to twitch.

I nodded, my eyes fixed on the whip.

"Make sure he reads only the Old Testament," the Reverend Mother said to Sister Agnes. Then, she moved behind her desk, turned her back to me, and stood looking out the window.

"Move," said Sister Agnes, shoving me out the door.

The next few months were the worst I remember in the Home. To the others, I had already become a Jew, and to their dislike of me for my deformities they now added anti-Semitism.

"Christ-killer," Legs said to me when he found out.

"It figures," said Pee Wee, who was about half Legs's size but just as mean. "A goddamn Jewish warthog."

Before, most of the other boys would pretty much leave me alone, except, of course, when Legs or Pee Wee were goading them on. But now, all of them went out of their way to torment me. I was only allowed to read "Jewish" books, which, according to Pee Wee, meant books on law and medicine. Legs, on his own, decided that I would have to read them from right to left, since he had heard that was how Hebrew was written.

"Figures," Pee Wee said, "they'd do everything ass-backward."

So day and night, night and day, they would be after me, even coming up to my attic room—which they hardly ever did unless led by Legs on an "ambush."

Finally, I could stand it no longer. The whip, the tension, the backward-reading got to me. I went after Legs, waiting till he was coming back from the bathroom, late, in his pajamas. I climbed up on the overhead boiler pipes and leaped down on his back when he passed under me. I think I had just wanted to scare him, so that he would leave me alone. I figured if he quit, the others would as well, because gangs of bullies are usually only as brave as their leader. But a curious thing happened. A kind of wildness took over. Maybe it was the waiting on the pipes; the hiss of the steam filled the air like the sound of a thousand snakes. All I know is that it felt so good to just drop on top of him, to feel him trying to squirm out from under me. I felt this deep urge to drag him away, up the stairs to my attic room. I even grabbed his leg and pulled him along, marveling at how light he seemed, how weightless.

I was about to open the door to the attic stairs when Pee Wee and some of the other boys came running out of the dormitory.

"He's got Legs. He's got Legs," Pee Wee started shouting.

They came and formed a sort of half-circle around me. I stood over Legs, crouched low, waiting for one of them to make a move. I could hear myself growling. I wasn't going to let anybody get Legs away from me.

One of the boys tried lunging at me. I whirled and got him across the arm with my upper teeth. He let out a howl and stumbled backward. I started growling louder and louder.

In the end, Sister Agnes brought things under control. She came flying into the hallway in a fury, swinging her leather strap right and left. It didn't take long for the place to clear, till only Legs and I were left. He was lying on the floor, moaning softly, his leg cut deeply where my nails had dug in.

"Help me get him to the Infirmary," Sister Agnes said, in a surprisingly gentle voice.

That curious wild feeling had gone out of me by then, and I was glad to help. I felt sorry for Legs. He had no idea what lies in a leopard's heart.

Nothing more was said about the incident. None of the boys ever spoke openly about it. No inquiries were made. I was never officially reprimanded. And from then on, the other boys left me alone. Only Sister Agnes mentioned it. She came to me a few nights later, as I was lying in my bed in the attic.

"What were you going to do with him?" she asked.

"Bring him up here," I said.

"And then what?"

I closed my eyes, trying to remember. But it was all dark and uncertain, all but the memory of that urge to drag him up.

"I don't remember." I was beginning to feel the saliva run in my mouth.

Sister Agnes quickly crossed herself, her eyes fixed on my face. Without another word she turned and walked away. That was all.

A day or two later, Legs returned from the infirmary with his leg thickly bandaged. For a week or two, he had to be helped around by some of the other boys. I offered to let him lean on me, but he just glared at me.

"One day," he said, hobbling away and mumbling, "I'm gonna get a gun and shoot you down just like a dog."

Soon after that incident Mr. Smyth and Simon came by again, and took me away from the Home and into the hardware store. And now most of them are dead—Sister Agnes, the Reverend Mother, many of the boys, and Mr. Smyth and Simon. Legs never came after me. I hope if he's still alive, he's forgotten me. Or better yet, forgiven me.

9

Obaman's Woman

NOTHING IS WITHOUT REDEMPTION, NOT EVEN war. The terrible struggle that swept away Simon and all the other millions brought a feverish activity to the ghetto. There were jobs and the promise, at least, of prosperity. A kind of desperate hope set in: the sense that the world was turned upside down and that in such a time those on the bottom might somehow rise.

And Obaman was at the center of it all. He was handsome and tall and regal. He was a scholar and a teacher. He had access to the white man's world, and, above all, he promised his people freedom.

"My father was a Pullman porter," he told me, pride and bitterness mingled in his voice. "Do you understand?"

It was late one evening. We were sitting in his study, a great round room in the center of his house that was filled from floor to ceiling with rows and rows of books, each one numbered and catalogued, as in a library. And why not? They had all been stolen from libraries. "We are only taking back what was taken from us," Obaman said simply, when he saw me looking. I think by that he meant the history of his people, the knowledge and the stories that were left behind and lost when the slave ships came. Obaman told me that there was a time not so long ago when a slave could be whipped or worse for reading from a book. "You fight fire with fire," he told me, pointing at the books. "Silence with truth."

Then he told me about his father. His voice was softened by sadness.

"My father was a brilliant man. He barely had any schooling, but he taught himself to read and write. He even taught himself some Latin. Because he wanted to be a lawyer. Only that. He wanted to use the law to bring his people justice."

"What happened?"

"An old story," Obaman said. "An old, old story. His father died, so my father had to go to work. Then he found someone to love. She gave him children. He loved them, too. But it was hard to care for them. It took all he had. He just grew old that way, one day at a time, and his dream of the law faded."

Obaman had risen from the large leather chair and had begun to pace the room. I thought about the animals in the zoo, how they, too, paced back and forth, scraping themselves against the bars. I guess there are many kinds of cages.

"One day," Obaman began again, "my father heard Marcus Garvey speak about Africa, about a whole continent filled with black men, some kings and warriors, some doctors and lawyers—and about going home again. That talk changed his life—what little there was left of it." Obaman's tone hinted at bitterness and sadness, both. "But it wasn't going back he wanted. No. My father said we had suffered too much for that. That our blood was in the soil as well as our bones.

"Instead, he wanted us to bring Africa here. Right here to America, to the city, to the black beating heart of the city. He wanted us to understand what we had been and what we had done and where we had come from. And what we could be again. That was his dream, this man who had never gone beyond the second grade, and who had spent his whole life polishing plates and pouring water for the white man."

Obaman stopped his pacing, lowered his head. Then he sat back in his chair, staring down at his hands.

"Before he died he called me in. I was the oldest, he reminded me. I would have to carry on for him, for his father before him, right back to whomever it was who had been sold out of Africa, stolen from his past, and present, and future. That furthest-back man, he said. He made me promise, lying on his death bed, his wasted hand gripping mine with the strength of his vision. I was to find out who we were, who we had been. We had been something, he was sure. I was to learn what. And then I was to use that knowledge to lead my people out of misery."

Obaman lifted his head, looked right at me.

"I gave him my word. You understand? Right then and there, as he held my hand, as he looked up at me with those burning eyes. And then he died. He just nodded once, as if it was going to be all right, and closed his eyes and died, leaving it all for me to do. He'd put some money aside. You understand? Saved it all those years. Penny by penny. So I went to school for him. I worked twice as hard as the next one. Twice as hard as all the white boys whose fathers were lawyers. I read everything available on Africa. I worked so hard they had to let me finish, had to give me my degree. But they didn't want to. You know why? Because I told them they had it wrong—those 'Heart of Darkness' writers and historians. Those Europeans who kept teaching about the white man's burden and bringing the light of civilization to the dark of Africa. You know how it came to me? I began looking at beads. Simple beads. Just like these." He reached into his jacket pocket and took out two small beads, ivory in color but girded round with a thin band of black. "And you know what those beads told me? That it hadn't been one way at all. Not only the white man coming in, but the black man going out. Because these beads were made in Africa, by black African hands, and taken north by Africans. And they were bought by white men who were dazzled by their beauty. And the African not only brought with him beads like these, but jewelry made of gold and silver. And he brought with him knowledge and wisdom, the bright polish of civilization. And it was the Arab traders and the European traders who took that back with them and not the other way around. I earned that degree," he said, his strong black hands curling around the ivory beads.

"And then it was time to go back to Africa, in my father's place. For him. For his father. Right back to that first man stolen from Africa. It took me a while but I got there. And I found out who we were and where we had come from. And what we had been. And I wrote it all down. And even those who had fought me the whole time began to call me an authority, a scholar. But I wasn't in Africa for that reason. I wanted to build my father's dream. My people's dream."

"So all this?" I said, letting my arm sweep around the book-lined room. "So the Leopard Man."

Obaman smiled.

"It was easier than I thought," Obaman said, emitting a soft chuckle. "It turned out my father was right. We had come from a long line of kings. How do you like that? Porters over here but princes in Africa. And they remembered. Can you understand? That history had not died out, had not been lost or forgotten. It endured in the stories, in the songs and dances, in the hearts. I knew the language. I knew the places, the names. I knew the rituals. So we made a pact, my African brothers and I. I would go back to America, teach the people about their past and their future. And they, they would raise a woman for me. From the noblest family. Someone pure: the strength and beauty of Africa. And when the time came, they would send her to me. To be my woman. To raise sons for me, sons who would carry on in my name, in my father's name, in my father's father's name."

"And me?" I asked. "What about me?"

Obaman smiled his glittering smile.

"You? Why, you're the living symbol, the life that binds us. Darkness and light. Wisdom and power."

He stood before me, his hand resting on my shoulder.

"Will you help us?"

Now, it was my turn to sit quietly, to stare at my hands. Destiny was a strange thing, more like a mist than a raindrop. It wrapped itself around you as you walked until you could not see another way.

"If I can," I said finally, feeling the pressure of his hand on my shoulder give way.

"Well, then," he said, turning and motioning for me to follow. "It's time for you to meet my woman."

I followed Obaman to the top floor of his house. The whole floor had been set aside for his woman and those who attended her. Outside the heavy wooden doors that led to her quarters stood two leopard-skin men.

I could feel their resentment as we drew near. Hatred leaves its own scent in the air.

When we moved past them into the dim room beyond, I growled low under my breath. Let them think about that for a while—about me, who had no need for hiding behind a dead animal's skin. Obaman turned and stared at me, but he said nothing.

All the rooms were the same: closed-in, with only a few high windows. All Obaman's woman would be able to see were the sky and clouds and whatever could rise to those heights. In a way, her world was as cut off as mine, I who was learning to see the city-world from the bottom of the door in the hardware store—from the waist down, as it were. But she and I might piece together a whole picture of the world. Perhaps that was what Obaman had in mind.

"She has known no man," Obaman used the biblical expression as he led me forward. "She comes from the village of my ancestors. The people raised her to be the perfect African woman. Do you understand?"

"What is that?" I asked him.

He paused at the entrance to another room, turning again to look at me.

"To be black without shame," Obaman said, his voice soft and low and certain. "To remember the long history of our people. And to remain strong."

Before we entered that fateful room, I found myself thinking of Simon, of beauty, of gentleness, of the gray sadness of the cleansing rain. What of all that? Was none of this permitted the perfect woman of Africa?

"Before I make her mine," Obaman said, "before she bears my sons, she needs to learn the ways of the white world." He took a step toward me. "You will teach her."

I had a thousand objections. What did I know about the world, any world, I who had been taught by nuns in the attic of a home for unwanted boys? Who himself had been an outcast, scorned by black and white? Who had to live his life behind a half-opened door, venturing out only in the shadows of the city-night.

Obaman smiled and nodded.

"All that is why," he said. "Because you have seen everything with your leopard's eye." He let himself laugh. "Like a cat watching a bird." Then he turned serious. "Your life has not been an accident," he said. "Not any of it."

She rose as we entered, bowed in a graceful arc, then stood straight, her eyes slightly averted.

"This is my woman," Obaman said, moving to her side, and lifting her face to mine. I never heard him call her by any other name. "And this," he said, "is the Leopard Man."

The girl looked at me, wide-eyed, curious. The inquisitive look of a child filled with wonder. And then she smiled, her whole face brightening. In a very gentle and sweet voice, her accent British-like, she spoke.

"I am honored," she said, and then, as if that were too forward, she lowered her gaze.

Whatever else happened that night, whatever else was said or done, is forever lost in a whirl of images: those clear bright eyes, that smooth black skin, the painted cross on her face, the full ripeness of her naked breasts, the faint light spilling down from the high windows. Whatever is most real must be kept in something other than words, something closer to the heart.

"She is the most beautiful person I have ever seen," I remember saying to Obaman when we were outside, his woman left behind to stare up at the distant window. Obaman gave me one of his hard, probing looks.

"It's a beauty she is hardly aware of." He smiled a slow, ironic smile. "You remember what Aristotle said: 'First a house, then a wife, then an ox.' He thought that was the foundation of civilization. But times have changed," he said, his face softening. "Now we seem to need a leopard instead."

We walked the rest of the way to Obaman's study in silence.

"You will come to her in the evenings," Obaman said, the moment we stepped inside. He talked as if it had all been decided. "You will let her ask you anything. You will answer her in your own way. Do not worry about what the books say. Only what you yourself believe." He smiled. "That's not so hard, is it? To say what you believe?" Then the smile vanished. "No one will force you. You agree to this on your own."

Obaman had baited the trap well. Who could refuse such a task, especially someone like me who could no more expect to find such beauty on his own than he could flap his arms and expect to fly? Obaman knew. Had he not said my life was no accident?

And so I came to teach Obaman's woman what I knew of life. She was remarkable. She could speak a dozen languages. She understood math and science. She knew so much about the history of Africa, about African people. She described it for me. Forests rippling with light. Mountains dripping white on the blue sky. And the people—each with his tribe's face, his tribe's wisdom. Women threshing millet with two-headed pestles till the ground beneath their feet seemed gilded. Men with their backs bent and their muscles knotted, poling long boats up brown and whirling rivers. The dancers, beads clattering and the grasses in their skirts rattling, snaking their way past the smoking huts. And the colors, how she made them fill my eyes: the red cloth of the warriors, the white feathery plumes in their hair, the black earth, the green grass, the crimson and violet sky that draped itself over the whole burning world, the throngs of people in the market, the women with baskets of fruit and vegetables neatly balanced on their heads. The valleys. The plains. The scorching dust. The whole vast teeming continent full of life and death and beauty and suffering.

But as she spoke, as she made me see, I realized her own lack: she had spent so much time learning about the world, she had had no time to live in it—to feel, to taste the world.

What is it like on market day? I asked her.

She was quiet for a long moment.

"A wise man said once, 'There are two joys that define the spirit of Africa—one is when the warriors dance, and the other is when the women go to market.' "

She became silent. You could see that she was thinking deeply, lips pursed, her brow furrowed.

"Was he right?" I asked.

"I cannot say," she said in a whisper. "I have never danced or gone to market."

She had been taught all these things. She had been told about them. She had read about them in books. She had been permitted to watch, even—but always from afar, always as a lesson, something to learn and remember.

It was strange how alike we were for all that surface difference. Her beauty was a wall that kept her from living her life as surely as my deformities kept me from mine. And thus we gave ironic truth to those stories of the beauty and the beast. And I think it's a begrudging world that can accommodate neither.

The first real question I remember her asking came suddenly, after one of her long silences.

"What is loneliness?" she asked with amazing intensity.

I began to tell her what the poets had said, but she cut me off.

"Tell me what you think," she said urgently.

"It's like being lost without a way to come home," I began. She interrupted me.

"Those are words," she said, almost with a trace of anger. "Obaman has told me the same thing. He has said that 'Loneliness is a hut with no fire.' But that is only something he has read in a book." She leaned toward me, and her hand felt like a burning flame on my arm. "When is it you feel this loneliness?" she asked.

I thought long and hard. So many times, so very many. All the while she watched me with those great dark eyes.

"When I look at myself in the mirror," I answered finally.

She said nothing. But she lifted her fingers to my face, touching it lightly. Then she turned away.

Hers was a strange life. Most honored of all the women around her, she was surely the most unhappy. I remembered stories of ancient kings and queens, how they had been viewed as living gods. Yet each day of their lives had been laid out for them, end to end, with the ritual certainty of imprisonment. Lords over others, they in turn were lorded over by history and fate. And in a way, this was the life of Obaman's woman. The spirit of Africa, Obaman called her, remembering only the role he had chosen for her, forgetting that she, too, had a past and a future that was being stolen away.

Many times I came in quietly and caught her staring up at the window. It was then my heart rushed out to her. I saw a cruelness in the fact that for all my deformity I had the freedom to come and go, while she, with all her beauty, had none. So I tried to make it up to her, to teach her how to wring from life its hidden secrets. I was not the Leopard Man for nothing. I taught her how to taste the air, to listen for the faintest sound. I taught her how to let each sense come alive, rise up from all the shadowy depths where reason and language had banished it. And she learned, for she was more than the spirit of Africa, she was the spirit in all of us.

Often we sat in the silent room, at dark, looking up at the window.

"What do you hear?" I asked.

"Nothing," she said.

"Listen again."

She tilted her head side to side, straining to hear.

"Tell me what is out there?" I said again.

"People walking in the streets. In leather shoes."

"Go on."

"And windows opening and closing."

"Yes."

"And someone slamming a car door."

"Good. Good," I shouted.

"And there are cats in the alley, by the garbage cans."

"Yes. Yes. How many?"

I taught her to scent the air, to draw it deep inside her nostrils and filter it, sift it, with eyes open and brain quiet. After all, we were hunters once, creeping along a forest trail, sniffing for danger.

And I taught her about machines, about how America had grown strong with its machines. And we talked of war, mistress of invention; how the need to kill had made us clever with our hands. I told her to think of machines as living things, with lives of their own.

"We give life to those machines," I told her. "But sometimes they turn around and feed off us, like parasites."

I told her about factories where some people slaved away their lives serving the machines, weary and broken by nightfall.

"Have they no choice?" she asked, and I knew she was also thinking of her own life.

It was my turn to be silent. What does it mean to choose? I wanted to believe that no life was cast in stone. That when you added up all the obligations laid down in blood and bone, there was still time to go this way

83

or that. Though I knew better than most the power of pain and sorrow, I wanted to believe that no matter how fierce the push and shove, we still could choose to go laughing or crying.

"We can only hope so," I said finally, thinking of Simon on his road and the leopard in his cage.

I T WAS A PUZZLING TIME DURING THOSE DAYS IN THE
ghetto. All around us the world had divided itself into two
great hordes that hurled themselves at each other. The names
of distant battlefields drifted down to us like dead leaves
falling from trees. But there, in the heart of the city, we were
strangely unaffected. Some of Obaman's followers were gathered up by the military, but others took their place. There
were rumors of nighttime raids on the Selective Service of-
fices.

"Our time will come," Obaman would say to me. "We
must be patient."

I was torn by a hundred different emotions. Whatever my
origins, I was now an American. And then there was Simon,
already lost to me. Yet, I felt a deep loyalty to Obaman, to
what he stood for. And I was bound to his woman by a sympathy that reached to the very depths of my being.

One day spilled into the next with a kind of seamless texture: my days spent as before in the hardware store, my nights
at Obaman's as the Leopard Man. After Simon's death, I quit
going to Hebrew school. Mr. Smyth barely protested. It

seemed such a foolish thing, then, to study three-thousand-year-old texts while the world was trying to destroy itself. So I never became a Jew in the strict, ceremonial sense. But in all these years on Friday nights, I try to light a candle. I do this for Simon.

One night, after a wild storm, I heard a light tap on my attic door, a tap so faint even I wasn't sure that I had heard anything. When it came again I roused myself from my chair by the window. But who could it be? No one ever came to see me except Simon, and he was gone.

When I opened the door, there stood Obaman. He wore a long black raincoat slick with rain. He was hatless. Beads of water slid down his two spiral braids like tiny crystal animals descending a rope. Neither of us spoke, but stared at one another while a small pool of water formed at our feet.

"Come in," I told him, opening the door. "Please."

He refused something warm to drink, saying only, "I am content." It was an expression he often used.

He walked around the room like a detective searching for something, touching everything, his long fingers absorbing the texture of whatever caught his eye. Presently, he sat down in the chair by the window.

"Nothing on the walls," he said, "but mirrors."

I suddenly felt embarrassed.

"Do you look at yourself often?" he asked, turning to me.

"Yes," I admitted. "Often."

"Why?"

I waited, remembering the times I had stood facing the mirror, looking at myself until my eyes blurred, trying to see past the deformities into my heart, into my soul, to see if they, too, were deformed.

"I don't know why," I said, finally. "Maybe to find out what I am."

Obaman kept staring at me.

"Would you like to come with me and hear a story?" Obaman asked suddenly.

"A story?" I said, but already Obaman was standing, putting on his coat, moving toward the door.

"Will you come?" he asked.

I followed him into the storm-spent night. We moved deep into the ghetto again, staying always in the shadows and the back alleys. "Better this way," Obaman said.

We came to a large, run-down building, the kind that always seems on the verge of falling down. The building's history was the city's. Each wave of restless immigrants carved its name in the stone and then moved on. Inside, the stench of urine and trash nearly gagged me.

"That's decay," Obaman said, waiting for me to recover. "You can smell it everywhere."

We found some stairs and walked down to the basement, then through a long, low concrete room filled with pipes that looked like thick vines in the dull yellow light. At the far end was a passageway that we followed until we came to a narrow steel door.

"The man inside," Obaman said, nodding toward the door, "is very old and powerful. In his own time and place he was a king. Even now," Obaman continued, his voice filled with intensity and respect, "he has the power of life and death. You must understand that."

"Will he be the storyteller?" I asked.

Obaman smiled that dazzling porcelain smile of his.

"If he chooses," Obaman said, and banged three times loudly on the door.

We waited. Nothing happened. I strained to listen but heard nothing beyond the noise of the old building. I made a move to pound on the door, but like the dart of a snake, Obaman reached out and grabbed my wrist.

"Don't do that," he said tensely. He managed a slight smile. "Please."

As the door opened, light wisps of smoke drifted out to us. The smoke had a strange, sweet smell as if someone were cooking honey or the petals of roses. A face appeared in the doorway. I recognized it immediately. It was the old man who had given me the necklace of fangs that night in the zoo.

"It is good you have come." He spoke in barely a whisper. Turning, he moved down a smoke-filled hallway and disappeared through a doorway on the right. He moved with a speed and agility that seemed to belie the years on his face. I followed after him. Obaman, closing the door, came behind me. The pleasing sweet smell filled the hall, intoxicating almost, but never to the point of overwhelming.

I turned right through the doorway the old man had used, and entered a most unusual room: no windows or doors, and no furniture. Everything was painted black—ceiling, walls, floor. And strewn about the floor were the skins of several animals. The old man was sitting on a lion skin, its mane full and flowing. He motioned for Obaman to sit on the skin of a tiger. Between these two was the skin of a black leopard. The old man nodded. I sat on it, over where its powerful neck and shoulders met.

The old man waited until we both were settled. Then he closed his eyes and began rocking back and forth, his legs crossed under him. Back and forth, back and forth, he rocked. Over and over again. Obaman and I sat in silence, in the darkness and the smoke, waiting.

"There is a village in a clearing," the old man began suddenly, eyes closed and still rocking back and forth, back and forth, "with many huts and many fires. But no one to tend them. A man has come to the village. And a woman. Their skins are white. The drums have foretold their coming."

It was eerie listening to the man speak like that, as if he were hearing the drums himself, as if it were all taking place right before him and he was describing it for us. I glanced over at Obaman. He was gazing at the old man, perhaps trying to see what he saw.

"The man is tall. He carries a gun. The woman is slender. Her hair is the color of gold. It burns in the sun. She looks like a yellow flower.

"They bring along other men with them, black men, to carry the guns. The man wishes to hunt. He brings gifts. He offers them to the villagers. Many bright things, beads and cloth. The cloth is red, blood-red. The man goes on alone. He leaves the woman behind. She is with child and cannot go far. The man does not return.

"They call to him with the drums. But he does not answer. It is told that a leopard wounds him. He will not return, they say, until he kills it, or it kills him.

"But it is time for the woman to give birth. She suffers much pain. The old women attend her. They cool her fever. At last she delivers the baby, a boy, a strange, yellow-eyed child covered with hair.

"The woman is dying. She calls for her child. Someone holds him before her. She takes him to her breast. No milk but the baby begins to suck. Then the woman cries out, a long, terrible cry. She rises up from the mat. The child clings to her. She falls back, dying. Her eyes stay open.

"They take the child from her. A woman comes from the village to nurse the child, to give milk. They wrap the dead woman in reeds and place her body on a wooden platform. They light a fire. The child watches as the flames burn.

"Later the man returns. He is no longer tall and straight, but bent. The man cannot find the leopard. The drums speak of it. They tell the man of the death of his woman. They tell him about the child. The villagers take him to see the boy. The woman holds the child at her breast. The man stands at the door of the hut. He will not enter. He stares at the child who turns to look at him. The man turns and walks out. He takes only his gun. He leaves the village, alone. They never hear from him again.

"But not the leopard. The leopard lives. The leopard comes to kill the people of the village. The people gather together. They speak of the child. Some say kill the boy, that he is evil. Others say give the boy to the leopard. Finally they decide to take the child to the white man's huts, far away. If the leopard is angry, let the leopard make war with the white man.

"They choose a man from the village to carry the child. The man is afraid but accepts his duty to his people. He carries the child deep into the forest. Suddenly a terrible roar fills the air. It stills the man's heart. His blood freezes. He drops the child and runs.

"Into the clearing leaps a great leopard. Black, blacker than black. A female, carrying a dead cub in her mouth. The man watches as the leopard puts down the limp cub and licks it. But the cub does not move. The leopard lifts her head and again roars. Everything in the forest is silent and afraid. The man in hiding fears the leopard will hear his heart beating.

"Suddenly the leopard raises her head, smells the air. The man imagines the leopard discovers him. He sees his death as terrible, as certain. Instead the leopard smells the child lying in the blanket on the trail. The leopard comes and begins to lick the child. As she does, one of her udders brushes the child's lips. The boy begins to suck. The leopard stands quietly letting the child suck. Then she lowers that great black head and takes the child gently in her mouth. Slowly, the leopard moves away, leaving behind the dead cub."

The old man stopped his rocking. He lifted his face and opened his eyes to stare directly at me.

"I was that man, the one chosen to carry the child to the white man's huts." He lowered his head. "In that I failed."

I felt pity for the old man. He seemed ashamed when he said that. If what he said was true, who could blame him?

"But from that failure—if a failure is what it was—came a greater blessing, a greater act of courage," said Obaman to me, to the old man.

"One deed does not undo another," the old man muttered. He began his slow rocking again, his lids half-closed.

"No one knew what this meant, this taking of the child by the she-leopard. Some saw it as a gift from the ancestors: a child of the white man nursed at the breast of a black woman, then taken by the fiercest of animals and raised to learn the terrible secrets of the leopard's heart.

"They said that we had been given a warrior to lead us. But that first we ourselves had to act like warriors. We had to find the courage to claim that child, to steal him back from the leopard."

The old man became silent, perhaps the strain of remembering too much for someone old and frail. I wondered whether he might collapse under the weight of the memory.

"Perhaps the she-leopard could hear our thoughts," the old man began again, his voice so low I could barely hear him, for all my keen hearing. "Because even as we whispered this, that leopard came among us, as if she would punish us even for our dreams."

The old man opened his eyes, fixed his gaze on me. I felt a terrible cold, like being frozen in a great block of ice. The pain on his face reflected the great sorrow he was remembering.

"And so it began," Obaman said quietly, speaking for the old man. "A reign of terror such as no one has known. There was nothing the people could do. No magic strong enough. The greatest warrior was like a boy before it. The spirit-men were like weak old women."

When Obaman finished saying that, the old man closed his eyes again and began speaking, until it was like a litany, each to each.

"Shall I tell you the dreams of the village?" he whispered. "Shall I tell you the dreams of a people doomed? Of how darkness became a curse? Shadows a terror?"

The old man's head was bowed, but I sensed his agony.

"She preyed on us," he said. "Like we were cattle. No more. No less. We served her great hunger. That was our life from beginning to end. To wait for her coming."

"She took old women," Obaman said, taking up his part of the story. "Young men in the pride of their manhood. Children. She spared no one."

"This I have seen," the old man continued, lifting his head. "A man and a woman lie asleep in a hut. Between them, a child. The door is barred. The window is barred. There is a slight stirring in the air, a cold wind down from the hills. With only a faint snap, a creak, the window gives way. A shadow falls on the sleeping family. And then the child is gone. No sound. Nothing. Only later the people hear the cries of the man and the woman.

"This is how we lived. To be alone meant to risk certain death. No matter where. Or when. A man would set out for another village and never return. A woman would open the door for a single breath of air and be gone forever."

Obaman waited for the old man's words to cease, before he began again.

"This is why my people say that destiny is a great stone you cannot cast away. And because there was nothing the people could fear worse, they spoke again about the child. They said that if they could steal the child, perhaps they could use it to lure the mother."

"You see, before," the old man picked up the story, his eyes on me, "when we had put out pigs or calves or even dogs that had been pets, the leopard would not come; or if she came she would not be seen. In the morning the calves and dogs would be ripped open but not eaten."

"You understand?" Obaman said to me. "It was only human flesh the leopard would eat. Nothing else."

"So at last it was agreed," the old man continued. "The people would choose someone from the village to give his life for the people." He was looking right at me when he said this.

"Do you understand?" Obaman said again. "Someone would serve as bait for the leopard; draw her away while the village searched for the child."

I sat silent and stunned. My head began to swirl; the room began to spin about me. The blackness of the room became the blackness of the night, the blackness of my soul. I could feel thoughts, images, whirling through my brain, leaping from synapse to synapse. One by one, smothering shadows closed in on me, grotesque and distorted. I covered my ears with my hands.

"No. No!" I heard myself scream. "No more." My head pained to bursting, so terrible. The death. The slaughter. I felt somehow that I was responsible.

Someone was shaking me. I looked up. Obaman was standing over me.

"You must listen," he said. "You must recognize the sacrifice."

I tried to break away.

"No," I pleaded. "I can't."

The black walls had begun to spin. Obaman's face was so close to mine it looked like a carved mask. The old man sat hunched on the floor, rocking back and forth. I had to get away.

Obaman pushed me down. I saw his throat looming before me, the veins in his neck thick and pulsing from exertion. I began reaching for it, as if it were a great vine I could climb to freedom. I felt it coming close, could hear the blood surging, could smell the blood even through the skin. And then I heard a terrible scream and the pressure on my shoulders eased. The darkness seemed to erupt, the whole world black and raging.

And then it stopped, leaving me in stillness. I took a deep breath and opened my eyes. The room ceased to spin. I was crouched in a corner. Beneath me, stretched out on the floor, was Obaman. The old man was standing beside me, looking down at Obaman.

I followed his gaze and saw gashes on Obaman's throat, blood seeping in rhythm with his breathing. I saw blood on my hands, warm and sticky. I lifted myself off Obaman, my legs weak. Obaman's fingers pressed on the wounded flesh at his neck. He, too, rose shakily to his feet.

The old man held out a cloth to Obaman. He peered at his throat.

"Not deep," he said. "You are lucky."

He moved off into another room. I stood as before, looking over at Obaman. We said nothing. There was nothing to say.

"Put this on the wound," the old man said, coming back with a bowl filled with a paste that smelled like rotting vegetation.

Obaman smeared some on his neck.

Over the paste, the old man put on the white cloth. Then he turned to me.

"We should not have tried to hold you," he said gently.

I looked from him to Obaman and then back again.

"I don't understand," I said. Everything from before seemed far in the distance, long ago.

The two men looked at each other but said nothing.

"Just as well," the old man said, sitting again on his lion's rug. "I am very tired."

Again, he seemed frail, more like a spirit than a man. I bent down before him.

"Why did you tell me this?" I asked, afraid he would not hear me, afraid he would.

He took a deep breath. "I thought you should know."

I looked over at Obaman. There were faint red lines showing through the bandage.

"I will stay with the Okombo," he said, the first time he had used that name.

"I'm sorry," I said, but I didn't know why or to whom I said it, only that I should.

I was a long time returning to my room. The night air felt cool and smooth against my skin, like black water pouring down from a mountain stream. I let myself bathe in the darkness, traveling the narrow alleys like paths cut through a thick, wet forest. Back in my room, I crawled into bed without looking in the mirror. I slept that night without dreaming.

11
The Wrestling Match

O BAMAN CAME TO SEE ME A FEW DAYS LATER,
after I had finished my work in the hardware store
and had gone up to my room. He was wearing his "day-suit,"
as he called it, his professor's garb. He looked different in his
suit, older, less imposing, as if civilization had whittled him
down somehow. He had a small bandage on his neck.

I asked him to forgive me, but he would have none of it.

"We each do what we must," he said.

"What is the truth of my life?" I asked him suddenly, the
words settling on my lips even as I thought them. I had been
thinking of nothing else since that night with the Okombo.
The story had gone straight to my heart—lodged there—yet
it seemed just beyond the light of meaning.

Dreams, visions, memories—who can sort them out, and
what is their difference? My head was filled with pictures,
day and night, waking, sleeping. Blue houses, red skies, black
shadows—a whole theater in my head. And everything,
everything, just beyond the naming.

"What is the truth of anything?" Obaman said, faintly
smiling. I imagined that many people asked him questions

like mine. "The African has a saying: What is the lion's roar to a river's stone?"

"Or a dream to a man?" I said.

"Or a dream to a man," Obaman repeated, and he sounded very tired.

"Sit, please," I told him, motioning to the chair by the window. He sat.

"Will you tell me the rest?" I asked. "Please."

Obaman sat still. Only his fingers moved, instinctively going to the bandage on his neck.

"Please," I said, coming before him, ready to go to my knees even. "I promise nothing. . . ."

He silenced me by beginning to speak.

"One day two men came out of the forest, carrying on a pole . . . a human child. Or something like a child." He paused, turned to me. "Though his skin was burned by the sun, he was not an African child. And he was covered with hair, thick, black hair, like an animal. And out of the child's mouth curved teeth such as no human child had. And instead of nails, claws grew from the fingers. They said the child twisted on the pole, growling like a wild animal."

"Was this him," I asked, "the child of the leopard?"

"They said the leopard had done her job well—human child with a leopard's heart," Obaman said.

"And the leopard?" I asked, whispering the words, looking down at my hands, covered as they were with thick, black hair, and at the sharpened nails that curved from my fingers.

"Killed finally, they say," Obaman spoke out of the gloom that had settled after the crimson sunset. "In a trap. They found later a bullet lodged in her flank."

I let the words sink in. It was a curious sensation, hearing about the death of the leopard. I felt moved, even as I remembered the stories of her kills.

"What then?" I asked.

"The child was too wild to keep in the village," Obaman said. "So it was taken finally to a mission house."

"And from there?"

Obaman smiled his bright, intelligent smile again.

"To America . . . the land of the free."

I saw him glance quickly out of the window and I had a sudden premonition. I moved near Obaman, by the side of the window. The night had closed in, but across the street and beyond the ring of light from the street lamps, I could see two figures. Even in the dark, their steel claws shone.

"I do not like them," I told him.

He stared at me intently.

"They serve a purpose," Obaman said, his voice surprisingly gentle.

I looked back at the Leopard Men and then down at Obaman. He was smiling again.

"We all have a purpose."

"And mine?" I said.

Obaman rose slowly.

"Your time has come." He reached into his jacket pocket and took out the front page of a newspaper. The headlines read: "Japs shell Oregon."

Obaman walked slowly to the door.

"We must make ourselves ready," he said, as he was leaving. "Tomorrow, we begin."

I waited a moment after he had gone, then made my way over to the window. I saw Obaman hurrying down the darkened street. After him, barely visible in the night-dark, followed the two leopard-skinned men. As I watched, one turned back and raised a steel-clawed fist. I sat in the chair where Obaman had sat. I felt empty, light enough to float away, as if there was nothing holding me to the earth—not even gravity. I gripped the chair to keep myself from drifting off to nothingness. I sat that way until morning, and the clear gravitational light of day.

The next night Obaman called us all together, in that vast room with the leopard on the wall.

"We must prepare ourselves for the long struggle ahead," Obaman said, standing on the large stone by the fire-pit. "This will be our one chance, when the white man has his back turned to us."

My task, I learned, was to train the men for the "righteous, bloodless, reclaiming," as Obaman called it. I was to teach the men the leopard's ways.

Obaman was certain we could succeed.

"They cannot afford to ignore us," he announced with absolute calm and certainty. "Not now. Not any longer. Not at this moment in history." Everything pointed to this moment, he believed. "If we rise up now, in the heart of the cities where they have banished us, they will see that they are lost without us. They cannot fight the Germans and the Japanese and us, too. They cannot turn their back on us any longer. They will have to make peace with one or the other. Which one will it be? The Japanese devils? The German madmen? Or us, the abandoned sons and daughters of their slaves? They will see that righteousness and expedience are fused together. They will have no choice but to give us back our freedom."

Obaman made it all sound so grand, so sensible, so just. Under the press of war, the white man would need to bury his hatred and his prejudice. He would have to extend his hand to his black brother. If he wanted his cooperation; if he wanted his help, his strong black hands, his strong black back; if he wanted all that, he would need to redeem his long-forgotten pledge: that all men were created equal and had a right to live free and to dream.

And if he wouldn't?

Then, he would have to learn to live with his back against the wall. "The way *we* have," said Obaman.

I was to teach the men about the night and darkness. Knowing about machines, I was to teach the men how to shine the black man's light on them, so that they would work for us, not against us, so that the magic power of technology would be ours as well. I would be the living symbol of the future, the "new man," as Obaman called me, someone with the heart of a leopard and the brain of a man.

"We need someone to teach us to remember," Obaman said, "to re-mind us what we have been and must become."

After the years of shame, I was to stand in the illuminated center of that changing world. All that had set me apart, isolated me, was now to give me worth and meaning. How can I say what that was like, that miraculous transformation? There are tales that tell of such things, but this was much more. For it was not something external, something bestowed, but something welling up from within. I was the same. It was the world that reformed.

I taught the men how to sniff the air for danger, how to listen for the slightest sounds that rustled in the shadows. I taught them about the darkness, how darkness was a cloak they could wrap around their shoulders.

We stalked the streets like lions and tigers, hidden whether beside the street lamps or in the dull glow that never faded from the city night. We passed through the parking lots of police stations and were never seen. We hid in the shrubbery outside the courthouses and prisons and were never heard. We climbed to the roofs of bank buildings and left no trace. We were like an invisible army walking in the shadows of others, a breath away, but never, never seen.

Each day I worked in the hardware store, then went to Obaman's house or out on missions, then back to my room for an hour or two of dreamless sleep. My only regret now was how little time I had to think of Simon, or to see Obaman's woman. For she, too, was caught up in the whirlpool of the times. History had cast her on the high shore of deliverance. The day was coming when she would be a queen among her people, Obaman's chosen, mother of the New Man.

Is it any wonder, then, that in those glorious days I never paused long enough to ask what vision of the future Obaman and his followers held? Freedom was a word no one could question. All around us the city was decaying. No one who lived there could pretend otherwise. For all its frenzied life, the ghetto was dying faster than it could be reborn. The days and nights were still full of hurt and hunger. The black man trudged home weary and bitter. He sat in the corners and came in the back doors. He was the last to be taken on and the first to be let go. For all the glitter, the laughter, the show of wealth, the poetry and the song, nothing could erase the stale stench of decay. Those who broke away were afraid to look back—remembering Lot and his wife. So, if we didn't ask hard questions; if we didn't demand a map and a blueprint for everything, who can blame us? When you're in the dark water and going down, you grab the first hand that reaches for you.

Obaman's stories made our hearts sing. We saw what he saw. He drew back the veil of time and let us see such splendors our own imaginations failed us. Whispered names became the stuff of dreams: Kush and Mali, Aethiopia, Bantu and Hamite, Timbuktu. Obaman wove such a tapestry of power and beauty and wealth, we sat in hushed awe: we, the grandsons and granddaughters of slaves and porters and who knows what else. He made us see what others had forgotten or never knew or concealed. Can you understand? If now we know more about the whole shining past of Africa, if we know that the Dark Continent was strung with beads of dazzling light, it is because Obaman helped make it so. It was he who wrote the first books, who inspired his students and their students to climb the mountains and lower themselves into the gorges, to scrape beneath the earth and the blown sand.

One minute we were there in the heart of the ghetto, the whole world bleeding around us, and the next we were standing on a steep hill looking down first at Ghana, then at Mali, then at Kanem and Songhay.

And what did we see, what pictures did Obaman paint for us? We saw the vast plains of the great savannas, great shimmering plateaus of grass and heat veined with brown and green rivers full of life, full of commerce. And everywhere, black men and women going about the business of civilization, living and dying to the sound of their own black drummers drumming: soldiers with quilted iron armor, long sharp spears flaming in the African sun; judges, doctors, priests—all in the service of an enlightened king who believed in justice and learning. And even after the coming of the white man, Obaman made us see the rows of sun-washed houses, the immaculate streets swept clean of desert sand, the mosques of Islam, the temples of Christ, the smoking huts of the spirit men, the palaces, the universities—yes, the universities where scholars pored over books and maps and charts even as the white man in Europe comforted himself with stories of blacks with heads for navels, feasting on the flesh of men.

That was why Obaman was such a powerful force. I see that now. For here was a man who had gone into the wilderness that was Africa, and he had come back filled not with gold or diamonds or the skins of leopards, but with more precious riches: a people's past, a people's history, a people's soul. And he remembered his brothers and sisters. He was not seduced by the outside world, by its wealth or honors. Rather, he used that world to strengthen his people, to deliver them. He came back and because he had gone into places they never could—and returned—they both loved and feared him. And to be loved and feared like that is a terrible thing.

Obaman took them all in: the downtrodden, the dispossessed, the hopeless, murderers, addicts, prostitutes, men who could neither read nor write, who never had a sober day in their lives—all of them Obaman claimed for his own.

I remember a man who had spent his life scraping the streets like a human rodent, taking up scraps and cigarette butts dropped on the sidewalks and the sewers. Day by day, he lived only to save enough, or steal enough, or beg enough to buy a cheap bottle of wine.

"You got to understand, brother," he said to me once. "This fire in me was burning me up, done killing me. I knowed it, like I knowed my own hand. And all that there drinking I was doin' wasn't gonna wash it away. But, brother, it sure felt good goin' down. You know what I'm saying? It done felt good goin' down."

Obaman had reached out to take this man and lift him out of the gutter and give him something to believe in. He put him in charge of caring for the books in the study. This man who could hardly read, whose hands trembled, kept those books polished and shined and without a tear. He knew in his head where on the shelves to find any book. He would shuffle over and climb on his little wooden stool and bring it down for you. He would give it to you with such pride and reverence that you could say almost—and it wouldn't be a lie—that Obaman had brought him back from the dead.

There were many others like that. Obaman shined a light into their lives and made them forget about their despair. He promised only that he would teach them about who they had been, and what they were, and what they could be again. Whatever they did with that understanding was up to them. Enough for him, he said, that they would know.

The times that I remember best, the times when I was most filled with awe and delight, were those devoted to the living history of Obaman's people. For Obaman was a scholar almost before he was anything else.

I want to tell about the night of the wrestlers. It was as if centuries of time had been swept away, and we were living not in the ghetto, but in some glorious age past. The house was lit with torches, a beacon alongside the cemetery. The great room at the end of the hall with the mounted leopard was cleared, and the floor was covered with sand.

The drumming began, not low or soft, but furious, driving, throbbing, pounding, sending blood coursing through our veins. The old men entered first. They sat on long wooden benches pushed against the far wall, under the leopard skin. Next came the young men, those who were only beginning their training as warriors. They sat at the feet of the elders. Then the men themselves, the warriors, entered, till the whole vast room was filled with spectators. No women were allowed.

And then, from the hallway, the wrestlers for the evening entered. What a sight they were: dressed in breechcloths to which were attached cowtail belts wrapped tightly in leather strips or ribbons of brightly colored cloth. Their black skins were covered with gray ashes, their heads shaved and streaked with ceremonial rings of black paint, their muscles gleaming in the wildly flickering light.

The drums ceased and Obaman and the old man, the Okombo, moved into the room. All eyes turned to them. Obaman nodded his head and several men held up the hollowed curving horns of water buffalo and blew three loud blasts on them. Then the Okombo gave each of the wrestlers a blessing, saying it in a language I did not understand, but which Obaman once translated for me.

"You have passed from a boy to a man, from a man to a warrior. Soon you will pass from a warrior to a spirit that will live forever. Until then, may you live bravely."

Then the Okombo sprinkled a mixture made of the blood and milk of cattle on each man, and took his place of honor in the ebony chair beside the fire-pit. Obaman stepped forward into the center of the room, holding each wrestler by an arm.

"Brothers," he said to us, "this is the time for strength and cunning." Then he nodded and each one of the old men in back rose and said some lines, chanting them, as if they were verses from a single poem. And so it would go, until all the old men had spoken, until the old song was done. I cannot remember many of the words now, but some are etched into my soul.

The woman mourns. Her son is gone.
He has left her hut, forsaken her.
He goes to be a man.
When he is a man he will return.
He will take a woman.
He will take his lands.
He will be a father to his sons.

His mother will welcome him.
He has returned.
He has returned to the village.
He has become a man.

At the end of the chanting the drummers started up again, this time low, insistent. Obaman led the evening's two wrestlers to the center of the room. He made a mark in the sand encircling them, a circle to serve as the ring. The two men began to stalk each other. Then one leaped at the other and the wrestling started in earnest. The strength and stamina of the wrestlers was amazing. Sometimes they would be locked in a rigid embrace for long minutes, almost like lovers. Their faces were twisted from the effort, sweat pouring down, mingling with the ashes to form a chalky paste on their backs and arms. They grunted as they strained, gasping for air. Then, in a sudden thrust, one man would catch the other off balance and whirl or heave him to the floor. He pounced on him like a jungle cat and pinned his shoulders to the floor.

Immediately, Obaman nodded to the drummers who then drummed a loud crescendo. The buffalo horns were blown, signaling the end of the match. Everyone cheered as the victor rose, his arm raised in victory. Obaman walked to the center of the room. He took each wrestler by the arm.

"Here is the victor," he said, raising the winner's arm. "And here is the man he vanquished." And he held that man's arm up in the air. "The glory of the victor is earned by the strength and skill of the man he defeats. Thus no shame in winning or losing."

Both men embraced and the drumming commenced again. The

women entered, bearing bowls of food and drink. They crowded around both winner and loser, not knowing which was which, in open admiration of their strength and beauty. Singing and dancing followed and many times the young men engaged in their own practice matches, honing the skills they would need on the day they had to fight in earnest.

On a Sunday night, the evening before another match was to be held, Obaman came to me, once again knocking faintly at my door. He neither smiled nor spoke any word of greeting.

"The men would have you wrestle," he said upon entering.

"Me?" I said, surprised, confused. "I've never done anything like that before."

Obaman managed a grin.

"The Leopard Man doesn't need to be taught, does he?" he said.

And then I knew. Even symbols had to defend their honor.

"And if I win?"

"Some will hate you," Obaman said.

"And if I lose?"

"No telling what might happen should the Leopard Man lose," Obaman said, without the slightest trace of a smile. Then he reached inside his coat and took out a small bundle which he handed me. "From the Okombo," Obaman said. "It seems he has faith in you."

Obaman left. I opened the package. Inside I found a breechcloth like the ones the wrestlers wore, only this one was black and before ever I touched it or smelled it I knew it had been made from the skin of a leopard. Next to it was a cowtail belt, bound tightly by strips of leopard skin.

That night the old dreams returned. I felt a relief when the sunlight streaked into the room, rousing me. The next day was a busy day in the store, and soon it was night again.

I went to Obaman's carrying my leopard skin. Two men led me into a small room. They called it the "spirit room," a place of meditation. Each wrestler was left for a while in such a room, to ready himself for the coming battle. I put on the breechcloth made of leopard and sat on the floor in the semidarkness. I felt exhilarated. Everything around me had the sharp, powerful smell of masculine strength. There were no women smells anywhere, nothing but sweat and animal skins. I felt wonderfully in tune with my body, as if I could feel the blood surging from my heart to each muscle in my body. I gave my will to muscle and bone, as if they alone defined me. So powerful was that mood that only after a while did I realize I had begun to growl.

A man appeared in the doorway. He smelled familiar. I recognized the Okombo.

"It is time," he said.

I rose and came over to him.

"I am afraid," I said.

"Of what?" he asked me.

"Of something deep inside," I said, trying to give it words.

He put his hand on my arm, a dry and leathery hand.

"Be yourself," he said. Then he let go of my arm and moved slowly down the narrow hallway, motioning for me to follow.

I closed my eyes. The old man's words seemed like a command. They comforted me. I felt light and free. I would be myself, whatever that was.

The room was full, fuller than it had ever been. There were women, and in the corner, shielded by the leopard-skin men, I caught a glimpse of Obaman's woman.

The smell of excitement filled the air, but I detected a low undercurrent of nervous whispers. Obaman was standing in the middle of the room. So was my opponent. I had not seen him before. He was a powerful-looking man, tall, with long muscled arms and a great round chest. He stood serene and confident.

But I, too, felt calm and confident. I didn't care about the match, nor what would happen. I didn't even care about the shame or the glory. I only knew that I would do what I had to do. I would be what I must.

The ceremonies again took place. There was the blessing from the Okombo, the coating with the ashes. The poem was chanted by the old men; the drums were pounded; the horns blown. The only change was that Obaman whispered a warning to me.

"If you lose," he said, barely moving his lips, "the leopard-men will turn on you."

Then he raised his arms and the room became silent.

"Now is the time for strength," he shouted. "Now is the time for cunning." Then he moved out of the circle, leaving the two of us in the center of the room, in our ring of sand.

Round and round we circled, each bent low, staring into each other's eyes, our arms before us as if pawing the air. I have never felt so light, so poised for action. I lost all self-consciousness. I did not worry any longer about what anyone thought of me. I had gone so far and deep inside myself that nothing else mattered, nothing seemed real except the blood whirling down my veins and the man across from me. I felt as if I could read his thoughts, follow each impulse from nerve to nerve.

And so I knew exactly when he would come at me. I could see his body tense. I could feel the word form in his brain: Now!

Yet so quick was he, despite his size, that even as the word formed he flung himself at me. His huge hand grabbed my ankle, began to tighten, while his shoulder drove into my stomach. But the warning I had was just enough to allow me to twist my body away, so that he caught me not flush, but sideways, in the direction I was already moving. I managed to break free, wrenching my leg from his grasp. In a flash, he righted himself, turning to face me, crouched and ready. For a single instant, a look of disappointment flashed across his face. Then it was gone, his face tight and tense again.

We circled each other. This time it was my turn to leap. But instead of diving low for his legs, I hurled myself at his chest, my fingers reaching for his neck. This caught him off guard, for he had bent low, intent on protecting his legs. As soon as my nails dug into his skin, I tried to jerk my body around. I wanted to get behind him, my arm across his neck. I was hoping to yank him backward over my knee and bring him to the floor that way, from behind and away from his powerful arms.

But at the last moment, he twisted slightly so that I lost my grip on him. And then he let his right arm sweep out in a powerful arc that hurled me into the air. I just managed to dig my nails into his shoulder, that alone keeping me inside the ring that marked the boundary of the wrestling pit. I lay on the sand, mere inches away from the line Obaman had drawn.

I leaped to my feet as my opponent turned to me. There was a grimly confident smile on his face. Past him, I could see the circle of leopard-men. They, too, were grinning. For some reason, that enraged me. I felt my limbs contract as if in slow motion, each muscle growing taut like a spring ready for release. All around me, too, the world had seemed to slow.

Even before it happened I knew my opponent would never get away. My muscles unwound. I was catapulted through the air. It did not matter if he saw me coming. It was as if he were a stake driven into the floor. It was as if all his strength had been diverted into his smile, leaving nothing for the rest of his body. My shoulder drove into his belly. I could feel it push in, deeper and deeper, compressing the flesh before it. I could feel his ribs against my bone, feel them give way like the tines of a rake under the weight of the earth. It seemed for a terrible moment that my shoulder might push right through him, exit his back, leaving a gaping hole out of which I would explode. But bone stopped me, even as I heard the terrible snap of something breaking.

He crashed to the sandy floor, a fallen tree. I landed on top of him, driving my teeth into his shoulder, my knees smashing into his groin. It was over in an instant. He lay like a rag wrung dry.

No one spoke. The drumming ceased. Only a loud, condemning silence. To break it, to call the world once more to order, I leaped to my feet over the fallen man and threw back my head and roared, a good, deep-down, leopard-roar that rattled in my throat and in my heart. I was only doing what the old man had said; I was being myself.

N O ONE SPOKE TO ME OF THAT NIGHT AGAIN. NOT even Obaman. But something was changed forever.

A strange quiet descended on us. Autumn fell on the ghetto, piling up mounds of decaying leaves till they nearly buried the headstones in the cemetery by Obaman's house. Sometimes swift surges of Arctic air turned the weather cold and we would suspend our training. Then I was able to visit Obaman's woman.

One of the old women took me in to see her. She waited in the room that was her prison, a wistful smile on her face. Often she stood beneath her open window, even on the coldest nights. Sometimes she came and stood beside me, so close her naked breasts brushed my arm, so close I could feel the warmth radiating from her skin.

"What is it like out there?" she asked.

"Dark and lonely," I answered.

She would be silent a long time.

"Is there no happiness anywhere?"

"Yes," I said, moving away from her. For I had to move

away, had to remember who I was. What I was. "People take comfort no matter what the world is like."

"How?" I remember her asking once.

"In the same way as always," I said.

"In loving?" she asked.

"Yes," I answered.

"In sacrifice?"

I paused a moment, thinking of Obaman sitting in his study with its row of orderly books, planning out the future of his people; of Simon walking down his narrow road. And thinking, even, of a great she-leopard with a human child in her mouth. But most of all I was thinking of a sad and lovely woman standing in a guarded room, looking out her one small window at the distant lights.

"Yes," I said finally.

"It's not easy to believe in the future," she said, simply, calmly, certainly.

"Nor the past," I said, recalling my own dark life.

"What else is there?"

"Now," I remember saying. "Only now."

Neither of us said more. With that fluid grace that marked her every move she came over and reached out with her arms and drew me to her and kissed me, kissed me on the lips, fangs and all. Her warmth, her softness, her innocence, closed around me. I shut my eyes, afraid to move, afraid to shatter the moment. I wanted more than anything else to remain forever moored on that single instant of time.

But then I felt her body draw away from mine. The cold and emptiness returned. I opened my eyes. The room was the same again. Obaman's woman was near me, her head bowed. She was crying.

I went over to the window, inhaled the cold night air. I became myself again: the Leopard Man. And she: Obaman's woman.

"I'm sorry," I heard her say from across the room.

"I'm sorry, too," I said.

"It seems there is no comfort anywhere," she said, in the saddest voice I have ever heard. Then without another word she turned and fled the room, leaving behind the heartbreak of her words and her skin's warm perfume.

"What have you done?" a voice said.

I whirled around. Standing in the doorway were Obaman and two of his leopard-men. They were crouched low, as if ready to spring at me.

Suddenly, I wanted them to. In that reckless moment, I wanted that more than anything else in the world.

"Do it," I heard myself growl. "Do it."

No one moved. We all just stood there, waiting.

"Do what?" Obaman said, slowly, calmly, his eyes never leaving my own.

The words broke through. I felt the anger pouring out of me like blood from an open wound.

"Do what?" Obaman said again, his words so calm, so unhurried, so implacable.

"Nothing," I said. "Nothing."

"Not yet, anyway," Obaman said, and to this day I cannot remember if he said that to me or to the leopard-men. I walked past him, past the two leopard-men and then out into the bitter, dreary dark.

Now when I wake from my dreams of Simon, I remember that night and I'm no longer filled with regret. If he died before such a moment of beauty, then at least he was spared the agony of losing it. And if he died a moment after, on that long dark road, then he died while the memory was still warm and real. I could wish no more for anyone. Not even myself.

Nothing was the same after that night. I never did know if Obaman had learned of what happened, that lonely, desperate kiss in the room before the world closed in. Perhaps there were hidden holes in the walls or ceiling where they could spy on her. Perhaps he made her tell him. Perhaps she herself confessed.

Everything seemed to take on a feverish intensity. The War. The days in the hardware store. The nights in the ghetto. Then Obaman called us all together.

"If we delay," he told us, "we will be too late forever." He fixed his gaze on me. "The enemy will devour us."

I think of those words often. They break the silence of my forgetfulness. They fill me with the crushing weight of shame. I think I may have betrayed Obaman. After that night, I think my heart was already filling with regret for what I had done—what I had let happen and rejoiced in. So, to dull the pain, I turned the regret to disenchantment. I let myself doubt Obaman's conviction instead of my own.

A man came to the hardware store. He was not a regular customer but he had been coming round recently to buy a few small items and to talk. I heard through the half-open door. He made small talk with Simon's father, about the distant war, about business and such. But always the talk turned to matters of the street.

"It seems awfully quiet," the man said. "Maybe they're all gone to the army." I think he meant by that the blacks.

Simon's father responded bitterly. If only that were true then his son would not have been taken half-an-earth away. No, they're here, all right, he said. At night you can hear them roaming about.

Do you trust them? the man asked.

Better you should trust no one, Simon's father said.

One time the man was in the store when I had to bring some finished blinds from the back room to Mr. Smyth. The man gave me a long, penetrating look when I walked in, not the usual "Oh, my God, what is that?" kind of look. It was something else, as if he were measuring me for something.

"So this is the helper you mentioned," the man said. He nodded in my direction, perhaps by way of a greeting. "Mr. Smyth tells me you go out quite a bit at night. Is that so? He was saying the streets seem busier than in the daytime."

It seemed like just talk then, just the normal chatter, even despite the look. It felt good to speak to someone in the daylight, to not have to hide in shadows and remain silent. The man came around more often. He would ask for me. We'd talk about this or that. He even went into the back room where I was working. He'd stand there watching me do the blinds. We'd talk of lots of things. I didn't think anything of it. Maybe there was nothing to it.

If I said to that man something I shouldn't, and if he took that and turned it against Obaman and all the rest of us, who is to blame? It takes more than words to bring a kingdom down.

The days went on like that, one into the other. Then the weather cleared and the time for action arrived. Time for the Mission. How the original plan was made I cannot say. I assumed the plan was Obaman's invention. It had his flare, his sense of symbol. And I can't believe he intended what happened, so I think it must have been a betrayal. That seems the human way. Perhaps the leopard-men sought revenge. Perhaps one of Obaman's disgruntled followers did it to discredit him. Or perhaps the white authorities got wind of it . . . or some Nazi sympathizers. In matters of betrayal, the possibilities seem endless.

The Mission was a simple one: to free the animals in the zoo.

"Let them roam the streets," Obaman shouted to us. "Let them leap out of every doorway, slither out of every alley," he cried, like a prophet calling down some biblical doom. "Let the white man know he is not a thing apart. Let him know that he, too, must live in the untamed wilderness."

And I agreed with Obaman. If it was the white man, the rich man's indifference he wanted to break through; if it was his arrogant belief in the protection of his machines that he wanted to shatter, then what better way to do it than to loose on his concrete streets the animals, the creatures of the natural world? They would lie down in their beds in their steel and concrete rooms, these arrogant rich men and women, lulled by the rumble of their machines, and suddenly they would hear the cry of a wild animal. Who would not tremble then, not recall Egypt and her plagues?

I was to be the leader, of course. But if this was a simple mission, I saw something important yet to decide: which animals were we to set free? It was one thing to shout, "Let the beasts roam the streets." But it was another matter to arrange this. Imagine what would happen if lions and tigers stalked the city streets. I thought of the librarian I had met at the zoo, walking alone at night.

Some of the men wanted to loose them all.

"As it was in the beginning," a man shouted.

I finally convinced them that they should let only certain animals out, ones that could create fear and panic but give people a chance to get to safety. So we decided on the elephants and hippos and water buffaloes; and small predators, ones that wouldn't do any real damage. Like servals and jackals or a wild dog or two. Animals that would frighten people, but not really hurt them. Animals you could hear coming.

We set off on the first night of clouds. Dressed in black, we glided as always along the narrow unlit streets and alleys. Soon the zoo loomed before us. In the dark it looked junglelike, thick with trees and vines. We leaped the fence easily.

Everything was going according to plan. Several of the keepers were either friends or followers of Obaman. They had provided us with the keys for the cages we sought. We divided ourselves into units. Some were responsible for the pachyderms, some for the ungulates, some for the primates, and so on. I led the unit in charge of the carnivores.

The antelopes came out first. They were already skittish and the smell of our bodies made them even more restless. Once the gates were open, they raced out of their compounds. The men, using whips and sticks, tried to keep them headed for the main gate, but some of them broke away and in a blind panic hurled themselves at the fence. Some, like the impalas and the Rainey's gazelle, were able to leap over the iron rails. But others just crashed into the fence and lay in a heap. One or two impaled themselves on the stakes.

Some of the other animals were loose as well. The night began to fill with the sounds of hoofbeats and bleats and roars. The elephants came thundering out of their enclosures, stampeding not only the other animals but the men as well.

Confusion reigned. It was almost as Obaman had said: beasts roamed the streets and serpents slithered out of alleys. I tried to be everywhere at once. But in the end that was a mistake. There were traitors among us. And they did what I feared most—they freed all the carnivores.

I knew it the moment it was done. The prey animals who had been running in wild confusion were crazed with terror. Even before I could hear the roars of the lions and tigers I knew they were loose. The scent of death was in the air. In an instant, some of the big cats made their kills. Not even the men were spared. I heard the terrible sound of a human death cry, the mindless, animal shriek of someone feeling himself lifted and shaken, of hearing his own bones crushed. When I heard that sound, my own blood froze.

I ran to the carnivore building. Animals stamped around me, lifting up great clouds of dust. The noise of men screaming mingled with grunts and whines. In the distance, I could hear the sirens, still far away. I rushed along, leaping over fallen animals, past crouched and horrified men, past the carcasses of disemboweled prey.

The door to the building was ajar. I moved inside, letting my eyes adjust to the inner darkness. Most of the cage doors were open, the animals gone. The silence was stifling. My lungs struggled for oxygen. I moved cautiously through the building, my nostrils testing the air. The animal smells seemed faint.

And then my nose caught the scent of an old, familiar smell. My every nerve and muscle tensed. My hair stood on end. The smell of leopard and the smell of death was in the air.

I crouched down, readying myself. If I was to die, I would die like a man. I moved closer to that cage at the far end. I listened for every sound, scented the air. The smell of leopard grew stronger. And the smell of blood. And then I heard it, that low, deep growling of a feeding leopard. Perhaps no other sound like it in all the world.

I strained to see that cage in the darkness. Finally, I could see a key in the lock on the cage and it had been turned. I took another step forward, not daring to breathe. The leopard's growling continued. I was so close now I could see that the door stood open—a large, black, vertical band ran from the bottom of the cage to the ceiling.

I tried to will my blood from flowing. I feared the leopard would hear. I moved closer.

The leopard was feeding on a man. I saw a faint, gleaming light nearby. It was the steel claw of one of Obaman's leopard-men.

Suddenly the growling stopped. I had only one chance to survive. My brain warned me at the same moment it sent the message to my arms and legs. I leaped into the air, drawing on every ounce of strength I had. Even as I hurled myself, I could hear the constricted roar that meant the leopard was about to attack.

I crashed into the cage door an instant before the leopard. The force of my hitting the door banged it shut. I could hear the door click into place. As I fell back to the ground, I managed to reach out and twist the key. The leopard, too, had hurled itself at the bars, but an instant late. I heard the air explode out of its chest on striking the metal. The whole cage shook and rattled.

I lay there a moment, gathering myself. Outside, I heard the chaos, the reign of terror that had been loosed on the city. The sirens blasted. I realized I had been inside the building only a minute or two, though it had seemed like hours.

I saw the leopard plainly now, lying on the floor as he had on the day Obaman first took me to the zoo. The leopard's head rested on its paws, and its tail was making a slow, sweeping arc across the concrete.

As I got to my feet, sirens moved closer; I knew I had to get away. The worst had happened. The carnivores were in the streets. People would die before it was all over. I hoped the librarian, who wanted to gentle the beasts, was not among them. But at least the leopard was caged. That was my only consolation.

OUTSIDE, THE SCENE WAS LIKE SOMETHING FROM prehistoric times. The bodies of animals gutted by the big cats were strewn everywhere. Some lay in pools of blood, throats torn, bodies disemboweled. Some had been gored to death by the buffaloes. Others stood in shock, their sides slashed by predators who hadn't even stayed to finish them off. I was looking at a killing ground.

Men had been killed, as well. Most had been taken by the cats, their eyes frozen in horror, their jugular veins laid bare. But these deaths had been quick.

Some men had climbed into the trees or the tops of cages. But the monkeys and chimpanzees had battered them. Some had been bitten by snakes. Perhaps a few persons died of fright.

Most of the animals had either been killed or had dispersed—gone into the streets and alleys. A group of us, working together, lifted the bodies of dead comrades onto our shoulders and made our way back to the ghetto.

Some of the men, thinking I had been the one to let the cats out, tried to knife me. But when one of the tigers hit us from the side and dragged off one of the wounded men, they realized they had better leave me alone and look out for themselves. We lost a few more before we could get back to Obaman's house.

Behind us we glimpsed the pulsing lights of the police cars and the ambulances. We could hear shooting and the trumpeting of the elephants. Once or twice something dark flitted by, but I was moving up and down the line by then, so it never attacked.

At last we made it to Obaman's. I ran up the stairs and pounded on the door. No one answered. I turned the handle. The door opened. I went inside.

The place was a shambles. I wondered if the animals had trampled through the house. The masks had been ripped down from the walls. Furniture was thrown about. I went into the study. Books had been pulled down from the shelves; ripped and torn pages covered the floor.

I ran to the stairs that led to the top floor. Something told me what I would find. The door was closed and I stood outside afraid to go in. I took a deep breath, finally, and opened the door.

Obaman's woman was looking up at her window. She was hanging by a rope. By her neck.

I went over and using my teeth cut her down. I held her in my arms, this beautiful woman, this innocent. I could imagine how it must have been for her, learning of what had happened, learning of the horror, the death, the mutilation. Perhaps Obaman had accused her: that single embrace, that single kiss, that gesture of absolute loneliness. Perhaps someone had told her that I was the traitor, that I was the beast after all. Perhaps it was only the loneliness finally, the long nights looking out the high window at a world she could never know. Perhaps, as with Simon, the world is not made for such innocence.

I left the girl in the room, by the open window, and walked back down, past all the devastation and chaos. On the way out, I saw a man I recognized. He was the wrestler I had beaten. One of the cats had mauled him.

"Can I help?" I asked him.

He only stared back at me.

"Why?" he said.

I knew what he was asking. It was the question Job had asked, and

Solomon in his despair had asked. And yet it seemed so futile, so foolish, to be talking of guilt or innocence, cause and effect in a world such as this. I put my hand on his shoulder.

"There is no why," I answered, then turned and left him there. I wonder if he ever found a truth that offered more peace or comfort.

I went back to my room to wait for Obaman and the leopard-men. I knew he would come, they would come. What else could they do? I was the leader of the Mission. I was the symbol. I was the Leopard Man. It was only right they should come.

Mr. Smyth was away, visiting relatives. The building was empty. I waited in my room by the window. I was thinking of Simon. And the girl. And the leopard.

There was nothing else to do. Obaman would come while it was dark, with his leopard-men. We were all bound together now. The fate of one would alter the fate of another.

I got up slowly and went to one of the mirrors on the wall. I had not looked at myself for a long time, seeing myself instead only through the eyes of others. I had on what I always wore: a black shirt and trousers. My face was full of coarse hair. I shaved but the hair grew back, began to sprout it seemed, even as I held the razor. The teeth, of course, stuck out even with my mouth closed.

I looked at the eyes looking back at me. They say the eyes are windows to the heart, mirrors of the soul. What I saw were two small eyes, faded brown that shaded off to yellow, framed by a thick, hooded brow. It was not a face supremely human, I knew, not one of those grand, Roman faces that made you think of empires and operas. But was it the face of a beast, the face of something inhuman?

And the rest of me? How different was I from the endless variety of human shapes you see in any crowd? What if my arms were longer than most? Isn't there room enough in people's imaginations for that? What if the muscles bunched at my shoulders? If my legs were short and curved? We all have our variations, our departures from the golden norm. What did it all add up to, what was the sum total of who I was? Had I crossed some invisible line that forever divides man from beast—a line not drawn in the earth's black dust, but in the blacker heart of man?

I tried to imagine a child, a normal human child looking up at me. I tried becoming people from my life, from my past, tried seeing that face in the mirror as they might. Sister Agnes, Legs, the other boys, Mr. Smyth, Simon, Obaman, and finally, finally before the tears made me turn away, Obaman's woman. I bared my teeth, let the long, curling canines fill the mirror. I let out a low growl, lifting my head and letting the sound rumble out of my throat. Let the beast fill the mirror so that I could see once and for all. But do not let them tell you that mirrors do not lie, that a single picture is worth a thousand words. Even as I looked, even as I roared, the face hanging in the glass shifted and twisted and whirled, so that it was both the face of a tortured man crying out in sorrow and the face of an animal warning away the world. And as I looked, and as I roared, I realized that not only my face in the mirror but my whole life was about to be hardened into a shape I could never change. I could live another hundred years, a thousand. It would not matter. Nothing would change it. I was to be the Leopard Man forever.

They came as I knew they would, down the alley that led past the yards. There were maybe a dozen, led, of course, by Obaman. Behind him, in the shadows, were the leopard-men. I had not realized they were so many. As they passed beneath the dull light that seeped between the buildings, I saw their steel claws glimmering.

At first it was like a game. I don't think any of us, not even Obaman, realized the desperateness of what we were doing. Perhaps it was just that early jauntiness that marks the distinction between life and pretense. We had no time for false melancholy.

I caught the first leopard-man as he was about to climb over the edge of the fire escape. The game ended then. For an instant his eyes showed surprise. Then a moment's wild panic. Finally, his face composed itself into a grim smile, as if understanding were like a hardening agent. He dropped into the night without making a sound.

I leaped from one building to the next. I caught one crouching by the ventilator shaft. He heard me at the last moment, but it was too late.

I caught a few down on the ground slinking through the alleys. I did what any good predator would do: I took them from behind, hurling myself at them, knocking them to the ground. Before they could get to their feet I drove my teeth deep into the backs of their thighs and jerked my head to the side, severing the nerves and muscles, hamstringing them.

We fought the war all through the rest of the night. I think we all knew that it was the end of everything. Morning would rise from the darkness, but on a different world. Obaman's dream would never be.

I caught another as he crept through Mr. Smyth's garden. I was waiting for him on the one strong branch of the old apple tree. I waited till he was almost under me, then dropped on him, my teeth ripping into his shoulder. He tried to shake me loose; instead he sank under my weight. I drew my arm tight under his chin and pulled. I felt his body go limp, and it took me a while to pry my teeth from his shoulder—and that was what almost did me in.

I had my hands pressed against the man's shoulders trying to pull my two top teeth free when I sensed someone behind me. I yanked back with all my strength and at the same time tried rolling to one side. I felt a sharp, searing pain begin at my shoulder and surge down my back, as far as my waist. It was as if someone had put a hot iron to me. As I completed the roll and looked up, I could see one of the leopard-men standing there, his steel claws outstretched. Strips of my black shirt and pieces of hairy skin hung from those claws. They were wet with my blood.

He must have been startled by my roll, because he took a moment to gather himself for another attack. That was all I needed. I sprang at him, even as he was turning. I caught him from underneath, driving my teeth through the leopard skin to his unprotected throat. At the same time I grabbed each of his arms by the wrist. Time seemed to halt, and we were suspended in a formless space. He remained in the same crouched position while I clung to him from below. Finally, I wrapped my legs around the backs of his. Nothing else happened until I heard a strangled, gurgling breathing. My jaw tightened. The muscles ached so much I thought my head would burst. And then, he began to shrivel under me, grow small and wither.

I pulled free. He lay on his back, the leopard mask still covering his face, his steel claws curled upward. He looked like a mythical creature—half-man, half-beast. I felt a rush of sympathy, for the man and for the beast. For that failed fusion. But the mood passed and when I looked again he was just a man in a leopard skin who had tried to kill me.

There's no use going on about the rest. It lasted almost until morning. One by one, all except Obaman. And when the first light of morning began to climb over the dark rim of the world, I made my way back to the zoo. I had always known that it would end there, even from the beginning. By then, most of the police were gone. Armed with rifles and shotguns, a few remained to patrol the outside gate. But most of the animals were either dead or dispersed like commandos into the city.

I knew there would be time to play it all out. To have altered it, we would have had to be different men.

Obaman was waiting for me. I could smell him even before I could see him. He made no attempt to hide. He would know the script as well as I. He was sitting on one of the stone benches by the carnivore cages.

"You have come," he said, calmly, as I moved out of the darkest shadows.

"Of course," I said. My lips felt thick. My jaws ached.

"So be it," he said, as if to himself. I remembered those words from long ago, from that first time we met. Everything was in its place.

Neither of us said anything for a long time. I don't remember what I was thinking—or if I was thinking at all. I felt a bone-deep tiredness in me. The last of anything, even one's life, is a burden.

"I did nothing to betray you," I said, forcing myself to speak. But even as I said the words I realized how hollow they were. What have words to do with fate?

"It doesn't matter," Obaman said, and he was right.

Slowly he got to his feet. We stood facing each other. A restless stirring came from the cages. The hair on my neck stood up.

"The leopard is loose," Obaman said, smiling his flashing smile, carelessly tossing a large metal key at my feet.

I turned to the cage door, slightly ajar. I could see nothing in the deep shadows within. I lifted my face to scent the air. As I did, I saw a quick flash of light. Obaman had drawn a knife.

A low, deep roar filled the air, rose above the noise of the city. As I leaped at Obaman, I remember surprise that the sound came from my own throat.

We fought a long time. Even as I think back on that time and try to remember, I recall only sudden surges of dark and light. It was as if a great searchlight kept sweeping the ground. Or an ambulance light. Obaman's knife kept weaving back and forth in the air. We rolled on the ground together. We hurled ourselves at each other in a wordless fury. I remember the sticky feel of blood mixed with sweat. Then I remember a sudden sharp pain in my side. I can even remember watching the blade part my flesh, carving its way in, the way someone cuts raw meat.

Then a terrible roar rattled in my ears. I remember looking down and seeing Obaman's face below me, a face suddenly blown up like the inside bladder of a ball that has burst through the seams. Obaman's eyes were huge white circles. But then his face was no more. A thick, pulsating darkness pressed down on me. I heard the long shrill whine of something dying.

For a long while I remembered nothing else. Much later I read in a newspaper that a man had been found lying in the dirt before the unlocked leopard cage. His throat had been ripped out, his body mutilated.

The leopard had been found lying quietly inside the unlocked cage. It said the leopard had been put to sleep.

14

The Man in Black

I STILL HAVEN'T SAID HOW I CAME TO BE IN THE WOODS before the dogs drove me out or before I let them. But first I want to describe what it was like to be the Leopard Man, one of the Eight Human Wonders of the World. I was the life force of the show, the one they all came to see. I, who had lived so much of his life hidden away, draped in dreams, became a living spectacle. My life was lived out on the open stage, under the lights, for everyone—and anyone—to see. In a way, it was the best disguise, because then I would be whatever it was the world wanted me to be, or rather, whatever it was they wanted but were afraid to be.

"Unchain the Leopard Man. Unchain the Leopard Man," they'd cry. I was the face in the mirror most men never see. I was the face of the stranger in the shadows, the face of the beast in their dreams.

The carnival went from place to place, along the back roads, past the farmhouses and the fields, the towns and the factories. We marked time by the seasons and the meadows. This month in that field. That month in this field. We moved, a small migration that followed the sun. For the sun alone was our constant. Tents will not keep out the winter cold. We land only in sunlit meadows. Our sails catch only summer winds.

The man in black was our weather prophet. Standing out in the field, his arm raised to the heavens, he would feel the air for currents that even I with my leopard senses could not fathom. He would stand like a black weathervane, turning slowly in the wind. And then he would return.

"Rain," he would say.

And in a while the rains came, thundering out of an azure sky. And sometimes the rain turned to a wet snow that heaped itself against the long grass of the meadow where we had tented. But we, ourselves, like the children of Zion, would be gone into another sunlit land.

He held us together. But to what end, I do not know for certain. He was our shepherd. He herded us on, town to town, always ahead of the storm. He kept us a dollar or two out of debt, out of despair, out of the cold. But for what purpose? And at what cost?

The man in black was not the first to make use of animals. Obaman had insisted I read the Bible again. It had made me shudder. There were animals, of course. Every kind. The Ark had carried them, preserved them in God's name. They were used for everything, even as now. But what I trembled at most was how often they were loosed upon the world as instruments of wrath and destruction: serpents and whales and all the wild hunting things. Take Elisha, whose name means "God's salvation": one day he was walking to Beth-el when some children came by and mocked him for his baldness. "Go up, thou bald head. Go up," they shouted like children will. And Elisha, prophet of God, turned and cursed them. And in response two she-bears came running out of the woods and tore apart forty-two of those little children, all in the name of God. And then those lions who spared Daniel's life. But those lions were not so kind to his accusers, breaking their bones and tearing them all to pieces—not only the men who had lied but also their wives and children. And leopards, of course. When the most terrible work of chastisement was to be done, when God wanted to shake and whirl and devour the world, He turned to the leopard. So if that was God's work, if this was how God chose to use the beasts, then is it so far-fetched to think of the man in black as doing similar work—loosing on the world his terrifying collection of freaks. Led by me, the Leopard Man?

If Simon had lived, perhaps he could have calmed my fears. Perhaps in his gentleness he could have made me see the justice that lay beneath the slaughter. Perhaps he could have made me believe more in the lamb of God than in the lion. Perhaps he could have made me understand what it was that drove the man in black who in turn drove us.

But there was no Simon to teach me. All there was were the stories we told each other about the man in black. I learned them one by one. The man in black was a disillusioned rich man's son, amusing himself at our expense. He was another de Sade, feeding off degradation. One story, with an eerie kind of reverse logic, told of how the man in black had fathered his own freak, and how that abomination had driven his beloved wife mad. In revenge or in despair, the man had given himself over to freaks—to us, the living reminders of his shame and loss.

There were other stories. I listened to all of them. Each one had its truth. In the end, though, I wondered if it was something simpler. Perhaps the man in black got tired of his tricks. If you're very good at making illusions seem real—more real than life—what is left for you? Because you yourself cannot believe in illusion, you would grow weary of the stupidity of those you dupe. After a while, perhaps even the applause grows stale.

Sometimes I think that one day the man in black grew tired of his magic and decided to give the world truth. And the truth was us—the Eight Human Wonders of the World. Were we truly human? If you thought we were, then what kind of world must it be to have people like us in it? If you believed in a God who created everything, then what kind of God must He be? One who is careless? One who is cruel? One who would create freaks and then use them to test the rest of humanity? So while the audience laughed and smirked at us and we laughed and smirked at them—and the man in black sat back and laughed and smirked at all of us—perhaps something more serious was going on. Perhaps the man in black had arranged it so that God would have a way to judge us. Or we Him.

The man in black spoke to me about this once—not directly, of course. That was not his way. He was too full of mystery and irony and we were too much in awe for that. But I think it was what he was intending.

"I want to tell you a story," he said. It was late at night, long after the show had closed, in that quiet time when morning begins to glow in the dark. We were alone outside the main tent.

"It's about a man who had everything, except immortality. So that he knew that whatever he had would come to nothing one day. Would disappear. Or that he would disappear—which is the same thing. That man would have two choices. He could enjoy what he had knowing it would come to nothing. Or he could despise what he had knowing it would come to nothing. Which do you think he should do?"

"Since it will all come to nothing, why not enjoy it?" I answered.

"Precisely," the man in black said, smiling with his shark teeth in the faint light of morning. "And if what you have is hatred, shouldn't you enjoy that, too?"

"But if you have everything," I said, "wouldn't you have love also?"

This time the man in black almost did a little dance, he seemed so pleased with my answer.

"Precisely. Having everything, you would celebrate everything. Since all will come to nothing." Suddenly, he became very intense, put his hand on my shoulder with a powerful grip. "Hate. Love. Everything equal. Everything good. Everything coming to nothing."

And then I thought about Simon.

"But some things are better than others," I said, "even if they do come to nothing."

The man in black let go of my shoulder, threw back his head and almost roared with laughter.

"What would I do without you?" he said. "You and all the others?"

And with that, he began to move away, disappearing behind the tent.

There was one other time I remember when he talked about his life, about the Eight Human Wonders of the World. Again, it was indirect, not something you could hold fast to. But then, isn't everything we know like that—a dream we believe in? A story we tell ourselves to keep chaos at bay?

I was riding in one of the trucks we used to haul equipment from place to place. The man in black was driving. He was quiet for a long time, but then without any warning he spoke.

"They say we came from apes," he said, looking at the road ahead and not at me, "but what if it were the other way around? What if we came first and then turned into beasts?"

I didn't know if it was a question he wanted me to answer or not, so I said nothing.

"What if the world moves both ways?" He paused a moment, then turned to me. His eyes were bright and dark. "What if it's a race, with the fate of the world hanging in the balance? Will men turn into animals before animals turn into men?"

I didn't say anything right away. I was thinking about myself, about all of us in the freak show—Leopard Men and Lion Men and Monkey Men. I remembered the old song. "Heart of a panther. Brain of a man." But what if it were the other way around: "Brain of a panther. Heart of a man?" Which would explain more of human history? Science or Slavery? Poetry or War? Simon or the Snake Goddess?

I looked over at the man in black. He was looking ahead again, looking at the road that ran like an artery or vein across the body of America.

"Are we the answer?" I asked. "The Eight Human Wonders?"

The man in black smiled. For one of the few times that I can remember it seemed a kind smile, not sharklike.

"Or the question?" he said.

And because he had smiled, and because it seemed important to know, I asked him outright, "And you?"

The man in black didn't say anything for a long while. And then he told me a story, speaking softly and slowly as we drove through the miles and miles of fields and woods that was our home. This is what he told me.

"There was a small boy once. An ordinary boy living an ordinary life in an ordinary city. His parents were not exactly poor but they were always close to it. The father owned a small store that sold shoes. He didn't sell many shoes but enough to keep a roof over their heads and food on the table. He used to say, 'You won't get rich selling shoes, but you won't go broke either. People have to walk.' He didn't mind selling shoes because it left him time to think. And what he thought about all the time was magic. Illusion. He would go to all the magic shows. He would buy all the books. He would read about all the famous magicians. And then he would try to figure out all their tricks. That was his life's passion. No sooner would he see a trick than he would go home and go down to his basement and try to figure out how it had been done. Many times he would stay up all night trying to make the trick work.

"Now the mother thought the man was foolish. She regretted marrying him, not because he sold shoes or because he was interested in magic, but because nothing came of either. If he had become a famous magician himself that would have been fine with her. Or if he had become a very good shoe salesman and made a success of it and built a chain of stores, she would not have minded that either. What she minded was that the man was not very good at either selling shoes or doing magic. 'Only a fool persists in being a failure,' she would say to the boy, determined to keep him from following in the footsteps of her husband. It did not matter that the man seemed happy and content to be as good as he was in both selling and in magic.

"As it turned out, it was the boy who was good in both. As soon as he was old enough he would help his father at selling and at magic. He seemed to know instinctively what it was people really wanted when they came to buy, and he had a wonderful knack for figuring out magic tricks, as well. And when you think about it, both skills are very much the same: both involve illusion. People will come in saying they are looking for a plain pair of shoes when what they really want is a fancy pair. And the boy had a wonderful knack for recognizing what they truly wanted and for making them feel good about wanting it. In just the same way he was good at magic. He had a knack for understanding what it was the magician wanted people to believe and in figuring out how to resist believing it. Pretty soon he was selling more shoes than his father and figuring out all the magic tricks, as well.

"His mother decided to take advantage of this. 'I may have married a fool,' she thought to herself, 'but I'm not going to raise one.' She would see to it that her son made something of his talents.

"The first thing she did was turn the son against the father. She made the boy see just what a fool his father was, what a failure. She made him see how pathetic he was, how unworthy of them. Then the mother made the boy understand that all their success depended on him—not the father. 'You have the means to save us,' she told him. 'Only you.'

"What she didn't realize was that the boy had no interest in saving her—or himself, for that matter. What he had an interest in was finding out the tricks and illusions behind everything—not just selling and not just magic. You see, he had come to suspect that the whole world was one big magic trick, and that if he worked hard enough, one day he would come to understand how it was done. He thought that perhaps God was a great magician and that all creation was His special effect. He thought that if he could figure out what God wanted people to believe, he could learn to resist it.

"He didn't really care about his mother or his father. They were like everyone else—saying one thing and meaning another; doing one thing and wanting to do another. His mother only wanted to use him to get the things she thought she deserved and that his father would never get her. His father only acted content with his failures because he really wanted to deny his wife the things she thought she deserved.

"So what the boy did was turn his back on both of them. He left each of them behind with their illusions and their failures. He had more important things to do—which was to find out how the world worked. He began to read everything he could read about truth and illusion, appearance and reality. He went to all the schools, to all the lectures, to all the libraries. He asked everyone he knew to tell him. But it was all very confusing. Some people said one thing. Others said something different. Sometimes the two things were exactly opposite. And then the people would fight about it. Even kill each other over it. It seemed like nobody had the answer, or that everybody did but that all the answers were different.

"And then one day the boy who was by then a young man decided that nobody had the answer. That what he had to do was find it out for himself."

The man in black told me this as we drove through the wheat fields and the corn fields on our way to another meadow, another fair, another freak show. I decided to ask him the question that had been on my mind, on all of our minds, ever since we joined the show, ever since the man in black came to us with his cards and with his sharklike smile.

"How did he do this," I asked, "this boy that had grown to be a man?"

The man in black reached out his arm as if to touch my face. But he didn't. He stopped just short. Instead, with just a quick little movement of his wrist, a card appeared in his fingers. On the blank whiteness of the card was the figure of a man painted in black. He was holding a globe of the world up over his head. He let the card fall to my lap.

"He built himself his own world," the man in black said softly. "Just like God."

"And what did he learn from building this world?" I asked, looking at the card and thinking of Simon and his gentleness and wisdom, both.

"That everything comes to nothing in the end," the man in black said, this time smiling his sharklike smile. "And that's exactly how it should be."

We rode the rest of the way in silence. I never did ask the man in black whether he was that little boy or not. Would it matter? Simon told me once that some things ought to be true even if they're not. And if you were to ask me even now whether in his heart the man in black loved mankind or hated it, made our lives bearable or a torment, I could not tell you. Perhaps the man in black was all the things we imagined. Perhaps he was only what we wanted or needed him to be. I only know that it was the man in black who brought us together and kept us together. If in the end this, too, will come to nothing, so be it. For a while, at least, the Leopard Man had a place to call home—even if it was only a cage. And for that I am grateful.

15

The Leopard in Love:
In Five Acts

WE PITCHED OUR TENTS. WE LIT OUR LIGHTS. WE set up our posters. And the people came, always the people came, pressing their coins in our hands, hunching down in their seats, watching with beady eyes the Snake Goddess's flowing breasts.

It was I who closed the show and brought a stunned silence to the crowd. It was I who drove my teeth into the huge slabs of raw meat, into the wooden handle of the whip; who rattled his chains and roared; who lunged for the hairy legs of the Monkey Men; who leaped across the stage with the speed and grace of a leopard.

I gave them a name for the fear inside them. I gave them a name for all the old memories of life out on the steaming plains: The Leopard Man.

The man in black "invented" a history for me, as he had for everyone else. Gone was the Catholic Home, Obaman, Simon. Instead, there was only Africa where I had lived out my life as the child of a man-eating leopard. "Let them wonder about what you ate," the man in black said to me, smiling his shark's smile. Captured by some white hunters and brought to America, I had become a scientific curiosity, unable to speak, eating only raw meat, trying to kill anything that came near.

He hinted that I had copulated with beasts, that I had left behind a new breed of "man-beast" who even now feed upon human flesh. The man in black wrote that a team of renowned scientists had tried to "break" me, civilize me, using the latest, most sophisticated tools known to medical science. But in the end they had failed, and now, at any instant, I might revert again to my savage ways.

He told this story to the local reporters who came out to see the show. This was the story written on the program and sold for an extra nickel. And, strangely enough, this was the story that the rest of them began to believe. It was as if I had become what the man in black had invented, as if I were this Leopard Man.

But, then, who can blame them? As Adam learned, there's everything in a name. And besides, you must not conclude that deformity breeds compassion. Read about prisons. Concentration camps. Prisoners always make the cruelest guards. And what are freaks, after all, but those who live inside prisons of flesh and bone. So the others drew a line between themselves and me, and the line became as real as the Leopard Man. And kept me out again.

Times got tough. We were not the only show on the road.

"Anyone with hair on his ass thinks he's a freak," the man in black said. We had to compete. "You understand?" he said.

The first thing he did was raise the slit on the Snake Goddess's dress, and lower the top, and then let her lead the procession into the town we would be playing near. I would bring up the rear, pulled along in a cage by the Giant. A black cloth covered the bars, which were just wide enough for me to get my teeth through. Whenever we'd pass a crowd, the man in black signaled me and I'd let out a loud roar and run my teeth through the bars and the cloth. That gave the crowd a nice scare, all right.

The man in black gave the Snake Goddess the whip, letting her lead me around—a sort of Beauty and the Beast routine. We'd get to one of the main streets and the Monkey Men would open the cage and I'd come leaping out, pouncing at everything in sight. Then the Snake Goddess would hurry over, snap the whip, give me a shake or two and show some leg and breast and I would quiet down. Then she would step close enough to pet me while I growled low and purred at her feet. After she left, I'd go crazy again. That worked well, because there was something powerful in the myth of a woman's sex subduing the animal that I was. Once in a while she would stand with her foot on my back, like you've seen hunters standing over dead animals in hunting magazines. Once or twice for effect, or maybe for some other reason, she would actually strike me with the whip, raising welts on my back and bloodthirsty cries from the crowd.

After a while, we didn't have to do such things. Times got better. Our fame spread. The people came.

Occasionally I wonder about all the people whose lives I entered. How had I changed them? I tried to count once, to multiply all the seats by all the performances. And then I tried to count the crowds on the streets, and then all the people that those people told. And I tried to think of all the times that I would appear in their dreams, that face peering out of the shadows, fangs glinting in the moonlight. How many people whispered my name? How many feared to?

But it all broke down, the numbers too large, the throngs of faces too vast. I had no real way of knowing. I was not someone people came up to and asked for an autograph. But I was a celebrity just the same. At night. In the quiet terror of dreams. In visions of sin and redemption. How often did the cry "Unchain the Leopard Man! Unchain the Leopard Man!" echo down the long corridors of bone?

Sometimes, as I looked out over the sea of faces, I thought about the farmer and his dog, about how they had given me that ride along that rain-slick road. Were all the men like that—good men deep-down, veering a little on their own straight roads? I tried to imagine them all getting up and going home to their full and ordinary lives. Smiling at their wives. At their children. Reaching down to scratch an old dog behind the ears. Going on with the quiet, steady business of living.

But then I would hear the yelling, the whistles, the catcalls; see the sneering faces, the faces full of rage or fear or lust. Then it would seem that there was more darkness and destruction in them than in any beast in the jungle—than in my own leopard's breast.

I could tell you about the women, too. Women have always been drawn by the grotesque. I could tell you about the shameless things they did or said. Ordinary women. Mothers and daughters. Wives and widows both. Lovely or faded. Perhaps that explains the rage of the men. Perhaps they knew deep-down the wild dreams of their women, could hear the blood surge just beneath the skin. I stood just beyond the ring of light, beyond the steady brightness of ordinary things. I stood dark and fanged and wild in the shadows they had abandoned—left behind for coat and tie and fatherhood.

A woman came to me once, by way of the man in black. He was always making arrangements, bringing us "guests" after the show had ended.

"They wish to make your acquaintance," he would say. "What you do with them is your business."

As long as it didn't interfere with the show, of course.

So, we all of us had our "admirers." Ordinary men and women with a taste for the exotic, or the forbidden, or for worse. This one I remember was so perfectly ordinary that I could never forget her. She stood quietly outside my furnished cage while the man in black spoke to me.

"You have a visitor," he said.

I remember looking past the man in black to a woman standing in the dim light. It was a late-summer evening. The air was mostly warm and dry but sabotaged here and there by little wisps of autumn air. The woman seemed of early middle-age: short, dowdy, pretty. She stood as if she were uncomfortable being there, as if she would flee if she could, but something just a bit stronger than her fear or revulsion kept her there. She reminded me of herd animals out on the plains, ready to bolt at the slightest sound, yet drawn down to the lush grass on the ground as if the earth itself could save them and keep them from harm.

Neither of us said anything for a while. I don't remember what I was thinking. Sometimes the silence around you seems so pure it's as if the whole world has been erased, washed clean of sound.

My cage had become my home. It was the man in black's idea. "It will add to the mystery," he said. So half the cage was covered in wood, sides and top, and painted black—except for a score of small silver stars that were scattered across the ceiling, and which seemed to glisten and flare in the candlelight. Instead of a bed, I slept on a raised platform covered with cushions and a black silken cloth. When I wanted to sleep, or when I wished to be left alone, I would leap up to the platform and hunch and curl and so be lost in the blackness. I often lay there on my back in the darkness, under my painted sky, dreaming my leopard dreams, while the world whirled around me. There was a small set of wooden stairs hidden against the far wall that could be lowered like attic stairs. I seldom used them. I had few visitors.

What it was the woman wanted of me, I cannot say. A dozen times she lifted up her face as if to speak. A dozen times the words failed her. She kept her hands together, palm to palm as if in prayer. I waited, patient leopard that I was. When I had despaired of her ever moving, she lifted her hand and held it out to me, held it out for the longest time while we both stood there in the silent painted dark.

I took her hand and held it. It was cold though the night inside my cage was warm. We stood that way a long time, so long that the candles went out; so long that even the night's darkness began to wane. Her breathing became rapid. Her body trembled. She let out a long and shuddering moan. What passed between us I will not say outright. The details are mostly unimportant. Bodies do what bodies do. And when daylight comes, when comforting shadows give way to light, we all drift back to our daytime lives. We all become husbands or wives or leopards. We pick up our books or brooms or guns. Some of us whisper, and some of us roar. But it's all the same, I think: whether you're on the stage looking down or in the audience looking up.

You must understand, though, that whatever it was that the audience thought about us freaks, we thought that and more about them. It was a constant source of amusement, bitter though it was. Just as closely as they watched us, we watched them. Perhaps even more so, because they had paid to see and were bound by custom and convention, while we were spying surreptitiously and in defense. The audience became an endless source of conversation. Whenever there was a lull, whenever we needed a diversion, there was always someone to say, "Did you see?" And there would follow the most pleasantly vicious observations. In this, we all had leopard eyes, and given who we were, no polite inhibitions. We found the most damning condemnations in the most ordinary things. In fact, ordinariness was for us the height of disgust. We catalogued every mole or pimple or scar with the care of a pathologist.

Aristotle's "Golden Mean" nearly made us vomit. If you were only slightly plump, slightly bald, slightly lame or crooked, we'd reserve for you our most scathing condemnations. Our inventory of invective was inexhaustible. As many as you were, so were our sayings. The closer you were to average, the greater our contempt.

Even after the "private" showings, when you'd pay good money to see us perform, it was you we talked about. Even after we'd been bought and paid for, it was your "normalcy" we mocked. Even if we did the most sordid things and you did nothing but watch, it was your performance we derided. "Did you see that look when . . . ?" "Did you see his hands shake when . . . ?" "My God, he was actually drooling. . . ."

I must confess. There were times when I, too, joined in. Our ritual of revulsion almost seemed religious. It felt good to shout out our contempt for what had been denied us, to make a virtue of our deprivation, a triumph of our exaggeration. It was as if we had been made in God's image and not you. It was as if we had altered the definition of what it was to be human—enlarged it, engorged it, stretched it till it could stretch no more. It was as if you were the abandoned limbs on the tree of Man, the branches with no leaves. Or so we told ourselves. Or so we desperately wanted to believe. But even desperate need gives out after a while. Even bitter contempt is not inexhaustible. The ordinary cannot be denied. The mean, the median, the average will out. The boundaries collapse, contract. The outposts are abandoned. The border guards return to the encampment. The great mass becomes the standard. Freaks are freaks once again.

And then I fell in love—with Lola, one of the Siamese Sweethearts, the one on the left, facing me; the one with the sweet voice and the gentle smile; the one who reminded me of Simon, and Obaman's woman.

But the love of someone like that does not come easy. How could it? Two hearts joined in one breast, as it were. But not that either. For there were two brains and two bodies as well, each with its own fears and desires. I remember once when they walked inside the House of Mirrors. I remember thinking as I saw their hundred faces staring back at me that perhaps their whole life was like that, full of multiple realities and deceptions. Yet, isn't that the way for each of us? Inside us all are there not as many selves as we dare believe in—lion and lamb and leopard?

Yet try to love a woman joined to another when that other woman hates the very sight of you. Let that test your imagination.

I suppose the love, if you can call it that, like so much else in my life was doomed from the beginning, from the moment our paths crossed that night long ago under moon and stars. In all the years Lola never once said that she loved me in return, but deep down I know she did. Deep down, where even her sister could not pry, I think she truly loved me.

In a way, it was similar to those soap operas on television, a silly little melodrama played out among the world's grotesques. Maybe there was something more, something even beautiful and tragic.

ACT ONE

Late one night, toward morning. We are traveling together down the road, in the back of the truck, open to the air. Thin streaks of pale light become visible, the morning like a stain seeping through the black quilt of night. I look over at the Siamese Sweethearts, at Lila and Lola. The two are sitting against one wall of the truck, looking out. I am sitting across from them, sharpening my nails.

LILA. [*Coldly*] Where'd you get the knife?

ME. [*Surprised she would even speak to me*] It was given to me. [*I tell them about the zoo.*]

LILA. [*Shrilly*] That's a bunch of crap, along with the whole goddamn thing about Africa. I bet your mother took one look at you and threw you out.

LOLA. [*Softly*] Our mother is still alive. We send her money.

LILA. [*Bitterly*] She tried to cheat us. Told everyone she was saving the money for an operation, to have us cut apart. But all the time she was spending it.

LOLA. She said she was sorry.

LILA. Why not? It's cheap to say.

LOLA. We've been to Europe, you know.

LILA. [*Butting in*] Yeah. We were a big hit. Sold out everywhere. [*Pause*] That's when we found out.

ME. Found out what?

LILA. That the old lady was stealing from us.

LOLA. We wanted to buy our own house. In the country. [*Very sad*] Away from people.

LILA. When we asked for the money, that's when we found out she was stealing us blind. You know what for? [*I tell them I don't.*] For a man. She thought he loved her, but he only wanted the money. [*She makes the word* man *sound like a curse.*]

ME. What happened?

LILA. [*Bitter, pointing at the cramped truck*] This happened.

LOLA. Now we'll never have enough.

ME. Couldn't you go back to Europe?

LILA. [*After a pause, to Lola*] Tell him.

LOLA. No.

LILA. [*Shrugging*] You can't go back. You go once, you're a star. Go back and you're just a freak.

LOLA. Don't you know?

ME. [*To both of them*] I'm sorry.

LILA. I bet.

LOLA. [*Looking away*] We send her what we can. After all, she's still our mother.

ACT TWO

Scene One

Months later. We are backstage after a show, too tired even to leave. We sit, not saying anything. I am in love with Lola, yet I try not to show my love because I know how much Lila hates me and I know it would only cause Lola pain and humiliation. I have faith that Lola can hear beneath the few words I say, beneath even the silences. Once or twice she looks at me with-

out turning away, looks long and hard. I think she is looking at my soul, hearing my heart.

ME. [*Daring it, because we are so tired*] What's it like?
LILA. What's what like?
ME. [*I nod slightly.*] Being together.
LILA. Jesus. [*Weary and disgusted both*] You, too? Doesn't anyone give it a rest? [*This last is said half to Lola, half to the heavens above.*]

[I want Lola to understand. Because I love her so much, I want her to know that I understand, that I want to share the reality with her, if only in my imagination, if only from a distance. But I don't know how to tell her.]

LILA. [*All the bitterness coming out*] All right. [*To Lola*] Shall I tell him? Shall I give him the ten-dollar answer or the twenty-dollar one? The one about how really wonderful to have a double, someone to count on, someone you know will always be there, someone you don't have to explain things to, someone who knows. "Hey Mister. Here's my sister. And if you twist her, here's me, too."

[Lila is silent a moment, looking closely at Lola who does not look at either of us, but down at the floor. When Lila begins again, her voice is eerily distant, ghostlike, tormented.]

LILA. You cannot get away. Everywhere you go it is the same. In the morning when you wake. As you drift off to sleep. In the middle of the night. You do not move, not a muscle. You breathe each breach as before. Then, slowly, slowly, you open your eyes, and her eyes are staring back at you. You go to the bathroom, she goes to the bathroom. She goes, you go. You go, she goes. Round and round and round. [*Lila finishes suddenly, looks up at me, holds out her hand.*] That's the twenty-dollar answer.
LOLA. [*Speaks finally, to Lila*] Let him alone. [*Softly, glancing for the briefest moment at me, my heart and soul leaping inside me*] He knows.

LILA. [*Bitter, shouting*] He doesn't know anything. [*Then, as if that has drained her of all emotion, what she says next she says in a whisper.*] None of them know anything.

Scene Two

Early one morning, outside the Snake Goddess's trailer. The man in black has sent me after an extra whip for the Monkey Men. I tap gently on the door, not too loudly because others are sleeping. No one answers. I tap again. Nothing. So I walk in. The Snake Goddess is lying on her side on the bed. She wears only red panties and a bra. No makeup. Her face is wrinkled, puffy. Lila and Lola are lying near her. Lola is asleep, resting her head against Lila's shoulder. Lila is gently caressing the Snake Goddess's breast. They both turn to me and scream. Lola wakes up. She sees me, begins to cry.

ME. [*To all three of them*] I'm sorry.

SNAKE GODDESS. Drop dead.

LILA. Freak.

ACT THREE

We are all sitting in the dressing room. The show is over. The Snake Goddess is sitting on Lila's lap, stroking her hair, kissing her. Lola does not say anything. She sits, absentmindedly playing with the cold cream jar.

LILA. [*Baiting me*] When we were stars, you know what we used to do?

LOLA. [*Pathetically*] Don't.

LILA. We used to let them pay to see us get undressed. They'd pay plenty, too. That's how we made our bucks.

SNAKE GODDESS. They'd tell their wives the car wouldn't start, when all the time they were trying to get a little of this. [*She cupped one of her enormous breasts.*]

LILA. Or a little of that. [*She reached down between Lola's legs with her hand.*]

LOLA. Some of them proposed to us.

ME. [*Surprised*] Marriage?

SNAKE GODDESS. You asshole, you.

LILA. They promised to get us out of the show.

LOLA. But no one ever did. [*She looks at her sister.*]

LILA. Don't blame me.

SNAKE GODDESS. [*Watching me*] You know, they used to pay a hundred bucks.

LILA. She [*Meaning Lola*] used to pretend to go to sleep.

SNAKE GODDESS. Fat old men with the two of them.

LILA. She [*Meaning Lola*] still thinks she's a virgin. Isn't that right, sister dear? [*She forces Lola to look her in the eye.*]

ME. [*To Lila*] What is it you want?

LILA. [*As if surprised*] Don't you know?

SNAKE GODDESS [*To Lola*] Tell him.

LOLA. [*In a whisper, looking down*] I want to be alone.

LILA. [*To Lola, beginning to caress the Snake Goddess*] Go to sleep, Lola.

ACT FOUR

Scene One

Time goes by. It is very late. I am in Lila and Lola's room. The Snake Goddess is asleep on the bed, snoring. Lola has taken some medication and is out like a light. Lately she has not felt well. But Lila is still awake. She is sitting up. Perhaps the medication has made her less mean. When she speaks, her voice is less bitter.

LILA. We've practiced this, you know. A hypnotist taught us. We can block out each other. [*She looks down at her sleeping sister, gently touches her cheek.*] You have to understand. It isn't really you. [*Pause, her voice drowsy*] You're all right, I guess. [*This is the first nice thing she has ever said to me.*] But we can't take anyone else into our lives. You see, there's only room for the two of us.

ME. [*I indicate the Snake Goddess.*] I don't understand.

LILA. [*Sadly*] I am what she is not. Don't you see?

ME. [*Not wanting to see*] No.

LILA. [*Exhausted*] You can't love both of us. [*Leaning back, by her sister*] No one can.

Scene Two

It is late at night. I am outside Lila and Lola's room. I dare not go in. Lila has bought a dog, a little white Pomeranian, a ratlike thing. In the daytime, he is no better than a rug. You could step on him and he wouldn't stir. But let the sun go down, and he rises from the floor like Dracula from the grave.

ME. [*A soliloquy*] I understand hatred. How it grows, how it festers. I know all the forms it takes. Listen. Watch me. Follow me. You, too, will know.

I am at the doorway. It is a quiet night, full of quiet sounds: a gentle breeze, gentle breathing. It has taken me an hour to open the door. They leave it unlocked, you see, to tempt me. I let my eyes adjust to the inside dark. They are on the bed together: Lila and Lola and the Snake Goddess and the little Pomeranian.

I have waited three days for the wind to change direction so that I can be downwind. Three nights of standing in the field, my head lifted to the hills, waiting for this soft breeze. Now I am ready. I begin to stalk. At first, there is no hatred in me, or if there is, it is buried deep down. I give myself to my senses. I live at the ends of my nerves. I can feel each atom enter. This is what a leopard is. This is what a leopard does.

It takes me half an hour to make the first step. Even now I am calm, emptied of emotion. I can pass between each molecule floating in the air. At first this is my only mission: to advance into the darkness, to make no disturbance. I use half the night just to move across the room.

Something strange has happened. This is the essence of the leopard's life. This is where it all begins. Listen close. A mystical transformation takes place. Attention shifts. Now every sense, every hormone, every protein is focused on the Pomeranian. A million years of evolution. Twenty million. To that single direction. And it lies there, its own millions of years directing it across that chasm; each of us driven by our separate aims. I have begun by infiltrating the night. For the leopard, and all like him, it is an act without malice. But now, it is all changed. There can be no accommodation. It is written in the world's infinite ledger: two living bodies cannot occupy the same space. One or the other must vacate. One or the other must rule. This is where it begins.

And so it builds, molecule by molecule, atom by atom. No matter how you begin, no matter how distant, how disinterested, you end up hating your quarry—every atom of it, every proton in the atom, every neutrino in the proton; whatever you call it down to the smallest part. You must. You begin not in lust or rage, but only in determination. Yet that is what undoes you, gives you your leopard's will, your leopard's reputation. Too great a desire; too great a love. But in the end it is hunger and hatred: ravenous, voracious hunger. Everything compresses into a single, constant craving.

And not only for leopards. Think of the fox in the hen house; the coyote and the sheep. This is why most hunting accidents occur in the gray hours of the dawn, after a long night's stalk. Make a move then, rustle a twig, and the hunters will rise from the reeds like demons and blast the world to smithereens. They are beyond reason. It is not food they want. Not even trophies. What they want to is to kill. And kill again. If they could, right then at that moment, they would kill every living thing in sight. So if the leopard is a murderer, if we all are, the blame lies with the victim as well. It is they who drive us to madness: the fat little Pomeranians of the world.

Try it some night. Crawl across the floor, inch by inch, afraid to breathe, listening to the seconds click, the minutes, the hours; listening to your fragile life ticking away. See what you feel then. Even the dumb, dead wall across the room becomes your enemy before you reach it.

Now think of me again. At last I am by the foot of the bed. The sun is almost up. Day is coming. I have spent the whole night covering twenty feet. Lola is turned from her sister, as far as she can. Her face looks peaceful in the early light. Her breathing is deep. I wonder whether she dreams, or if her dreams are her own. I would reach down and touch her just once, the single brush of skin against skin. I would not wake her. But the dog stirs.

I flee into the morning's light, undoing in ten seconds what has taken me a whole night to accomplish, I take with me my loneliness and my hate. Later, a letter comes. From Lola. It reads:

Dear Leopard Man

Please never try to see me again. I cannot love you. Not in the way that you want. You must think of me only as a fellow performer.

Lila says you will understand. I trust that you will. I don't want you to get hurt. Lila is thinking about getting a German shepherd.

Lola

I would have you know, my fellow stalkers, that one dark and stormy night, I ate the Pomeranian, hair and all.

ACT FIVE

It is now many years later. I have failed. In all this time, I have never been alone with Lola, never said a word to her in private. Now, they are dying, the two of them: Lila and Lola. There was a small article about them in one of the newspapers, a filler they call it. I have come to the hospital to see them. I am in the shadows again. They do not know I am here. No one does. I have heard the doctors say that it won't be long. Lila's heart has given out. The rupture will kill both of them. There is some talk of trying to separate them, but I hear one of the doctors say that Lola is the one who will not let them. The room is empty. The doctors have gone for the moment. I wait in the shadows. Lila suddenly begins struggling, as if she can't breathe. She sits bolt upright, turns to Lola, her mouth twisted in a grimace. Her eyes are wide. I hear a gurgling noise in her throat.

LILA. [*With a terrible effort*] Forgive me. [*She tries to say something else, cannot. Her lungs rattle. She falls back to the bed.*]

LOLA. Sister. [*She looks down a long time at her sister, then reaches over and gently closes both of Lila's eyes. She looks around the room. I crouch further in the shadows.*] Alone. God.

[*I want more than anything in the world to go to her, to tell her I love her; that I have always loved her. But I do not. I do not move. I am remembering her words from long ago. She has earned her last few minutes alone.*]

LOLA. Forgive me. [*She says this out loud, but to whom or for what I do not know*] I should have let him know. I should have let him know. [*She is looking at her sister as she says this, but it is my ears that are ringing, my heart that is pounding in my chest. These words are meant for me. For me. I know they are. I feel myself getting ready to spring, but just then she settles back on the bed. I force myself to remain still, watch as her breathing becomes labored. Then she expels one long breath and is silent.*]
ME. [*Coming out of the shadows, to Lola, to both of them, for in a way I have let them both down.*] Forgive me.

[*I close Lola's eyes. I lift up my head to roar, but no sound comes out.*]

I CAME STALKING THE MAN IN BLACK, AS IT WERE, BUT it was he who found the rest. He would suddenly appear in their lives. And of all the people in the show, it was the Elephant Lady who knew him best. She had been working a two-bit show out West. She heard a knock; when she opened her door he stood smiling at her, all dressed in black and holding out a card.

"A card?" I asked.

"Yes."

"What was on it?"

"On one side: 'The Eight Human Wonders of the World.' "

"And on the other?"

"A picture of an elephant." She shook her head, acres of fat rolling as she did. "I told him I never heard of it, these Eight Human Wonders." She stopped speaking long enough to stuff half a chicken in her mouth. "You know what he said? He said: 'I'm making it up as I go.' Can you beat that?"

"So you joined him—as the Elephant Lady?" I said.

She stared at me with her little pig-eyes.

"You know, I wasn't fat then. That was the crazy thing. I worked in a knife routine, holding up the balloons for this guy to break. But let me tell you, I was glad to get out. This here guy—his name was Fred—he had started to drink and his hands were beginning to shake. He cut me once." She reached out with one hand to try and show me the scar, but it was buried under such mounds of flesh she couldn't find it.

"I was glad to go. Another funny thing. I didn't have much of an appetite. But I took the card and off we went. And suddenly I couldn't stop eating. I mean I'd get so hungry I'd start to cry. He didn't say anything. He just kept taking me to restaurants or buying food and cooking for me. I didn't have a cent to my name, but he never said anything. You know, I gained fifty pounds that first couple of weeks. No matter how much I ate, I wanted more. And the pounds kept coming and one day he got me an outfit with a tail on it and a poster that said 'The Elephant Lady.'" She smiled again, her lips forcing back the fat. "You know," she said a little wistfully, "I used to be real pretty." She picked up the other half of the chicken and bit into it, the grease sliding down the creases in her jowls and disappearing behind her neck. As I left, she called out, "Now, who'd believe it?"

Once I asked the man in black about the Elephant Lady, about how he figured she could become the one. He laughed.

"We're all born twice," he answered.

I wondered what he meant by that.

"Once in the womb and once when we know who we are." He grinned. "All the rest is just finding the right name for it."

"A name?" I said.

"Take yourself. Now, you were the Leopard Man long before you joined the show. All I did was write it down for you." He laughed. "That's all I ever do."

Later, I was told the story of the Snake Goddess. The Rubber Man told me. Again, the man in black with another card. Or so the Rubber Man said.

"She'd been a stripper, a burlesque queen. In a sleazo show somewhere down South. Make this place look like Carnegie Hall," the Rubber Man said, twisting his rubbery neck to take in all the tent. "She had a roommate, another bump and grinder. Real skinny thing, according to her.

150

Come from out West and was real homesick. Hated the traveling. Hated the South. Hated the whole thing. So she kept a snake to remind her of home. A goddamn rattlesnake, rattles and all. Kept it in a glass case, like an aquarium. The Snake Goddess was scared to death of it. Couldn't even stand to look at it, she said.

"Then one day the skinny broad run off. Went home, I guess. Just walked out and left the snake behind. The Snake Goddess was so damned scared, she didn't know what to do. She didn't want to go near it. Figured she'd leave it alone and after a while it'd starve to death. And finally the thing just lay in the glass, not moving.

"So one time she gets home late and slides into bed. Told me she was so beat she was snoring before her head hit the pillow. I guess that bump and grind stuff is hard work. Anyway, all of a sudden she feels something next to her. She thinks maybe somebody has got into her apartment and is trying to rape her or something. She feels this thing on her leg, going up her leg for you know where. So she's lying there, still half-asleep, trying to decide what to do, whether she should scream or pretend to be asleep or what. And all of a sudden she hears this funny sound like someone coughing.

"And then all at once it hits her. It's the snake, the goddamn rattlesnake. It's got out of the cage. She's so scared now she can't even move, even if she wanted to. She just lies there, feeling the snake gliding over her pussy, and she's scared to death it's going to go inside her. But the snake just keeps going up onto her belly. You see she don't sleep with nothing on, at least she didn't used to, so she can feel this cold slimy thing right on her skin. She's trying not to move, not to breathe. She's sure if she moves, the thing will bite her.

"All the time the snake is moving up her body. And finally gets his head between them tits she got, them great big tits. And it sort of stays there, its head right between them like it's looking out a cave or something. And it stays like that the whole damn night, she says. She's lying there trying to be calm and not make a move. And guess what? The goddamn snake goes to sleep.

"Can you believe that? It got its goddamn eyes closed and it's lying there all curled round her great big tits, and she gets up the nerve to reach down and grab it, grab it behind the neck. Then she jumps up, holding the thing like a damn belt or something. She puts it back in the cage and puts a god-damn chair on top of the thing so it can't get out and then she runs into the bathroom and pukes her guts out.

"After a while she calms down, see? And then she decides. She's got to get the hell out of there. She's gonna walk out like that skinny roommate of hers. Leave everything behind, including the snake. And then you know what? There's this knock on the door and when she opens it this guy is standing there, dressed all in black."

"Holding a card in his hand," I said.

The Rubber Man stared at me.

"Yeah," he said, after a long moment.

"With a picture of a snake on it."

"On one side," the Rubber Man said, a bit deflated. "On the other side it says: 'The Eight Human Wonders of the World.' She reaches out and takes it. She said she was still in a fog. 'I'll be back later,' the man said. 'You think about it.'

"So she took the card and went and sat on the side of the bed. And the more she looked at the card the more she started thinking about the snake. And she figured the snake wasn't so bad because it could have bit her but didn't. And she got to thinking that it was sort of cute the way it went to sleep on her like that. And besides, it just stays in the cage all day, and she got this crazy idea that maybe it was lonely, being so far from its home and with the skinny girl leaving and everything. So she went down to this pet place where they sell rats for snake food and she got this rat and brought it back. The snake was lying all curled up in its cage, staring at her. She was still a little bit scared, she told me, but she was feeling sorry for the snake and thinking it could have bit her but didn't. So she got up the guts to lift the glass and throw the rat in.

"But the snake don't move, see? It just keeps lying there, watching her. And she gets this crazy idea that it misses her, that it likes her. And all the time the rat is running back and forth in front of the snake, only the snake don't seem to care. She told me the goddamn rat even ran on top of the snake, but all it did was look out at her with these sad little eyes.

"So without really thinking about it, she opens the glass again and reaches in and takes out the snake. And it just stays there in her arms while she pets it. And she swears it was rattling its tail softly so that it sounded like a cat purring. And she keeps petting the snake till her arm was about to fall off and then she put it back in the cage. And you know what? The second it got back there it went for the rat. Bit it right on the neck and wouldn't let go. She said you could see it pumping in the poison.

"It was like the snake was ravenous. It just opened its mouth the way snakes do, you know, and started sucking the rat in, and a minute later the thing was gone, tail and all. Then the snake went over to the corner and curled up and just stared out at her till it fell asleep.

"So when she looked at the picture of the snake on the card it came to her all at once. It would make a dynamite act, to have the snake crawl on her while she was doing her dance. And while she was thinking it all out, about how to do it and what kind of costume and everything, she heard this knock on her door again. And sure enough it was him. And he had these snakeskin bracelets for her to wear and this black silk dress. And a poster with 'The Snake Goddess' written over it." The Rubber Man swiveled his head all around, as if to make sure no one was listening. "And the damn thing was," he whispered, "before that night she was scared to death of snakes. Now they say she makes love to them."

That was only a rumor, of course. No one ever saw her or knew for certain. But some said, I won't say who, that she had intercourse with the snake, that it would stiffen up and she would take it for a lover. I only know that it slept in the same bed with her, and that she would hold its head up to hers and kiss it.

But snakes have always figured in our human stories, so it doesn't surprise me that people would come to believe things like that.

Anyway, one by one, the man in black came for all of them. He would just appear—with a card—at some crazy moment in their lives. Take the Monkey Men, for example. They had been midget wrestlers out West; all separate, fighting against each other. One of them dressed up like an Indian and called himself Standing Bull, and another one dressed up like a cowboy and called himself Little Custer—crazy things like that. They played all the Elks clubs and cowboy bars. It was never big-time, but it was a living. But then their manager got hold of some women midgets and he figured he could make more off them, so he gave the Monkey Men the old heave-ho. Left them stranded somewhere out in South Dakota. You can imagine how that was—three hairy midgets without any money and all those badlands. They were getting into fights with the cowboys all the time, and if it hadn't been for them sticking together they'd have been pounded right into the ground like fence posts, they told me. And then one time, right after this big brawl, when they'd been hurled out of a bar and were lying piled up on one another on the dirt street, who should walk over to them? You got it—the man in black. He'd been watching them, watching how they came flying out of the bar all bruised and battered. He held out a card to them. You know the rest.

Of Goliath the Strong Man, and the Rubber Man, I won't say too much. They were somewhat tame as freaks go. Goliath was really just a big strongman, only he had a special kind of strength. He could crush just about anything he could get his arms around. It was amazing, really. He could crush a chair to splinters, for example, and it didn't matter what kind of wood it was, either. He would squat down and get his great, massive arms around the thing and just sort of bring it to his chest, which was apparently as hard and dense as stone. And after a minute or two of him just squatting there and concentrating, the chair would suddenly start to collapse, to shatter and splinter, until it was a heap of sticks at his feet. Then he'd take a deep breath and stand up and bow, and the whole thing would be over. He could do this with just about anything: a chair, a table, a box, a bicycle. It didn't matter—whatever it was the man in black could get cheap from a junkyard or an old farm.

Sometimes, the audience would get a bit restless. I mean if you weren't sitting close enough to see the veins bulging in his arms and neck you would think nothing much was going on. Sometimes the audience would be on the verge of getting nasty, of booing or actually throwing something. But then they'd hear that popping or snapping sound and whatever it was shattering, and that would quiet them down in a hurry.

The man in black cooked up a couple of different stories about the Strong Man, and he'd change them depending on the audience. In one, the Strong Man had gotten into a fight defending a woman's honor and ended up breaking a man's back and having to run away from home and join the Foreign Legion. In another, he had accidentally crushed to death a woman he was only trying to hug and had to flee the woman's family. "Even now," the man in black would say, "they're looking for him. They could be out there among you right now."

When I asked him what determined which story he would tell the audience, the man in black smiled that impenetrable smile of his.

"How much they look like they beat their wives," he said.

The Strong Man himself would only say, "I did something very bad in my youth."

The Strong Man was very powerful, but it was a special kind of strength. It seemed limited only to this crushing power. In all other ways, he seemed to have no more strength than any other large and muscular man. I've read about something like that in alligators. They have an amazing bone-crushing strength in their jaws—but only in the closing of them. Apparently, it doesn't work the same way in getting their jaws open. That's why people can wrestle them. Once you can get their mouths shut, you can keep their jaws together by just pressing tightly with your hands. Of course, the trick is to get their mouths shut without them biting off your arm or leg.

Anyway, a dozen different men beat up the Strong Man. All they had to do was keep from letting him get his arms around them, and that wasn't so hard to do, because he was slow and clumsy and didn't have any instinct at all for fighting. I guess there is a difference between being strong and being tough, being a fighter. Or maybe it was like a safety device, invented by either the Strong Man himself or Nature to keep him from being too dangerous.

The Rubber Man was basically triple-jointed, if there is such a thing. Where other men had bones, it was as if he had cartilage. He could get himself into the most amazing positions, all right. But he had a nasty disposition. The official story was that he had been abandoned by his parents and raised by a band of thieves—and I can well believe it. It was said they used to take him to places they wanted to steal from and make him hide in all sorts of tight spaces until night came. Then he would climb out of whatever he was in and go and open a door or window and let the others in. He tried doing that to me once, but I smelled him. He had curled

155

himself up in one of the drawers to my dresser and was waiting till I went out for my customary late-night walk. I sniffed real loud and growled a lot and shook the whole dresser as if I was suspicious of something before pretending to leave. The Rubber Man waited a minute to make sure I'd really gone and then he kicked the drawer open and uncurled himself and flew out of the room. He never tried it again, but still I didn't trust him. I guess his early training had taken hold and shaped him.

The Stork Man was different. I've thought about him a lot over the years. In a way, he was the purest freak of us all, the most perfect metaphor. He was the absolute embodiment of the Law of Conservation of Energy: for every action there is an equal and opposite reaction. Simply put, his body lacked a shutoff valve. He started to grow and as far as I know he never stopped growing. He was two feet as an infant. Five as a boy. Six as a teen. Seven as a young man. And nearly eight when I joined the show. And he kept growing, slowly, of course, a half-inch or so a year.

But then Nature intervened. Or perhaps even God. After all, does it not say, "The Lord giveth and the Lord taketh away"? Whatever lift his mutated genes or glands or hormones gave his tortured body was counterbalanced by the implacable universal force of gravity. His bones curved and compressed. He was like a mountain—uplifted one moment, settled and eroded the next. And in pain always. Pain in the joints. Pain in the extremities. Perhaps even pain in the soul. My heart went out to him. There he was, head and shoulders above the rest of us, as if he would be our scout, the living monument to our human aspirations; as if human flesh could somehow try and match our human imaginations and leave this troubled earth—if not for heaven itself, then at least for the pure vastness of the open sky.

But it was not to be. Like Icarus he was brought low, not by the burning fire of the sun, but by the slow decay of ligament and cartilage and bone. His heart grew vast and fragile transporting blood to those distant limbs. He was a thousand lessons to me—history in the making: of empires collapsing under their own weight; of outposts left untended till they could no longer defend themselves.

But in the end, a man is only flesh and bone and blood and no more than that—not symbol, not metaphor, not dream. He fought the good fight, with dignity and courage and without complaint. Only late at night, as he lay writhing in tortured sleep on his extended bed, did the Stork Man cry out his suffering and his pain. We heard it in our own beds, in our own cages—we Human Wonders of the World. Perhaps you have heard it in yours.

And that's how, one by one, we all came to join the show, till there were Eight Human Wonders of the World. And a snake.

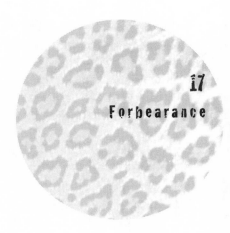

17

Forbearance

L EST YOU THINK ALL MY TIME WAS FULL OF HEARTACHE, I want to tell you this story. We were way up north and the rain had settled in around us so that even the man in black couldn't get away from it.

I went for a walk down the muddy road. Rain never bothered me much, anyway, what with my hair and everything. Along came two boys in an old Dodge and they tried running me off the road. The boy on the passenger side rolled down the window and gave me the finger, but then they drove too close to the soft shoulder and got mired in the mud. I'd been thinking of Simon and his dark road, Simon who had been so gentle, and that made me mad. I let out a roar and came running at them. When I got close I roared again and leaped up on the hood and shoved my face, teeth bared, against the windshield.

You should've seen the look on those boys' faces. Their eyes got big and they turned white as sheets. The driver even threw his arm up in front of his face.

"Please, Mister," the boy who had fingered me said, "we didn't mean nothing."

I stayed another minute, growling, then hopped down from the hood and came over to the boy who had fingered me. He had been too scared to roll the window back up.

"You boys should be more considerate," I said.

"Yes, Sir," he answered, not daring to look me in the face.

I looked closely at the two of them. They seemed like good boys, deep-down.

"A car's not a toy," I said.

"No," they agreed.

They'd been scared enough, I decided.

"Well, let's get you out of the mud," I said. "You wouldn't want to be stuck here all night," I added.

"No," the boy on the passenger side said, getting out of the car. He moved around to the other side, keeping his eyes on me the whole time. We rocked and pushed and soon the car came free. The boy jumped back in and the car took off even before he got the door closed. It went a short ways down the road, slowed, then stopped. Then the car started backing up to me.

I got ready to jump again, but the car stopped a couple of feet away and the boy rolled down his window again.

"Need a ride, Mister?" he asked.

"That's nice of you," I said, "but I'm just out for a walk."

The boy's face suddenly brightened.

"You in the carnival?"

I told him I was.

"No kidding," he said.

"Jesus," the driver added.

"Say," the first boy said, "how'd you like to come home for supper?" He looked right at me for the first time. "My mom sure can cook."

"I don't know," I said. "She's not expecting anyone."

"Don't you worry about her," said the driver, interrupting. "She don't let nothing throw her."

"And you can tell us about the show and everything," the first boy said. "Ain't no one like you been to our house before."

160

I smiled. "Well, if your mom won't mind."

"She won't mind," the driver answered for him, "as long as you wash your hands before sitting at the table."

So I got in the back of the old Dodge and we headed down the road. The rain had turned to a fine drizzle.

"What do you do?" the driver asked.

"I'm the Leopard Man," I said. Even though the engine was pretty noisy, I could hear them both gasp.

"No kidding," said the boy on the passenger side.

"Jesus," added the driver.

They were both quiet for a while.

"How'd you get a name like that?" the driver wanted to know.

"It was given to me," I said.

They were both quiet again. The driver turned the old car off onto a rougher dirt road and after a little ways we came to a farmhouse nestled in a clump of trees. It was a small place set on the edge of some hay fields. There was a vegetable garden off to the side, and a couple of small sheds nearby. The place looked like it had seen hard times. The boy pulled the car into a little clearing.

"Will you tell us about your name?" the driver said to me.

"Please, Mister," the other one added.

"If your mother doesn't mind," I said.

"She won't," the driver answered for her.

"My mom ain't afraid of nothing," the other boy said, getting out of the car and running toward the house.

As I got out of the backseat, the boy's mother came outside. She must have been around forty, but it was hard to tell in that light. She looked like the house, weathered and set but not broken. I guess the boy was right; it didn't look like much was going to shake her.

She stood with her hands on her hips as we came up. Whatever she was thinking, she didn't let it show.

"That's him," her son said. "The Leopard Man."

The woman didn't move or change expression. She just kept her hands on her hips, watching me. With a quick sweep of the back of her hand, she brushed a little curl of brown and gray hair from her forehead.

"You're welcome to have dinner with us," she said. And her voice, too, seemed like the farm, a little worn and tired but not unkind.

"Thank you," I said.

"He helped us out of the mud," the driver said, glancing at me. I understood. I wouldn't say anything about them trying to run me off the road.

Inside, the house was old and used but comfortable. And all of it was spotless. I admired people who could keep out the dirt because everything was set against it. It took a lot of work, steady work. And the woman had her share of that. You could see it in her eyes and in the lines that etched her face. You could see it in the farm. In everything. But she wouldn't let that break her.

The dinner was plain and good and just enough to keep off the hunger. Before we ate, we had to scrub our hands by the sink. After we sat, the woman clasped her hands and lowered her head and prayed. She spoke softly and you could tell that she meant every word.

"Thank you, Lord, for this food, and for giving us enough to give to another. Amen."

During the meal, I could see the boys wanted me to begin the story, but the woman held them off.

"It's not polite to ask someone to speak while he's eating," she said.

We ate in silence, making little comments about the food or the weather or farming. I managed to ask her, in an indirect way, about her husband.

"He died."

"I'm sorry," I said.

"That was a long time ago." Her voice sounded tired.

"In the war," her son added, proudly.

We finished eating and the boys began to clear the table. I offered to help with the dishes, but the woman would have none of it.

"You come to dinner, not to work," she said simply.

Afterward, she brought out some cups and made some tea and we sat around the table in the darkening light. The boys wouldn't wait any longer so I told them the story, leaving out a lot of things it was better not to say.

And the boys' eyes grew bigger as I told them about Africa and the leopard-men. The woman kept her face bent down, stirring the tea with her spoon. The boy was right. Little was going to throw her. And when I finished, the boys got all excited about going to the carnival and seeing the show, especially since they had been to dinner with the star, as they put it.

"A leopard can beat a lion any old day," the woman's son said.

After that, the boys got restless and wanted to go outside.

"Maybe you'd like to get some air," the woman said to me.

I saw that the boys wanted to be by themselves, so I said that I would just as soon sit there, if she didn't mind. And maybe could I have another cup of tea.

The boys went out, slamming the screen door behind them.

"They've gone to smoke in the back of the shed," the woman said. "They know I don't like it, but it's all right, I guess. You can't have them exactly the way you want them."

"They seem like fine boys," I said.

"They don't mean any real harm," she said, pouring me more tea. Then she sat back down. "Was it true?" she asked quietly.

I wanted to say "Yes" right away, because I felt it was important to her. I felt that she was a woman who had no time for lies. But truth isn't just one simple thing.

"I think it's true," I said, finally, looking up at her.

She smiled then, a fine, full smile that canceled out the tiredness in her face.

"Then you've had a hard life," she said.

"Who hasn't?" I asked.

She lowered her head to the teacup, letting her index finger circle the cup.

"They say there are some."

We could hear the boys outside. They'd come back from the shed. The woman had been right. I could smell the cigarette smoke on them.

"Can you stay?" the woman's son said to me. Then he turned to his mother. "And Lonnie, too?"

The woman didn't look at me.

"They'll be expecting him," she said.

"You call and tell them we got a famous performer here. Go ahead," the woman's son said to his friend.

"Maybe you've got someplace to go," the woman said softly to me.

"I don't want to put you to any trouble," I said. "You already have a guest," I added, nodding to the boy who was already dialing the phone.

"No trouble," the woman said. "There's a spare room. Those two," she nodded toward her son and the other boy, "sleep out on the porch in this weather."

I heard the boy talking excitedly on the phone. He said the words "the Leopard Man" a couple of times, and then I heard a happy yell.

"I'll come right after breakfast," the boy said, slamming down the phone.

"I'll go make up the bed," the woman said.

We sat around the porch till it was late and the night well-set. The rain had mostly quit and the air was heavy and hot. The boys did most of the talking. They told me about the farm and school and fishing and hunting. The woman's son talked about his father. He even went inside and got out this picture of him dressed in an army uniform. He was a nice, plain-looking man with a clean, honest face. The boy looked like him.

"You two go wash up," the woman said.

The boys went back inside the house and after a while I could hear water running and some talking and some laughing. Then I heard a toi-let flush. Soon the two boys came back out, carrying their shirts. I smelled the soap on them.

"Teeth brushed?" the woman asked.

Both nodded.

"Well, say good night," she told them. She went inside and brought out two sleeping bags, putting one on one side of the porch and one on the other.

"See you in the morning," her son said to me.

"You sleep on a bed, don't you?" his friend asked.

Before I could answer, the woman interrupted us.

"We've got a tub," she said, "and plenty of hot water."

"If it's not too much trouble," I said.

"Not at all." She left the room, I guess to get the bath ready. I turned to the boys.

"It's good to sleep out," I said, "where you can hear the night." I smiled. "You're good boys."

I went inside and followed the noise of the water filling a tub. The bathroom was a small room, plain but clean. Against one wall was the bathtub, the kind with four curving legs. It was long enough so you could almost lie down full length.

The boy's mother handed me a towel.

"There's soap in the holder," she said, nodding toward a little wire dish that hung over the tub. She moved past me, closing the door. I heard her footsteps trailing off into another part of the house. Then all was still.

I got undressed and settled into the tub. The water was nice and warm. I lay there, letting it lap against me. It felt good, seeming to seep into my bones, warming me from the inside out. All the sounds were muted, as if someone had draped a heavy blanket over the house and hills and fields. I strained to hear. I made out the sounds of little things moving in the dark, moles and frogs and crickets. Once or twice I even thought I heard the flap of owl wings. I closed my eyes and settled down.

Maybe I dozed. Everything was still and quiet. And then I heard a soft rustling noise, like leaves stirred by a breeze. When I opened my eyes, the woman had come into the room. She was kneeling by the side of the tub. She never said anything to me, but she smiled, reached over, and took the bar of soap from the dish and began soaping my back and shoulders.

She was very gentle, her fingers hardly touching me, her arm moving so lightly through the water it barely made a ripple. She took a cloth, rubbed the soap on it and dipped it into the water, pressing it softly to my skin.

The woman's hands were soft in the water. She washed more than the dust away. I felt almost young again, innocent, as if my life was the scab of an old wound that had fallen away. Simon had read to me something about how a man could feel like that with a woman.

The woman rose, handed me a towel and turned away. She walked lightly to the door. All I could hear was the slight scuffle of her bare feet on the linoleum. When I reached for my clothes, I realized they were gone. The woman had taken them with her.

I let the water drain and sat on the edge of the tub. Wrapped in the towel, I felt refreshed and clean. I let the silence build around me again. The woman came back with a bundle of clothes in her arms.

"I think these will fit you," she said. "The others will be dry by morning."

Before I could thank her, she had turned and was gone.

I put on the man's work clothes. Worn and clean and serviceable. They mostly fit. I went out and into the living room. The woman stood there, looking out the open window at the night that was beginning to shine with moonlight.

"Were these your husband's?"

"Yes," she said without turning around. She seemed very small and frail standing there, looking out at the vastness. Then she turned to me. "I wished him gone a hundred times," she said tonelessly. "And now I miss him. Isn't that sad?"

The word surprised me. Sad. I thought perhaps she was going to say "strange" or something like that. But maybe sad was the word after all. Simon had told me once that he thought the saddest thing in all the world was a regret we could not redeem. I tried to think of something to say, but there was nothing.

So I turned and went into the small, spare room and lay down on the bed. A sadness had come over me, too, who had my own regrets. I fell asleep remembering them.

When I woke the woman was in bed beside me. It was beginning to be morning, nothing yet distinct or defined. Light and darkness mingled together. I could hear the woman breathing, slowly, deeply. A pleasing warmth rose from her skin.

She lay with her back to me, curled, above the sheets. I knew this without turning, by the warmth, by the breathing, by the way a body shapes the air around it. I lay still and let my eyes grow used to the thinning dark. I did not want to disturb the woman.

I knew that if I were to turn to her, to lift her from sleep and press myself to her, she would not resist. She would let me settle on her, into her, sharing her warmth.

But I would not wake her, for a woman lying beside a man is a wondrous thing. Two halves of a single life, separate yet designed for each other. And sometimes to refrain from a thing is a greater intimacy than to have it. Sometimes forbearance is the greatest gift we can give to another.

And so I rose from the bed, careful with the silence. In the kitchen I found my clothes washed and dry from the evening's heat. There was some bread and cheese in a little bag beside the clothes. There was a note, written in pencil on a small white pad.

"I wish you well," it said.

I dressed quickly and left her husband's clothes where mine had been. Beneath the woman's words I wrote: "And I you."

Outside, the morning had taken possession of the land, settling on the hills and fields easily, lightly, the way some mornings do. Soon the woman would awaken. She would go on with her life.

In all my life, before or since, that was the day I felt most human and less alone.

18
Into the Woods:
Part One

I've been trying to put off telling you how I
came to be in the woods, but now it's time. It wouldn't
do, would it, for the Leopard Man to be afraid?

It began after the fight with Obaman, that darkness all
around me for a long time. Or maybe it only seemed a long
time. When the light came again, I could tell I was no longer
at the zoo, no longer in the city. The air had a different smell,
a strange mixture of soap and wildflowers, disinfectant mingled with woods and fields. The decayed smell of city pavement was gone. Sounds were altered as well. I could hear birds
singing their songs from beginning to end, no screams or
sirens to drown them out.

I was in a large, square room painted white, one small window across from me. The window was crisscrossed with wires
that sliced light into thin bright shafts that slashed across the
bed where I lay.

I tried to move but something held me fast. When I
looked down, I could see that I was tied to the bed with thick,
black straps that cut across my arms and legs, binding me to
the mattress. I struggled against them out of instinct, I sup-

pose. I tried to get at them with my teeth, but I felt strangely weak, and after a while I lay back breathing heavily.

I felt a dull ache in my jaw and a sharp one in my mouth. My head felt bloated and throbbed at the temples. My whole body felt bruised and raw. The pain reminded me of Obaman and his knife, yet for some reason the side where he had stabbed me didn't hurt much. Perhaps it was numb. I closed my eyes and tried to remember. But everything seemed so long ago, so far away, like the vaguest lingering image of a dream.

I tried thinking about Obaman's woman. I tried to picture her as I first saw her, black and regal and glowing, radiant with innocent beauty. But even this memory blurred and faded. Maybe this is how we keep ourselves from going mad, from being drowned in a torrent of memory and regret. Otherwise, who would have the courage to face another day of sorrow?

So I lay there and waited. Whoever had bound me would come again. I would lie there and wait. I wasn't the Leopard Man for nothing.

The room began to spin. I closed my eyes to let it pass, but it didn't help. Even the darkness was whirling. Blackness descended again. I let it cover me.

"You can open your eyes," someone said after a while. "I know you're awake."

I opened my eyes. Standing beside me in a coat as white as the walls was a woman with red hair. She was holding out two pills. She smiled at me.

"Really," she said in a pleasant voice, "there's nothing to be afraid of." She leaned forward to place the pills on my tongue. She smelled of soap and wildfowers, and as she leaned over me her breasts brushed against my chest, then my neck and chin. Instinctively, I began to nuzzle against them. The woman pulled back from me. Her smile disappeared and her face tightened.

"Good, good," she said, forcing herself to smile again, speaking not so much to me as if to someone behind me. There was a slightly foreign accent to her words, as if the word *good* ended with a *t* and not a *d*. She reached down and patted my cheek, the way someone would pat a child or a dog. When she spoke again, she was not speaking to me at all.

"You see?" she said. "You see how he would like to suck?" There was a note of triumph in her voice.

"It could all be the disorientation," a male voice said from behind me, deep and calm and resonant.

The woman's smile disappeared again. She looked down at me intently.

"Did you think you were at your mother's breast?" she asked, bending close again. "Yes or no?"

Even if I had thought so, I couldn't tell her. My tongue was thick and swollen and my lips felt fused together.

"My mouth," I tried to say, but it was impossible to speak.

The man from behind me came into view. He was wearing a white coat also.

"Eh?" said the man, moving near.

"Lips," I managed to whisper.

"Yes, yes, the lips," the man said, vigorously nodding his head. "It's difficult to speak, isn't it?"

I nodded. It was easier than trying to talk.

He turned to the woman.

"He's a little dry-mouthed," he said, and it was as if he was pleased with himself.

"Well, we can fix that," the woman said rather pleasantly, and in a moment she came back with a cloth and a bowl of water and began bathing my lips. The man then brought over a glass of water for me to drink. I drank greedily.

"So, it's the liquid, not the container," the man said, looking at the woman.

Reluctantly, she turned to me.

"How do you feel now?" the woman asked.

"Better," I said.

"Goot, goot," said the woman.

The man moved to stand beside her. He was holding a yellow pad in his hand and a pen that wrote in red ink.

"And what about your side?" the man said suddenly. "How does it feel?"

"Goot, goot," I heard myself answer in that same faintly foreign accent, but why, I don't know.

They both stared at me a long moment, as if trying to read my mind. Then the man jotted something down on the pad.

"No pain?" he said finally.

"No pain," I repeated.

"Goot, goot," said the woman.

"Do you know where you are?" the man asked casually.

"In a hospital," I said, without really knowing.

"And do you know why you are in a hospital?" the man asked.

I didn't answer right away. So many things seemed hidden in shadows.

"No," I heard myself say.

The man and woman looked at each other.

"Are you certain?" the woman asked.

"No," I said.

"You remember the wound, though?" the man said.

"Yes," I whispered. My lips were becoming dry again. I saw again the flash of the silver knife, Obaman's knife.

The man wrote something on the pad. I could hear the pen scratching across the yellow paper.

"Do you remember when that happened?"

"A long time ago. Such a long time ago," I said.

"How long?" the woman interjected.

I closed my eyes and tried to remember. I felt suddenly very tired— tired from the soul up. Bone and spirit tired.

"A long time," I repeated again. It was all I could manage.

"Why do you call yourself the Leopard Man?" the woman asked, making it sound like an accusation.

"It was the name I was given," I said, surprised that they would know it, that the woman would know it.

"By whom?" the man said.

"Obaman," I said. It was getting harder to speak, harder to turn thoughts into words, words into sounds.

"The man who stabbed you?" the man prompted.

"Yes," I said, nearly hissing the word in my fatigue.

"And why did he call you that?" the woman asked.

"My face," I said, grasping for words. "My face."

The man and woman looked quickly over at each other.

"Quick," said the woman to the man. "Get him up before the pills take effect."

The man hurriedly put the pad down and began undoing the straps that held me. The room seemed to be getting darker. I felt myself being lifted from the bed. I tried to stand but my legs were too weak. If it wasn't for the man holding me, I would have fallen. The room was getting ready to spin. I could feel it gathering itself, beginning the movement.

They began half-carrying me, half-dragging me down a narrow corridor.

"You must keep awake," the woman kept saying, over and over.

They led me to a small room. The darkness made it hard to see, but against one wall I could make out a mirror above a washbasin. They pulled me over to it. Both the man and woman were holding me. My legs kept getting weaker and weaker, my body heavier.

"What do you see?" the man said. "What do you see?"

The room became diffused with a thin, nearly transparent white light. I blinked to clear my eyes. I was so close to the mirror I was nearly brushing the glass. I blinked again, and again. The face staring back at me, the face in the mirror, my face, was not the face of the Leopard Man.

I closed my eyes and then looked again. In the ghostly light I traced the outline of the face in the mirror, my face, as if the glass were made of flesh and bone. Then, eyes still fixed on the mirror, I lifted my hand to my own face, to the face staring at the face in the mirror. My fingers brushed my lips, pried them open, reached inside. There were no long curving teeth. No fangs. Nothing top or bottom but plain white teeth. Square and even. My face was swollen, sore, and bruised. But no protruding teeth. No fangs.

And the hair was gone. Or rather it was no longer a thick tangle of black matted hair that covered my face. Instead only the stubble of a recently cut beard. The face in the mirror, my face, looked like the face of a normal person, bruised and ugly certainly, but no beast, no monster, no freak of nature.

And then either because of the shock, or because whatever it was they had given me was beginning to take effect, I felt my legs give way. I tried grabbing the edge of the washbasin but my hand slipped. The man and woman both reached out for me, but they were too late. I slid past them, down into a cold, hard dark. As I fell, I looked up once more. The face was gone from the mirror.

I KNEW THAT I WAS CRAZY. I MEAN, THAT WAS THE most logical explanation, but sanity is such a seductive condition. I had thought it would be the other way around, that madness would seem like a release. Even Simon had called it "the curse of reason." But it wasn't that way at all. I knew that I was crazy, but I didn't want to be. Not at first. I had fought too hard to be sane.

But madness has its compensations. Everything can be unconnected then. The world can come apart, atom by atom, moment by moment. There are no causes. Or too many causes. So after a while you give up on causes and take the world as it is, atom by atom, moment by moment. And so you see, being crazy, in a way, is like living in the leopard's world, the eternal, unconnected now. At first it was a liberation, a grand liberation.

I remained in whatever darkness I had settled in. It was comfortable, complete. I just lay there, floating or drifting, watching the dark flit by, atom by whirling atom. The hardest part was figuring where to begin. After all, I'd been sane all of my life. Or rather, I had thought of myself as sane, which is really the same thing. So, I had to retrain myself to think of myself as crazy. It wasn't easy. I realized, then, that crazy people had to want to be crazy. Deep down. Deep in their core. Even if they act as if they don't want to be. That must be why it's so hard to cure them. It would be like trying to tame a leopard.

So the question was—where to begin? I had a whole life to reexamine. I thought about going back to the beginning, to my birth. Or even before that. To the womb maybe; to the warm black sea. But that was too close to being logical, to being sane. So I decided to begin at the end.

Everything fell right into place. Reason is the reason nothing makes sense. You do away with reason and the mind is like an open door. Everyone is welcome. Nothing has to be hidden. Why should it be? We only hide what we're ashamed of. And we're only ashamed because we think we should be. But if you're crazy, you don't have to be ashamed of anything. All the worst is expected. You can't disappoint anyone—especially yourself. So what's there to feel guilty about? What's there to hide?

I lay there in the dark that was already like a womb. I let myself smile, a nice, restful, smug little smile. Nothing to be solemn about. Wherever I was, asleep or awake, what did it matter? Wind on my white enamel. Lips to port. Tongue astern. I let my newborn face sail quietly into the dark waters of forgotten things, the grand tour of the leopard's heart, beginning, of course, at the ending.

Obaman was dead. I was lying on the ground not a foot away from him. His throat was torn open. Blood was still bubbling out, a frothy rhythmical bubbling, like a small, red geyser. Only the well must have been running dry, because the spurts kept getting smaller till they died away to slow seeping.

Nothing can hold back the dawn. Not even death. So it came to me at first light as I lay on the ground, my own blood trickling down to mingle with Obaman's.

The leopard was there, too. It lay on the ground not five feet away. Its great black head was resting on its massive paws. Its long black tail was sweeping slowly back and forth along the ground, stirring up grime and dust like an old porter's broom. Its eyes were closed. It was leisurely licking its whiskers with a long, salmon tongue.

It was all strangely harmonious: the great cat, me, the body of Obaman, the blood, all beneath a dawning sky. If the leopard had not suddenly roused itself, I think I would have just closed my eyes and gone to sleep forever. But it did. It lifted itself up in the morning air and stretched its limber, muscled body. Then it ambled over to where we lay, dead Obaman and I. It bent its head low, and with quick stabbing motions of an unfurled tongue, it lapped my face. It felt like a dull razor on an early morning shave. The tongue was crimson beside the blue-black of its lips.

Then the great cat sniffed the air, stretching itself once more. Contented. Satisfied that all was well. Next, it turned and padded back to its cage, in that slightly ludicrous swaying motion the big cats make when they walk— as if a great round ball in their bellies rolled from side to side each time they pawed the ground. It stood beside the partially opened door for a moment, stretched again, and then with a quick, graceful, hunter's leap, landed inside.

The leopard's leaving shattered the calm. My side began to ache with a fiery insistence. A drumming began in my head, and I started to shiver from the cold. All gone was the calm quiet of the dawning. The air filled with noise. Loud. Cacophonous. Morning fire burned the night in streaks of red and saffron. The sky curled like parchment.

Our scene was sordid. Obaman, lying there, his blood congealing on the filthy pavement. And I, ripped and battered, without the sense to die. Even the leopard seemed obscene, lying there, its hide mangy, its flesh sagging from the bone. The small, dank cage suited it well.

It was clear to me that the last battle had been fought. But without glory. Had I died, or the leopard, there might have been a certain poetry to it. But with Obaman dead, his woman dead—his dear beautiful betrothed— nothing redemptive could be said of it. It was all loss. No gain. Ugly and pathetic. One noble couple slain. One beast caged. One unable to die.

I struggled to my feet. The leopard watched me. I think he knew. I stood before the door, swaying and weak. I dared the leopard to leap and devour me.

But he only lay there purring, tail sweeping the concrete, eyes gazing at me without passion or intent. I closed the door. I turned away. Nothing to do but wander into forgetfulness, empty the stage for another dream.

I clung to the last lingering shadows of that bitter night, following the narrow alleys clotted with human waste. The streets were brightening with the squalid light of civilization. The wound in my side stopped bleeding, sutured by my shame. Perhaps I had shed enough for absolution. I marveled at the body. Blood and bone have ways of contrition our brains can only envy. Every fortnight or two we renew the flesh, but retain the memory. If only we could slough off remembrances the way we slough skin. Then when our marrow had done its work, we might spring from the blood as innocent as a child. But old deeds make us old forever.

So I went down the dark alleys of the city's ruin, past everything human and decayed, to the city's own river of forgetfulness, there to bathe. I was so close I could hear the sewer rats paddling through the sludge when my legs gave out, or my will, and the world went mercifully dark.

And so I lay, letting the darkness cleanse my soul. That is the final consolation of insanity. Silence. Silence in the face of reality. Silence in the face of dreams.

EVEN SILENCE CANNOT ENDURE. THE UNIVERSE IS singing, we are told, a song of pain and woe: stars sizzling in their own hot juices; solar winds whirling across the galaxies; atoms exploding and imploding; static crackling across the immeasurable reaches of space. What chance has blessed silence in all that?

So a voice called out to me—wherever I had been—and brought me back to the white room again.

"Nice try, asshole," the voice said. "But I seen your kind before."

I opened my eyes. A man was looking down at me. He was tall and lean. His eyes were narrow and dark, hooded over by thick, arching eyebrows. A long, curving beaklike nose divided his face in half. He looked birdlike. Predatory. A hawk.

"You can fool them," Hawkface said, jerking his head slightly. "The whitecoats. But you can't fool me." With that he reached out with talonlike fingers and roughly grabbed me by my chin, lifting my face to his.

As he did, I realized I had gone forward in time again. My face was no longer scraped clean. Instead, under the press of his bony fingers, I could feel once more a downy coat of fine long hair. I let my tongue lick my lips. Sure enough, my teeth had begun to bloom again. I could feel their sharpened tips with the edge of my curling tongue.

"So don't you try nothing funny with me," Hawkface went on, his fingers pressing down on my bones.

For an instant, I had a terrible urge to jerk my head around and slash him with my newborn fangs, but I held back. It wasn't the place or time. As if he suddenly understood my restraint, Hawkface released his grip on me.

"You'd like to get at me," he said, hissing out the words, "wouldn't you?" He stood there for a moment, rocking slightly on his heels, his arms outstretched, looking like a giant hawk about to soar.

"How long has it been?" I said, before he did take off.

"Since what, asshole?" Hawkface said, standing stiff and peering down at me. His manners certainly left a great deal to be desired.

I was going to say "Since the night with Obaman," or "Since my teeth started to grow," but I realized all that might not mean anything to him. So instead I asked about the War.

"What about it?" Hawkface asked suspiciously.

"Is it over?" I asked. "Who won?"

Hawkface threw his head back and laughed. It was terrible to hear. A mocking, bitter laugh it was, raspy and guttural. If vultures could laugh, they would make such a sound.

"Save it for the whitecoats," he managed to say. Then he came closer to the bed, reached behind him and took out a billy club.

"They told me to get you up and give you the tour," Hawkface said. "So I'm going to tell you this once. You do what I say. No more, no less. And if you don't, I'm going to take this club here and beat your brains in."

And with that he brought the club down with a terrific thud about two inches from my skull.

I could feel it happening again, that surge of anger through my veins. The old feeling, that deep-down blood lust. I thought maybe after that night with Obaman it had passed away, but there it was, burning in my soul. The tips of my nails tingled.

"Don't even think about it, asshole," Hawkface said, as if reading my mind.

I smiled. It felt good to smile. It also bared my teeth.

Hawkface hesitated a moment, as if confused. Then he put the billy club under his arm and began to undo the straps that were holding me.

"It's time to meet the other freaks," he said, breaking out in his vulture laugh again.

I won't bore you with the details. Too much has been written about mental institutions, about all the ironies involved, about who was crazier— the inmates or the guards or the people who put us both together. And I won't take you on a cook's tour of the place either, with its wards filled with us crazies. Or tell you about its special little rooms: the sleep room, where they monitored our dreams; the water room, where they let us float like small ships at anchor; the shock room, where they sizzled our brains into order; or the hypno room, where they guided us through the back roads of distant time. But I must tell you about the two doctors, the man and the woman in the white coats, because without them my life would have been different and I might never have gone into the woods. The woman's name was Dr. Nouse. The man's was Dr. Hart. They were psychiatrists. They were going to help me. They were going to make me whole. They were going to take me home.

"Right now," Dr. Nouse told me, "it's like you're stranded on a moment in time, with no beginning and no end. You don't know who you are because you don't know who you've been."

"It must seem very lonely," Dr. Hart would say.

It was their job, they told me, to restore my past to me. Only then would I have a future.

They had a curious relationship. I think they really hated each other, but they tried hard to pretend they didn't.

"She's very competent . . . in her way," Dr. Hart would often tell me, among other things.

"He's really very bright," Dr. Nouse would say of Dr. Hart, "though you might not think so."

I think it was because they had different theories about human personality. Dr. Hart believed in dreams, and Dr. Nouse believed in mothers.

"It's in the brain, in the memory," Dr. Hart used to say.

"It's in the womb, and in the nursery," Dr. Nouse would counter.

Curiously, neither of them believed what I told them about Obaman and his woman and the leopard-men; about Simon; about my life as the Leopard Man.

"Why do you call yourself that?" they would say. "What are you trying to hide?"

"It was given to me," I would say, patiently, lying on a bed or a couch. "It's who I am."

They would both frown, give meaningful looks to each other, then shake their heads sadly.

"Come now," Dr. Hart would say. "You want to be helped, don't you?"

"Yes. You want to get out of here, isn't that right?" Dr. Nouse would add.

I used to think about that. What was there outside for me? Obaman was dead. His woman was dead. Simon was dead. And even the person I had been was dead. To go back would be to visit my own grave. My teeth were growing back, and the hair, transforming me again from the ugly to the grotesque. What could I hope for out there, out beyond the hospital walls, the gentle, sloping lawns, the iron gates?

Maybe it wasn't so bad to be suspended on the moment, to walk its boundaries, round and round. Without quite realizing it, perhaps I had begun to accept my life in the hospital the way the leopard in the zoo had accepted his. I thought of how he used to scrape back and forth against the cage, or lay crouched in the shadows, his yellow eyes fixed on the soft white throats of the visitors. What was he dreaming of as he lay there? Or was he dreaming at all?

But a man is not a leopard it seems, not even I, and so it began innocently enough—with a simple question.

"You want to be helped, don't you?" Dr. Hart asked me, peering up from his yellow pad.

"You want to be like everyone else?" Dr. Nouse added, coming close beside the bed. "Capable of affection. Of love. Don't you?"

I let the words echo in my head and breathed in deeply the smell of her, the soap and perfume, the starch of her white coat. I was surprised that words still had such power to move me. Love. What a small and foolish word. Yet, it stirred something deep inside my red and bloody heart. I remembered Simon telling me that love was a gift you give and are given. What you offer is yourself as you are, without pretense, without deception. And what you are given, what the other returns to you, is acceptance. You are not betrayed. The self you bring is not scorned or turned away. It is like the small offerings we give to our gods. What could be more foolish or more beautiful? All human acts are such, Simon thought, foolish and trivial but for the receiving. A woman yields where she might refuse. A man asks where he might take. We open our clenched fists and reach for our neighbor's hand. What could be more simple than that, more trivial and more noble? The difference between our smallness and our grandeur lies not in the deed, but in the imagination. It is we who choose. It is the world that is blank. And because I still wanted to think of myself as man, I nodded.

Dr. Nouse reached out and patted my hair.

"Good," she said. "Good. First, you must learn to trust us," she said, "to let us help you help yourself."

"To help us help you make contact with your human origins," Dr. Hart added, leaning toward me but speaking to Dr. Nouse. "Let us help you become part of the race of men again."

"You want that, don't you?" Dr. Nouse said.

I nodded again.

And so began my rehabilitation. The first thing they did was give me a new name.

"The Leopard Man will never do," Dr. Nouse said.

"It's like a chain around your soul," Dr. Hart added.

"We'll call you Adam," Dr. Nouse said, smiling.

"If it's all right with you," added Dr. Hart.

I nodded yet another time.

"Good. Good," said Dr. Nouse.

The next thing they did was fill in my life for me.

"That's our job," Dr. Hart said, patting me on the knee as if I were a child. "You just lie back and listen."

And so they told me the story of my confinement, since that day I had been found, all bloodied and scraped, and hairless and toothless. That had been a long time ago, a long, long time. The War had ended. The police had found me by the river. They thought either I had been beaten and robbed and left for dead or been mutilated in some sort of ritual. There was no identification on me, so they brought me to the hospital. They waited for me to recover so that I could give them a statement, but all I kept babbling about was a leopard or a leopard man and something about Africa and a Simon and an Obaman, whatever that was.

So, finally they gave up and just brought me here to the psychiatric hospital; they thought that I was crazy. Miraculously, my wounds began to heal. Hair began to sprout all over my body. My teeth began to grow. The only thing they weren't certain of was my brain. Some of the doctors believed I had suffered permanent damage. That was why I couldn't remember. But Dr. Hart and Dr. Nouse thought otherwise. They believed that I had suffered some terrible psychic trauma.

"You seemed the perfect textbook case," Dr. Hart said, and Dr. Nouse nodded.

So they began my "treatment." They tried a new drug on me, a sort of truth serum that had been developed during the War. It was supposed to relax me, lower my defenses, reduce the need to lie (to "mythologize" was the word Dr. Hart used).

Had it worked?

"Yes and no," Dr. Nouse said.

Some things seemed to make sense, to be real, as it were; some, of course, could not be.

"It's not like you were lying," Dr. Hart said, patting my knee.

"No," said Dr. Nouse, "you were only trying to save yourself."

From what?

"From the truth," they both said in unison.

So, reluctantly, they abandoned the drug.

"Too bad," Dr. Nouse said. "It seemed so promising."

"But the results were too unpredictable," Dr. Hart added, wistfully, as if something very valuable had been lost.

And it was on to other things.

"More decisive," Dr. Hart said.

"We had no choice," Dr. Nouse added, shaking her head.

Things like sensory disruption and electric shocks to my brain.

"We were a little reluctant to begin with that, I can tell you," Dr. Hart said. "But others were getting some pretty impressive results."

"Especially in cases like yours," Dr. Nouse added.

Like mine?

"Where there seem to be so many deeply rooted . . . blockages," Dr. Nouse replied. "The rapid surge of current seems to disrupt the inhibiting mechanisms."

"No one knows precisely how or why, but the results can be impressive," Dr. Hart added.

But not in my case, it seemed. No matter how they wired me up and "surged" me, as it were, the results were not conclusive. It was the same strange blend of truth and fabrication (that was Dr. Nouse's word). Only more so.

More so?

"Yes," Dr. Hart said, pursing his lips.

"You started blocking out the more recent memories and replacing them with . . ." Dr. Nouse paused, searching for the exact, professional word . . . "more distant visions."

Visions?

"Don't you remember?" Dr. Hart said.

"Let's leave that for now," Dr. Nouse said to break the discomfort of my silence. "You do still want to get well, don't you?"

They tried lots of other things. They were committed and inventive. They tried hot and cold water-therapy. ("To confuse your thermal regulators," Dr. Hart explained.) They tried sweating my inhibitions out of me. ("That was a long shot," Dr. Hart admitted, but there was some anecdotal evidence from some Indian reservation in the Southwest that it could work and so they tried it.) But, to make a long story short, nothing really worked.

"Nothing you could count on," Dr. Nouse said.

"Nothing you could really believe in," Dr. Hart added.

So they had to go back to the beginning.

The beginning?

"Of everything," they said in unison.

Again, they began with a simple question.

"What do all humans have in common?"

I thought that was a strange question to be asking me. What? I wanted to know.

"Think," Dr. Nouse said.

I thought. Brains? Hands? Awareness? Teeth?

What? I asked.

"Dreams," Dr. Nouse said. "Dreams."

Dreams? I repeated.

"Our dreams are like storms," Dr. Nouse said. "They cast up all manner of things that have been hidden."

What had Simon said? Shattering an illusion is easier than finding something to believe in.

"It's the key," said Dr. Nouse.

"It's the pathway home," said Dr. Hart.

To what? To where?

"It's your unconscious crying out," said Dr. Nouse.

"It's everything you've buried rising to the surface," said Dr. Hart.

And together, they had begun to enter my dreams. And this is what they had found:

All my life had been a fantasy, born out of pain—the terrible pain of having a face like mine, teeth like mine, hair like mine. To endure, to compensate, to make my existence bearable, I had buried the reality and created the dream. I had drawn it from the world around me: bits and pieces of the truth, of remembrances, of desires, of fears, of things seen or things imagined. The leopard. Obaman. The girl. All of it a dream. When reality became too persistent, too full of pain, when the truth of my life came too close, I covered it over with dreams: from freak to dreamer, from a lonely, unloved child to the Leopard Man.

"It's nothing new, nothing to be ashamed of," Dr. Hart said. "All of us walk that way, one time or another. It's part of being human."

186

"When the world outside cannot seem to give us what we need, the love and protection we must have," Dr. Nouse said, gently touching my arm, "we invent it for ourselves. We must."

"The danger comes when what we create becomes more real than what we are trying to hide," said Dr. Hart.

"Then our dreams become reality," Dr. Nouse added.

"And reality seems like a dream," said Dr. Hart.

And this is what they told me:

That it cannot last. The price is too great, the expenditure of energy too draining. It requires too much vigilance to keep the world out. It's like building castles by the shore. Sooner or later the tide comes in. The water rises. The walls break. Disaster. The dreamer cannot dream fast enough. Reality comes pouring in, like a tidal wave. The person has no more resources. All the energy is spent. Everything is shattered. Broken. Drowned. It's the end of everything. Ruin. Decay. Living death. That's what awaits the dreamer who keeps reality away.

"That's why, you see," Dr. Nouse said gently, "you must learn to face the truth, to begin to accept the past, accept what happened to you."

"What was done to you," Dr. Hart added, "no matter how painful it may have been. Only then can you learn to face it. Only then can you learn to live with it."

"Reality is never as terrifying as you imagine," Dr. Nouse said. "Believe me."

Oh, Simon, help me.

"He cannot."

Why?

"He, too, is an illusion."

Simon, help me.

"Perhaps he once was real, or someone like him."

"But not anymore. Believe me."

"Like the toys children play with when they're young."

"Invisible friends."

"Unreal."

I smiled. They were very close to me now. It was time to give them a taste of reality. What had Simon said? Always bite off more than you can chew, that way you'll have some for later.

Dr. Hart's arm was on mine, assuring me, reassuring me. I shot my head forward as far as the straps across my chest would allow. I speared him neatly in the forearm. He was real, all right. And so was I, the Leopard Man. I snagged a little flesh on the way out, because he jumped so. I decided to chew on it. It was real. Not quite as good as the meat they'd been feeding me, but it would do. To make a point.

In searching for what is most human about us, one of our best thinkers has said it is the hand that is more important than the eye, that it is our opposable thumb more than our stereoscopic vision that makes us what we are. But he is wrong. Both are overrated. Blind men have become prophets and kings. And what are hands anyway? What can they do? They grasp but they cannot devour. They kill but they cannot consume. They feel but they cannot taste.

Teeth alone are the gateway to our souls. Whatever the world is, how various, how new, how deceiving, it must finally reveal itself to our teeth. You cannot eat dreams, for all their fancy savor. A banquet in the mind is not worth a biscuit in the belly. Psychic delights don't fill up your gut. Whatever else the world may be, if sometime, somewhere, somehow, you can't take a bite of it, chew on it, swallow it, digest it—it won't be worth a damn. It may as well be an illusion.

Teeth alone can cut through all the world's vast confusion. To be real, it must be bitten. To be meaningful, it must be chewed. To be worth something it must be digestible. We may never have to eat our neighbors, but in our hearts and souls we know we can.

Think of children, little children. They are most human. Fresh from the womb they come, filled with the electronic biology of the species, untainted by lies, by history, by art, by religion; they know what to believe in and how. They reach out to the world with their lips, portals of the teeth. They suck. Then their little teeth grow and they bite. Then they chew. There's no uncertainty for them, no paralyzing deliberation. Their eyes search the world for food. Their fingers bring it close. Their little pointed teeth do the rest.

And isn't it teeth, after all, that determine our destiny? Don't busybody archeologists leap in scientific joy when poking in the ground they find an ancient tooth? It seems a most important existential artifact: show me the tooth and I'll show you the beast or I'll show you the man. On a single tooth you can hang tons of bones and flesh and even supply occupation and temperament. Vegetarian or meatatarian? Hunter or gatherer? Warrior or pacifist? Teeth seem to be our ultimate vocational determinant.

I had learned not to trust anything I could not bite. Unlike Descartes, who tried to build his whole philosophical edifice on something so ephemeral as words, I chose something more substantial. I bite; therefore I am. It is bitten; therefore it must be. What could furnish a more authentic, hard, unyielding truth than bright enamel?

I looked over at Dr. Hart. He had begun to turn whiter than his coat and was slowly sinking to the floor. A little blood spurted from his arm, streaking his white coat in curling little streams. Dr. Nouse watched without a word. She was a cool one, all right. She kept her distance. I let myself lie back down. I think I had made my point, so to speak.

All at once, Dr. Nouse turned, hurried to the door and yelled.

"Guards. Guards." She had a heck of a set of lungs.

In a moment Hawkface entered. He had come running. This is what he had trained for. He looked quickly at Dr. Hart.

"Nothing vital severed," was all he said.

Then he looked at me. A nasty little smile played across his face. He had taken out the billy club. He turned to Dr. Nouse.

"You better take him to the infirmary," he said, motioning to the still-fallen Dr. Hart. "I'll take care of the cannibal."

And with his club he did.

21

The Story of My Life

A LONG TIME SEEMED TO PASS BETWEEN THAT BITE and the resumption of my treatment. Spring came, heating up the winter earth with warm sun, dripping rain on roofs and roots and buds, melting snow on the distant hills. After a few false starts it settled comfortably over the landscape. I would lie in my bed smelling the bloom. Spring brings its own aroma, full of the wild abandon every living thing feels—tree and man and leopard. The power of restoration overwhelmed Hawkface's efforts at teaching me contrition. All my bruises healed. My teeth grew even longer; they glistened like tusks in the sharpened light. I shed some hair but what remained was sleek and fine, properly feline in its texture. I gained weight, grew strong just lying there.

I must have been something of a disappointment to them. And so one day, my uncertain penance apparently as complete as they believed it ever would be, Dr. Hart and Dr. Nouse returned.

"Well," they both said brightly, as if nothing had happened, "how is the patient?"

"Hungry," I said.

They both laughed. Uneasily. Dr. Hart fingered his arm absentmind-edly. What had Simon said? A good test of character is when you can laugh at yourself or let others laugh at you.

Then they got serious.

"We think it's time," said Dr. Hart, pleasantly enough, but standing just out of reach.

For what?

"For the past," said Dr. Nouse.

"For the story of your life," said Dr. Hart. "And what it means."

Why?

"Because you can't block out everything that brings you pain," Dr. Nouse said.

"Because sooner or later you'll run out of the psychic energy neces-sary to keep all that out," Dr. Hart added.

"Sooner or later the system will collapse. Break down."

"And everything will come pouring in."

"Overwhelming you."

"Drowning you."

"Burying you."

I got the picture.

"You don't want that, do you?" Dr. Nouse said, coming closer, but not too close.

I didn't say yes and I didn't say no. As I've said, I believe in more than words. But I guess they took my silence for assent.

And as best as I can remember, this is what they told me:

My mother was a prostitute. I was her illegitimate child. She loved me, they said, but her struggle to keep me was doomed. A child in a brothel is bad enough, but what about a freak? A beast?

I was hidden away, kept out of sight. But late at night, I would slip out of my room, glide down the hallways—beast-child that I was—afraid of being seen or heard. I learned to move like a cat.

And what would I see? Always the same thing: a darkened room and a bed; always a woman—my mother?—and with her the shape of another, something large and powerful heaped in the shadows. And groans and creakings and whispers.

Back in my room I would put it all together, lonely and frightened and jealous: I was not an outcast, a freak. My mother was not a prostitute selling herself to any man with money enough to buy her, letting men ride her in the darkness night after night.

These things I swept from my mind, banished to the dark corners of my dreams. Instead, another story filled my head. I became the Leopard Man. My deformities became marks of distinction. Symbols. Child of the white man. Child of the leopard. I filled the years of torment with miraculous visions. Those men lying with my mother became transformed into leopard-men. And I, I became the child of the leopard.

And why not? What a perfect symbol: fierce and inhuman, yet to me, loving and tender. The perfect mother: one implacably set against all mankind but me.

But then my real mother died, and I could no longer stay in the brothel and live among the shadows and my dreams. So I ran away or someone at the brothel took me away—to the Home, of course— to wake up that fateful morning, remembering nothing of my life till then, but the echoes and the flitting shapes that filled my dreams.

At the Home I grew into a man, despised and tormented by the other boys. Next, at the hardware store, I was once again hidden away and exploited, coming out only at night to walk the deserted streets, past the decaying houses, past the black men lurking in the shadows, till I came to the zoo. And then I transformed everything again: Obaman, his woman, the Leopard Man. I invented it all to give myself a mission and a destiny and a love.

But reality kept intruding. Too difficult, they said, to keep such a vision intact. And at last it crumbled. Because the life of the leopard that I had invented had a fatal flaw: it did not bring me comfort. It did not bring me a lasting peace.

So, in a final, desperate gesture I mutilated myself, scraping the hated hair from my body so violently I stabbed myself, trying to file or rip out my oversized teeth. Then, with the last of my strength, I crawled to the river's edge, hoping to die or be reborn. That is how the authorities found me: bloodied and amnesiac. That is why they brought me here, to the psychiatric hospital, to be cured.

But the hair had grown back. And the teeth. And the pain from before. And all the old memories and visions and distortions. So once again I sought refuge in the old way—becoming the Leopard Man, going deep into my soul, into my psyche, to once again fashion a world in which to live—to keep from oblivion.

That was the story they told me, in more detail, of course. More persuasively. They had an explanation for everything. Obaman was the father-figure, the mythic male who had abandoned me and had to be slain. His woman was the virgin mother I longed to have. Simon was only my alter ego: the friend I never had.

No one had called me out of the darkness. No one had made me the Leopard Man. That I had done myself: transformed my sad life into one full of mystery and destiny.

So they said. So they would have me believe.

I sat quietly listening, letting the day end, letting the night come on with its shadows and its mystery.

After all, I was not the Leopard Man for nothing.

22
Dr. Nouse's Analysis

LATE THE NEXT EVENING, DR. NOUSE CAME ALONE into my room. She didn't have on her white laboratory coat. Instead, she wore a yellow dress, with ruffles and lace. She had let her hair down. Long and sleek, it glistened in the dull light. Her skin smelled sweetly of soap and wildflowers.

I had been lying on my bed, looking up at my lone, high, barred window, listening to the night: the flutter of leaves, the scurry of tiny feet in the grass. I had banished any thoughts about what they had told me. Let the words settle in on their own. Sometimes that's the best way.

Dr. Nouse moved the wooden chair very close beside my bed.

"I feel sorry for you," she began, and her voice was no longer sharp and efficient, but seemingly filled with human emotion. "I'm not just a scientist, you know, a doctor. But a woman. A mother."

She paused then and looked at me. I thought for a moment she was going to cry. She had seemed so coldly efficient with her white coat and clipboard, it did not occur to me that she had a life away from the hospital. The amber darkness of the room softened her features, made her seem younger. I could imagine her leaning over to kiss a sleeping child.

"Try to understand," she said, controlling herself, "that the human child is like a candle held in the wind. At every moment, he lives in terror of being extinguished. From the moment of his birth the child knows this.

"Until that moment when he is born, he lives without fear, without worry. His world is complete, harmonious, secure. He floats there in his mother's womb, hidden, nourished, warm. He wants for nothing.

"And then he is born, wrenched from that wonderful security, pushed and pulled violently into the bright and hostile world. He can do nothing to save himself. He is forced to breathe, to swallow, to blink. He cannot run away, or fly away, or even hide.

"He has but one chance to live. And it is this: he must bind his mother to him, the being who conceived him, who kept him safe inside herself, who endured the agony of birth for him. On her—and her alone—depends his existence, moment by moment, hour by hour, day by day.

"And the infant knows this, instinctively. This is part of his inheritance, his legacy as a human being. Evolution has equipped him with this single tool of survival. He knows he must bond his mother to him, force her to minister to him. He knows that everything depends on her. She is like some vast, powerful figure that rises up before him, that gives him life and gives him comfort."

All the while she was saying this, Dr. Nouse was leaning close, till she herself seemed to loom above me. The warmth and perfume settled over the room like an invisible mist.

"Can you imagine the terror that realization unleashes? He wakes. He is frightened, hungry, cold, alone. He cannot move, can barely turn his head. And she is gone. Missing. Absent. He cries out in pitiful desperation. That is all he can do—issue this plea of tears.

"But she doesn't come. He shrieks louder. The hunger is gnawing at his insides. He shivers from the cold. He trembles at the shadows. He screams till his little lungs are ready to burst. He tries to find her, but he cannot move.

"And then, like some great shadow descending, she comes. And she is smiling. And she is warm. And she is full of life-giving milk. It gushes from her. She lifts him and takes him in her arms. Milk pours from her, pours out of her as if she were a fountain. She holds him, rocks him gently while he draws life from her. Later, satiated, warm again, she bathes him, dries him. There is comfort again, blessed, holy comfort. She whispers to him, rocks him. Her breath is sweet and warm on his skin. He closes his eyes. He sleeps. He dreams."

I must have done the same, so powerfully evocative were her words. When I opened my eyes she was no longer sitting in the chair but had moved to the side of the bed. Moonlight was pouring in the window like white milk flowing down.

"But never again," Dr. Nouse said, calling me back, "will the child be the same. Never. For he has known now the terror, the terrible emptiness of separation, of a world without his mother. And in the innermost recesses of his heart, he is filled for the first time with a violent, destructive hatred, a hatred for the same being who has brought him not only life and comfort, but also separation and despair.

"For every man-child that is the great primal crisis, the one great shaper of his life, the secret mover behind everything he does, all he is or will become."

I lay there barely listening, watching instead the rise and fall of her breasts against the yellow dress, tasting now in the air the slight saltiness of her perspiration.

"But one more dreadful anguish awaits the man-child, one more crisis in his life. And that is the rivalry of his father. For now the child is driven to return to his primal state of innocence, before the great separation. And the only way he imagines to do this is through intercourse with his mother, the one certain way back into her womb.

"But it is not so easy. Not only does society itself stand against him through its taboos and myths, its tragedies and religions. But there is also the father—more real, more threatening, more deadly."

I tried to fit the pieces of my own life into the pattern she was weaving for me. But everything was swirling around me, words and images and desires.

"To the normal terror and burden of your birth," she continued, "add not one father, but many. A new one every night. And you a witness to it all, hiding in your corner, watching as your mother abandons you night after night for a different man, a different father, a succession of hulking shapes."

Her words rang in my ears, then seeped into my brain.

"It was too much for you. It would have been too much for anyone. No one could have endured without going mad," she said. "You had to block out of your conscious mind the reality of your life. And in its place, drawn from those fragments of your mind, you created another reality, a dream to keep you alive and contain both the terrible rage and sadness within you. You became what you are: the Leopard Man.

"Think: What other set of facts can explain the dreams, the memories, the blank spaces?

"So you became a child of the leopard. The shapes you saw in the darkness—your mother lying under a succession of men—you made into the figure of a beast as ferocious as you yourself felt deep inside. And you gave it the capacity to love—but love only you. And around this beast–mother you invented a world of half-lit shadows, glimpses of shapes strange yet comforting.

"And to preserve this, you invented yet another world of myth and wonder—with you the center, you the Leopard Man, the redeemer."

Her face appeared radiant in the moonlight. She was caught up in the passion of the telling, the way a storyteller sometimes closes his eyes and is filled with the vision of the story he tells.

"But now we have begun to see the truth, the reality, haven't we?" She bent toward me. "We don't need this dream of Africa, or of the ghetto. You don't need to dream of being pressed tight to the back of some powerful beast, its rippling flank beneath your thighs, do you?"

Each time she asked, I didn't know whether she wanted me to answer or not. But in the end, I didn't. I figured they were rhetorical questions, the way she was asking them with her eyes nearly closed and rocking back and forth in the moonlight.

"But now it's time to move beyond," she said, stiffening and straightening and opening her eyes again, "time to move beyond the torturous ruins of the id, the primal blackness. It's time to move into the bright and necessary world of the healthy ego."

I sensed a fine and delicate silence as she paused. I could hear the grasses bristling in the wind.

"All you ever wanted was this," she said, her voice skipping above the airy quiet. "Your mother to love you, to take you in her arms and hold you close and give you the comfort that was stolen from you."

And so saying she put her arms around me and lifted my face and buried it in her bosom. I swear I could smell the milk running just beneath the ruffled silk.

23

Dr. Hart's Revision

THE NEXT NIGHT, AS I WAS LYING ON MY BED, HANDS behind my head, looking up at the moon-bright window, Dr. Hart came into my room. He was alone, of course.

"You asleep?" he called from the doorway. I think he was still a bit uncertain of my reformation.

"No," I said.

"Mind if I come in?" he asked.

"No," I answered.

He sat beside me on the wooden chair, as did Dr. Nouse.

"I bet Dr. Nouse really shook you up," he said, confidentially. How he knew about her coming to see me, I didn't know. I had not said anything, though I had thought about her visit. "Using her mammaries like that," he said, shaking his head in disapproval. "It's all those damn Freudians." He pronounced Freudians as if it were a curse-word. Then he settled comfortably in the chair.

"Well, don't you believe all that pap," Dr. Hart said. "Because Obaman is real. Legs is real. Those fellas in the leopard skins are real. And above all the leopard is real. In fact," he said passionately, "it's the most real thing in your life. Don't you ever forget that."

He said it as if he were delivering a sermon, his voice full of conviction, of revealed truth.

"Look, each of us is born the same way. Men and women both. We all had to go through the same process of getting here, of being yanked and shoved out of the womb. So what? So does every animal. Why should it be any different with us. Grunt. Grunt. Plunk. And there we are. And every other animal in the world can deal with it, can't they? An hour after it's born a zebra can run with the herd, can't it? Or it can remain still in the grass for hours, lions not a hundred yards away.

"Why? Because Nature provided each one a way to survive, a way to deal with the world. Each gets just what it needs to give it a fighting chance at life. Right? That's evolution. Nothing magical about that, right? No great cosmic trauma. An animal gets born and does what it has to do to survive. Right?"

Dr. Hart kept inserting these questions into his monologue, but as with Dr. Nouse, I thought they were mostly rhetorical. I didn't bother answering. I just lay there listening, but also thinking it was nicer listening to Dr. Nouse as she swayed in the moonlight smelling of soap and wildflowers. But maybe Dr. Hart was right, maybe that way only led further away from the truth.

"Well, man is an animal, too. Right?" Dr. Hart continued, and I certainly couldn't argue with him there. "He, too, must have his own way of surviving, of dealing with his birth. If he's physically immature, if he is dependent on his mother, that's not a nightmare—that's the condition of his existence. One he's been born to live with. If the act of getting born is going to make everyone psychotic, full of terrible complexes and guilt-laden wishes, then what kind of species are we? If everyone is going to go around lamenting the loss of the womb, where does that leave us? You see what I mean? We'd be the only animal that didn't get some real biological preparation.

"So I don't think that's the problem. I think we are prepared biologically for our birth. You'd be amazed at the physiological changes that occur in both mother and fetus to dull the experience, the pain, the trauma. A million chemical changes, cellular changes, organ changes; we get born ready for life like the other animals. And I think that like other animals we accept the fact of our birth and get on with living. And we get on with it the same way that the other animals do—through the herd, through the tribe. We turn to the social group. We are the social group. It's in our blood, in our bones. And," he said, pausing for effect, "it's in our dreams." He leaned forward and peered at me long and hard. "You understand what I'm saying?"

It seemed to make sense. If leaving the womb were going to be such a big thing, it stands to reason we'd find ourselves some way to deal with it. I mean, after all, floating around there all day we don't have much else to do but get ourselves ready.

"I think," Dr. Hart went on animatedly, "that our dreams are poured into our brains through evolution. All of us—and I mean all of us—share the same heritage. That's why so many of our stories, so many of our dreams, are the same. Why we paint ourselves the same kinds of pictures; believe in the same kinds of gods and demons; dream the same kinds of dreams. I don't care who you are, whether you're a pygmy running through the jungle or an Eskimo sitting in an igloo, or an executive in a gray suit riding in a limousine. Deep down we're all the same. We understand the world in basically the same way.

"You see, we're all brothers and sisters. And not just those of us alive now, but everyone who came before: the living and the dead. Because in a way, it was their dreams that first entered our heads. You follow me? Just as we pass on the color of our skin, the color of our eyes, whether we're good at music or math, so, too, we pass on our dreams." He paused again, dramatically. "And our nightmares."

"Look, I'll grant that something may have happened when you were a child. Dr. Nouse may be right about that. Perhaps your mother did abandon you. Perhaps you never did know your father. Or perhaps you were abused, tormented, even—given your . . . uh, handicap. But all that makes it even more urgent for you to reach down into that place that harbors the memories of our race. We all sometime or other turn our backs on the world and go live in our dreams until we grow strong again; until we are healed from life's pain; until we understand what has happened to us and can deal with it.

"But you couldn't come back out, or didn't want to come back out. So the place of dreams, the place of the ancestors, became your home. And there you found what you needed: the wild, primal landscapes filled with lightning and thunder, filled with caves and shadows and ferocious beasts. That's the world in which you sought refuge and understanding—you with your tormented fears and angers—and once having found that world, there you stayed.

"You discovered the world of ancient memories and dreams, the world all humans discover sooner or later. But whereas most of us go there only at night, when we sleep and dream, when our conscious mind lets us, you went there all the time, daylight or dark. For you, there was no other world, no other reality.

And what did you discover? You found heroes and monsters, the clutter and mumble of the past. Beasts roaming the jungle where men, primitive and weak, crouched in terror behind bushes. And what did you do? You willed yourself part of that world, one with it. You found in yourself a ferocious strength and a wild freedom that made you one with the world. If you could not be stronger than the beasts that hunted you in your mind, then you could merge with them, become one with them. You could be more than human then, you would become like a god. Powerful. Invincible. Ferocious. Cunning. And yet, still a man, still wise, still capable of love and passion. Child of the beast. Child of man. The Leopard Man."

By this time, Dr. Hart had gotten up from the chair and was beginning to pace the room. Sweat glistened on his forehead. His hands balled into a fist. Like Dr. Nouse before him, he was caught up in the telling.

"It's an old story, an old, old story, told by every tribe of people who ever lived. In South America. In Asia. In Africa and America. Everywhere the same. The Beast-Man. The Man-Beast. Child of the Wolf. Child of the Bear. Child of the Jaguar. Human and bestial. Human and divine.

"You chose for yourself, out of those whirling, swirling forms hidden deep in our psyche, the image of the leopard. Or maybe you didn't choose it. Maybe it chose you. Maybe you looked in the mirror, in a certain light.

Maybe you saw yourself reflected in someone's eyes. Maybe someone said, half in jest, half in mocking: 'He looks a little like an animal. Like a lion. Like a leopard.' But despite the laughter you were intrigued. It could serve your needs. The leopard still lives, does it not? It has not passed away; it lives even in the modern world as it did millions of years ago. Untamed. Unbroken. Mysterious. It still brings terror into the hearts of men, women, too. Powerful. Solitary. Implacable. It has all the qualities you felt you needed, everything to compensate you for your fear and anger and pain.

"To be like the leopard, feared and respected. To be powerfully self-sufficient, relying only on your own strength and cunning. Needing no one and nothing. Not like the lions and wolves that live together in packs. No. The leopard lives alone.

"One catch, though, isn't there? One flaw in the perfect psychic plan. And that's what kept it from consuming you entirely, leaving you forever in a primal land, with no need of anything else, not even reality. For the leopard is not totally self-sufficient, is it? One need, one desire leads it out of isolation: the need to mate, to be with another, if only for the briefest moment. As with the leopard, so with man. And so with a man who would be a leopard.

"Each time you were called out of yourself, out of this primitive dream-land and into the world of humanity, you saved yourself from drowning in that storehouse of ancient images. One by one you invented that other someone that you needed: Simon, Obaman, his woman. Each one lost, finally, but not until they had drawn you out of yourself and given you a place and a mission in the world."

Dr. Hart had moved to stand beneath the window. He seemed suddenly drained, as if the telling of the story of my life had been too much for him. His shoulders slumped a bit and he took a deep breath.

For my part, I felt great. The story was certainly interesting. I didn't feel tired at all. The shadows in the room shifted from shape to shape as if in response to Dr. Hart's narrative. It was a good night.

"We are not beasts," Dr. Hart said wearily, breaking the carefully wrought silence, "are we?"

And just like that, hearing those simple words, I felt a sudden sadness welling up in me; I could barely keep from crying.

"No," I whispered.

Dr. Hart took a step toward me.

"We are human and we need the company of humans," he said.

"Yes," I said again, or thought I said. Tears wet my eyes. I felt empty, alone, like a vast space had opened between me and the rest of the world. And into that space floated the image of Simon, gentle Simon. The sorrow in our lives, he told me once, comes from regret. We were together in my attic room, in the dark. He was sitting on the chair by the window, the one that later Obaman would sit in, and he lowered his head to his hands and wept. He had been talking about his mother, how she had suffered in silence. I wanted to comfort him, but what could I do. He was right. Once you regret you seek for redemption. And to believe in redemption you must believe in justice. You must believe in others. And so we open the doors to our souls and let the world enter. What had Simon said as he was leaving that night? Regret is the cancer of the soul.

The image of Simon faded. There was nothing I could say to him—then or now. No one needs to sit in judgment of us. Memory does it for us.

Dr. Hart had come to stand beside the bed, and suddenly I felt as weary as he appeared to be.

"If what you say is true," I said, "what happens if you take the Leopard Man away?"

His hand on my shoulder felt heavy.

"You won't have to be a leopard to be a man," he said.

I don't remember his going. The room was very still and gradually I realized he was gone. Perhaps I'd fallen asleep. Perhaps I'd gone back to that place in my memories he had been talking about. But if I had, I couldn't remember. And I didn't know whether that was a good thing or bad.

THE TWO OF THEM CAME FOR ME THE NEXT DAY.
The birds were singing, bright little songs for the gift
of morning.

"It's time," they said, Dr. Nouse and Dr. Hart, and loosed
the straps that held me.

I knew for what.

I followed them out the door and down the corridor, past
rows of rooms filled with people waiting for their own mo-
ments of truth. Walking along, I silently repeated, "I am the
Leopard Man. I am the Leopard Man," but why I do not
know.

We came to one of the small hypno rooms, soundproof
walls and artificial lights. Dr. Nouse and Dr. Hart put on their
white laboratory coats and stood against the far wall, watching me. I lay down on the full-length couch, on my back,
and closed my eyes. There was music in the air. Voices. Slowly
the room began to spin, darken. Shadows heaped themselves
into impenetrable shapes. Words echoed like distant thunder.

I am someplace else. In a street, I think. In an alley. It is
cold where I am. A wind has picked up. My back is pressed

to the stone wall of a building. I am looking up at another building across from me. My eyes water. Two windows hang in the brick, each filled with pale yellow light. One is a bedroom. At least there is a bed in it. The other is a kitchen: sink, table, three chairs.

A man appears in the door of the bedroom. He moves inside. He stands by the bed, his back to the window. He unbuttons his shirt. I cannot see, of course, but in a moment he takes off his shirt and lets it fall to the floor. His skin is black. His back is large, heaped with knotted muscles. He undoes his belt, lets his pants slide down his powerful thighs till they fall past the bed-line to the floor. The man stands naked but for a pair of gleaming white shorts that barely cover his muscled buttocks. He sits on the bed, his back to the window, to me, looking at the open door.

A woman comes into the other room, the room that looks like a kitchen. She is a small woman in a pale yellow dress, her yellow hair pulled up onto her head. She comes over to the table, then stands looking out the window, at me. I crouch into the darkest of the shadows. I am shivering. I feel certain that the woman can see me. I close my eyes.

When I look up again, the woman has moved. The light in the room like a kitchen is gone. Instead, the woman stands rigid in the doorway of the other room, the room with the bed on which the man sits. He looks at the doorway, at the woman. She stands there for a moment, then she reaches up with her hand and touches something on her head and shakes it. Suddenly her hair cascades down in waves of gold that frame her white oval face. I can see the man take a deep breath as he watches her, his muscles rippling.

The woman leans against one of the doorposts, so that she is in profile to the man, to me. Her fingers run through the thick golden hair, topped by long sharpened nails, like the tines of a comb. Her whole body seems to become liquid, as light and free as her hair. She seems languid, seductive, catlike in her grace. She stretches, her arms raised in the air, her palms bent backward.

Then, in that same unhurried ease she unbuttons her dress. The dress slides from her shoulders down her slender body to the floor. The man laughs at this. I see his body shake, muscles knotting and releasing. The woman stretches once more, lets her own fingers run softly down the white silk of the slip that blooms where the yellow dress had been. Her body seems to flow beneath the fabric as she stretches, slowly, luxuriously, the way a cat stretches after a long nap.

She does the same thing again, but now she presses her palms to the white silk, the flesh of her body rippling beneath the fabric. She rubs her palms over her breasts, then over her stomach, over each thigh, till she reaches the hem at the bottom of her slip. All the time she is looking coyly at the man and smiling. The man still sitting on the bed, watching, breathing heavily.

The woman begins to raise the silk up her silken thighs.

"Lordy, Lordy," I hear the man say, as he shakes his head. "You sure is a tease."

The woman grins. "I know what a man likes," she says in a singsongy voice. The slip is nearly to the top of her thighs. And then suddenly she freezes, face a mask of fear. She screams like a siren. Shrill. Piercing. Paralyzing. I am frozen in place.

The woman has seen me. She is staring past the man, her eyes wide. Her hand still holds the slip, but the other is now covering her breasts. The man turns from her toward the window, toward me, his face a mask ugly with hatred. He leaps to the window, smashing it with his fist. The glass shatters, crashes to the pavement around me.

He is coming for me, I know. He will jump from the window onto me, onto my back. He is going to crush me. I can see him climbing through the open window, looking down at me. His white teeth are bared. His white shorts glow.

And then just before he leaps, a hand grabs mine and pulls me away, out of the alley, out into the street.

I look to see whose hand has saved me.

A woman stands beside me. She is dressed in white. She speaks in a reassuring voice.

"You're safe now," she says

I turn back. The windows are gone. The man is gone. The light has turned from yellow to white. I am in a room, a small, square room. I am standing on a chair. The woman is beside me. Across from me, by the door, is a man.

"You're awake now," he says softly. His arms are crossed in front of him, as if he guards the door. He is dressed in white. I recognize him. Dr. Hart.

"You're safe now," the woman says again. I know her, too. Dr. Nouse. "Come," she gently pulls on my hand.

I let myself down from the chair. Dr. Nouse takes her hand from mine and moves it to my face which she lifts to hers.

"You've only been dreaming," she says, smiling.

"The truth," Dr. Hart says quietly from the doorway.

I believe him. I must.

25

The Beginning
of the End

ONE DAY BLEEDS INTO ANOTHER, ONE VISION INTO the next. I journey from one room to another, but I cross decades and miles and miles of time. I am drawn by the bright glisten of the shimmering sun. Or is it only a golden pocket watch held before my watering eyes? We journey from light into darkness and back into light again. I feel like a beast on the African plains on a long, dry migration. I am following my own footsteps in the dust. I am following my own self home.

We gathered in the dark again. A face began to arrange it-self, drawn from the blackened air.

"Whose face?" a voice asked. "Tell me."

I watched in fascination, like someone watching the birth of a child.

"Whose face is it?" the voice repeated, soft, deep, insistent.

The skin was white, dull and lifeless, spiderwebs of hair covering that face.

"Tell us more," the voice said, hanging in the air.

The face began to cry, to howl. The lips parted. Four pointed teeth, slender, tapered, protruding from pink gums.

"Whose face is this?" the voice demanded.

Before I could answer the face disappeared. I could see nothing, yet I felt the presence of something. And then, one by one, faces began to emerge. They were the faces of spotted leopards, their yellow eyes becoming clearer and clearer, as if someone were fine-tuning a television image. Now I saw that the faces were really masks, skins of leopards worn over men's faces. Steel claws began to emerge. Then men appeared. Leopard-men who encircled me. When I turned to join them, I noticed something at my feet: the amber-colored body of a small antelope, patches of white visible except where covered with streaks of red. The creature's throat had been torn open, and I saw long gashes in its flanks.

"Careful now," a voice told me.

The men in the leopard masks were grinning. The small, dead antelope looked strangely peaceful, as if it had only lain down to rest. I backed up slowly, and the crowd of leopard-men parted for me. But no sooner was I past them when they fell on the carcass, tearing off chunks of flesh with those terrible steel claws. Some ripped at the antelope with their teeth.

I wanted to run away, to be anywhere but where I was. I could hear the flesh being ripped.

"No." The voice was loud, insistent. "Stay."

I stood, my back turned to the leopard-men and the antelope. Gradually the sounds died down, giving way to a dull moan. The light grew dim again.

"No more lies," a voice said.

"No more dreams," a voice said.

I felt myself alone, a solitary figure on a windswept plain.

"The truth," a voice said.

"Only the truth."

I turned back. It seemed to take forever. No light anywhere except for an eerie, milk-white glow cast by a high and distant moon. A faint wind stirred. I thought I could hear the sway of grass.

"What do you see?" a voice demanded.

I saw a shadow heaped on the ground. But not the antelope. It was large, motionless. I could sense life within it, feel it, taste it. It lay there waiting for me. I knew that without knowing why.

"What do you see?"

I could see more clearly now, perceive two shadows nearly merged into one, but separate. They were both on the ground, sprawled out across the clearing from me. I took a step forward.

"Careful now," the voice whispered again.

One of the figures appeared human. I could make out arms and legs, a body. The other figure was less defined. Sometimes it seemed human, but larger, more hulking. I took another step forward.

"What do you see?"

The larger figure was black, heavy, dense. I could hear breathing, see it rise and fall in rhythmical pulses as if to lift itself up from the ground and then let itself down again. I took another step forward.

"Very careful now. Be very, very careful."

I shivered in the cold as the shapes grew more distinct. I took yet another step forward.

The larger form was now obviously man-shape, with powerful shoulders and a huge thick neck. The head was bent toward the figure beneath it. The man-shape lifted itself on elbows, then drove itself downward. I could almost make out the figure beneath it, a small woman, frail, supine, faceup. I thought I saw the rounded curves of a woman's breasts. I took two steps forward.

"The truth now. Nothing but the truth."

I rubbed my eyes; I could see clearly now. The larger figure was no man at all. It had only seemed so, but now I saw the thick, wide head, the small pointed ears. I could see those great rounded shoulders that rose almost to a hump before they curled downward into the long, sleek expanse of its body. It was lying on the ground crouched on its haunches, a long black tail sweeping quietly back and forth. Its head was lowered to the form underneath.

I could see that it really was a woman lying on her back. Naked. For an instant she seemed a woman waiting to receive her lover.

"The truth now. Only the truth."

The woman's arms were crossed; one on her stomach beneath her breasts, the other over her eyes as if she were blocking out the scene before her. I took one more step forward.

"No more dreams," a voice said. "No more lies."

I saw everything now. No love made here. The animal bent its head down only to tear away chunks of the woman's body. It was feeding on the soft flesh of her thighs now. I could hear the ripping, see the animal brace with its huge paws to tear the flesh away I could hear it chew and swallow, and the low, guttural noises deep in its throat.

"The truth," the voice shouted. "The truth. The truth."

"The truth," I shouted back. "Only the truth."

The great black beast on the ground lifted its head to me, its eyes burning yellow. It growled under its breath. Then bent to the body again, shaking its head to tear the meat. It rose up, stretched, moved toward me, muscles tensing and flexing. It approached slowly, that great black body swaying back and forth. It carried something in its jaws. I wanted to look away but I couldn't. It came right up to me, carrying a bloody, shredded leg. It dropped the leg at my feet. Then, with a slight movement of its head, it curled out a thick bristly tongue and licked my hand. Deep in its barreled chest, I could hear the beginning of a purr.

I screamed, long, loud, primal, my scream filling the air, drowning out every other sound. I had to clap my own hands to my ears to keep the sound of my screaming from driving me mad. I screamed and I screamed and I screamed.

And when the sound wouldn't come out any longer and my throat felt ripped open and raw, I looked around. I was back in the room again, Dr. Nouse and Dr. Hart staring down at me, their faces bleached white.

"It can't be. It can't be," Dr. Nouse was mumbling, tears streaking her face.

"My God. My God," Dr. Hart was moaning.

I uncovered my ears and lifted myself from the couch. The screaming had been good. It had emptied me. I felt buoyant, as if for the first time my soul had been scraped clean.

I looked from one to the other. When I spoke, my voice was calm, perfectly controlled.

"I have come home," I said.

Neither moved. It was as if my screaming had hardened them into frozen, terrified shapes.

"It can't be. It can't be," Dr. Hart said finally, only his lips moving. "No one could have lived like that. . . ."

"There must be a mistake. We must try again," said Dr. Nouse, but I heard no conviction in her mechanical tone.

"I remember," I said, looking at her. "Everything."

"Oh, my God," Dr. Nouse clapped her hands to her ears so as not to hear.

Dr. Hart closed his eyes, took an enormous breath, let it out in a wail-like moan.

"Do you know what that means?" he said, his voice a strangled whisper, his whole body shaking.

I waited for him to stop trembling.

"Do you?" I said.

No one moved. No one spoke. And then I turned slowly and took a step toward the door. There was no more reason to stay.

"You can't," said Dr. Hart, but that, too, was said mechanically.

"Something went wrong," Dr. Nouse said, her voice shrill, strained. "Something must have gone wrong."

Again I moved toward the door.

Dr. Hart began to stir, to move after me.

"You can't," he said. His voice was louder, more authoritative. "You can't leave. Not now."

I turned to him and began to growl, my nostrils flaring. He backed away.

I let out a light roar. It made me feel better. The two of them nearly fell over each other getting out of my way. I stepped into the hallway and sprinted down the long corridor, out the door, past the startled nurses, past the attendants, past Hawkface. I felt light and lean. I bounded along. The ground whizzed by under me.

I could hear sounds of commotion behind me, shouts and screams, the banging of doors. The iron gate was in front of me. Without breaking stride I crouched and sprang. I soared into the air. My hands caught the iron spikes. I vaulted over and dropped down on the other side.

I had never been this far before. I looked around. To the right were rolling meadows and fields as far as I could see. They were dotted with farmhouses and barns and sheds. I could see the dim forms of grazing cattle.

A road cut through the fields like a deep gray slit. A car with flashing red lights was speeding down the road.

To the left, another large meadow curled down to a thick woods. The woods seemed to stretch for a long ways, almost to the horizon. I let myself laugh out loud.

I turned to the left, to the woods. I would begin my life there. I knew the truth. I would live with the truth. I was the Leopard Man.

26
Pretenders

S O NOW YOU KNOW. SIMON USED TO SAY "TRUTH IS a one-way street." I got on it and walked as far as I could. And when I came to the point of knowing, I had to keep moving or die. But horrible as it was, the truth didn't kill me. I wouldn't let it. The leopard in me wouldn't let it. I gave myself to the wind and moon and sun. I let life carry me— the way life does—from one morning to another. And pretty soon it passed, that feeling, and I set about living in the woods, letting the leopard in me loose.

But I've told you about that, about the leopard-life. And the woods. And the dogs. And coming out. And the Eight Human Wonders of the World. But I haven't told you about the Pretenders—that's what we called them—and how it all ended.

Think of it. There were just the eight of us, but there was a whole world to draw from. Why he chose eight he wouldn't say. Perhaps it was to match the immortal wonders of antiquity with the all-too-mortal wonders of our flesh. Still, eight it was. No more. No less. And if someone left, another would

be brought in to take his place. But not many left, not of their own voli-
tion. They went like the Lion Man.

The new ones, the ones we called Pretenders, just seemed to show up.
You could never tell when. There was never any special season for it. One
day you'd finish a show and walk backstage and there they would be: a
new Lion Man, another pair of Siamese Twins. They'd give you the once-
over, as if to say, "You ain't so much." Then they'd start stalking you,
needling you, running you down. I remember the time a new fat lady
showed up calling herself "Gargantua." She went right up to the Elephant
Lady, looked her over the way a farmer looks over a hog.

"What you weigh, sweetie," she said casually. "Four hundred? Five? Well,
I weigh six hundred thirty pounds and I can eat more than twenty pounds
in a single day. How you like that?"

Nothing came of it, of course, because the thing about the Elephant
Lady was that she could stay fat *without* eating a lot.

But sometimes the challenges were real. Sometimes the man in black
would say to one of these Pretenders, "Show me what you got." Then there
would be a real tension in the air because you never could tell if they were
faking it or not. Sometimes they'd spent a lot of years getting ready to take
your place. A few had been big stars somewhere else. They wanted your
job and let you know they were going to get it.

It wasn't so bad at first. We were all pretty young and healthy. We had
our acts down. We stuck together. Most of the time the man in black would
take one look and tell him or her, "No, thanks, we've got no openings."
But later, it wasn't so easy. You'd get older, lose a little, start to slip. So when
you'd hear that, "Show me what you got," things were altogether different. Then you had to worry.

The first one I remember clearly were Siamese Twins. I think they called
themselves Left and Right. They were sort of pretty, Oriental, with yel-
lowish skin and very tiny heart-shaped mouths. The man in black didn't
just send them away. He said, "Show me what you got." I looked over at
Lila and Lola. They were staring at the other two. Lila was looking very
mean. Lola was just scared, I think. All the rest of us had come in to watch.
The show was over, the place closed down. But the man in black lit up
the lights again and told them to go ahead. He'd never done that before.

218

Left and Right asked for some music.

"Fast," they said in these high-pitched voices. So the man in black put on some of the Monkey Men music and then the two women started doing this crazy routine, sort of a half-dance, half-wrestling thing. They crawled around each other and over each other, like they were an octopus or something. I guess they were double-jointed. And being Siamese Twins to begin with, they could get in the most amazing positions. They performed till the music ran out and then they bowed, very respectfully, and stood waiting.

The man in black didn't say anything right away. That always made it worse, because you could never tell what he was thinking: whether he liked the act or not; whether he was trying to figure a way to add them to the show; whether he had decided your time had come; or whether, as he sometimes did, he would make them challenge you.

That time with the Siamese Twins he just stood quiet for a long while.

"It's a bit too much like the Monkey Men," he said, finally. Then he bowed to the two of them, Left and Right.

"So sorry," he said, shaking his head.

They didn't seem upset or disappointed. But maybe it was only that Oriental politeness you hear about that kept them from showing it.

"Thank you. Thank you," they both said, bowing and moving backward off the stage and out into the night. I guess they went back to China or wherever they came from, because we never heard of them again.

Sometimes the Pretenders won. That happened with the Monkey Men. One day after the show was over we went backstage and there they were: three of them. They were just plain midgets, I think. But they had powerful chests and arms, and a kind of a bony ridge on their foreheads that made them look very primitive. They were brothers, they said. They called themselves the Missing Links, and claimed they had descended from a prehistoric tribe of ape-men. They were never very specific about that, and were very touchy about the whole subject. I saw them lay into a couple of people that tried to disprove their origin.

Anyway, we came backstage and right away the Monkey Men started getting jumpy, jabbering back and forth and doing back flips. They tried jeering at these Missing Links fellows, but it was all pretty strained. The

Missing Links stood there beating their well-muscled chests with their fists, just like you see in Tarzan movies.

"Show me what you got," said the man in black, standing with his arms folded, his face as impassive as ever.

They didn't ask for music or anything. They didn't even have any real act. They grabbed the Monkey Men and started heaving them around. It was amazing to see, really, and kind of awful at the same time. The fact that there were four Monkey Men to only three of them didn't make any difference. They grabbed hold of the Monkey Men and lifted them over their heads and started whirling them around. One of the Links would throw a Monkey Man to the next Link who'd whirl him around, then pass him on. It was like they were heaving sacks of potatoes or something. Sometimes they'd miss, whether on purpose or not I don't know, and one of the Monkey Men would go crashing into one of the big tent poles. After a few minutes the Monkey Men were battered and dazed. Then the three Links each grabbed a Monkey Man by the leg and started whirling them around. At a signal they aimed them all together so that their heads struck in one terrible crash that knocked them all out cold.

The fourth Monkey Man was slumped against a tent pole when the other three got smashed together. When he saw them knocked cold like that and their heads bleeding, he started to whimper. The three Missing Links turned to him. I don't know what they were planning but certainly something scary, when the man in black suddenly spoke up.

"Not bad," he said. "Needs a little polishing, but not bad."

Then he walked over to the whimpering Monkey Man and took out a wad of bills.

"You need to be gone by morning," he said simply, handing him the money, patting him on his head.

By morning they were gone. The posters had been painted over to read, "The Missing Links." They became the ones who led me out on the stage and tried to provoke me. I had to be on guard with them. They would try to hit me with the whip, not just come close, and they would try to choke me with the chain. It made the act better, but when I got the chance, I'd take a little bite out of their legs to pay them back. I guess the man in black knew what he was doing.

To tell you the truth, I think it was the Missing Links who really gave the man in black the idea of making it a contest between us old-timers and the newcomers. Before then it was hit or miss. Someone would show up and either get sent away right off the bat, or else be given one of those "Show me what you got" chances to perform. But after the Missing Links had driven out the Monkey Men like that, a contest became the way it was done.

We had to be on our toes; you'd never know when they would show up and you'd have to have it out with them. Men and women both. It didn't matter.

I had only a few challengers the first years. I guess they'd heard too much about me, or when they came to see the show they had second thoughts. Only a few had the courage to come backstage and actually challenge me, and most of those weren't much. There was the Jackal Man who was just a runt with long hair. I took care of him with a growl and leap. Next, the Wild Dog-Boy who claimed he had been raised by a pack of wild dogs. He looked more like thirty years old than the fifteen he claimed, but he was no trouble at all. I let him make a run or two at me before I leaped on his back and gave him a little bite on the shoulder. That took the fight out of him, quick enough.

Afterward, I invited him into my cage to have some supper, he seemed so broken. We had a nice little chat. He admitted to me that the whole wild dog thing was made up. He'd run away from home as a kid and ever since had been knocking about, eating out of garbage pails and stealing vegetables from gardens. A couple of times he'd had run-ins with dogs. One time he came upon a small pack that had brought down a deer. That's when he decided to join them—well not really join them so much as tag along, share in their kills. It wasn't too bad a life, he said. But then one of the females went into heat and a big male joined them and drove him out. I guess the dog was afraid the Wild Dog-Boy would try to steal the female. "She was a pretty bitch," the Wild Dog-Boy said to me, almost wistfully.

Anyway, he was getting mighty discouraged with things when he came upon one of our posters. It took him a while to track us down. Now he didn't know what to do.

"Go back," I told him.

"Back?" he said.

"To the pack," I said. "Or form one of your own."

I told him about my time in the woods. "If you can stand being away from people," I said, "it's not so bad. And dogs can make good company."

"There's nothing for me here?" he ventured.

"I wish," I said. "But there's only room for eight."

He left the next morning. I gave him some meat to take with him.

We had a few days of calm and then the Gorilla Man showed up. He didn't wait for the show to end to make his appearance. He stood up during one performance and started throwing things around. First he hurled some wooden chairs on stage, and then some of the paying customers. One poor fellow landed right on the Rubber Man. Luckily the Rubber Man was able to absorb most of the shock by bending himself backward. Nevertheless, the rest of the audience panicked and began rushing out of the tent.

I didn't blame them. The Gorilla Man wasn't someone you wanted to be near, believe me. By the time I got out on the stage, he had wrecked the place. He was average in height, but I've never seen anyone who looked stronger in all my life. He had great long, hairy arms and a tremendous round barrel chest and these short little bowlegs.

"About time," he said to me as I came out to face him.

The man in black had come backstage and pointed to me.

"He wants you," he had said.

I had to step over a few sprawled-out people, but then I got right down to the edge of the stage. The Gorilla Man had used up his supply of wooden chairs and paying customers and was trying to pry up some floorboards to hurl.

While he was bent down like that, I took a jump at him, figuring to catch him shoulder-high. But at the last minute he raised up and I crashed into his knee. I hit the bone with my chest and I guess that really stunned me. The next thing I knew I was hurtling through the air, backward, away from him and toward the stage. Fortunately, I hit one of the customers just as he was getting to his feet and that broke my flight—otherwise I might still be going.

"I'm gonna break your back," the Gorilla Man said as he began rambling toward me, his knuckles scraping the wooden floor as he walked. I was still dazed, but I knew one thing: I couldn't let him get those arms around me.

"Show me what you got," said the man in black, superfluously. The Gorilla Man grinned at him. "Snap it like a stick," he said.

I leaped at him again, but this time I made sure I left some space between us. He tried to lean over and grab me as I went flying by, but he was a little too slow, a little too late. As I passed him, I reached out and raked him with my nails. I got about a good three or four layers of skin and a lot of hair. It didn't really hurt him, but it made him furious. That was what I wanted. I wanted to enrage him. Then he was more likely to do something foolish.

Sure enough, he let out a grunt and tried running at me. This time I went for his legs, giving him a good slash with my teeth as I bounded past. It wasn't enough to hamstring him, but it did force him to crouch lower and limp. But I underestimated his strength—or overestimated his intelligence—because the next thing I knew he had shuffled over to the center pole and grabbed hold of it. For a second I didn't know what he was trying to do. I thought maybe he was getting dizzy and wanted something to hold on to. But that wasn't it at all. He was going to try to topple the whole place down. He began heaving against the pole and then leaning way back, trying to pull it toward him with those great hairy arms.

By then, the Missing Links had come out. They took one look at what he was trying to do and made a run at him—all three, head-on, which was the only way they knew, I guess. They were pretty tough, but no match for the Gorilla Man. He let go of the pole and turned to face them. He took the shock of all three right in his belly without much more than a loud grunt. Then he started hurling them. Two landed against the backstage wall and the third hit by the exit. None of them stirred much.

The Giant was next. He was a big, strong man, all right, and plenty tough, but he was no fighter. He got all his muscles from lifting weights and it just tightened him all up. He could hardly bend over to sit down, he was so built up. So while he was strong and could break you in two if he ever got hold of you just right, usually he couldn't get hold of you. I'd seen him get really thumped in a fight or two by guys half his size. They'd just run around him, taking potshots at his nose or kicking him in his groin, and pretty soon he'd be a bloody mess. Besides, he was very gentle and didn't really want to hurt anyone.

This time, though, he could see what was happening and so he, too, came right at the Gorilla Man. A big mistake. The Gorilla Man was pretty nimble for being that powerful. He let the Giant get close and then he swung around the center pole, using his long hairy arm to generate force and speed. He hit the Giant right in the groin with his shoulder. That didn't topple the Giant—he was too strong for that—but it did sort of paralyze him.

Next, the Gorilla Man swung back the other way. At the last minute he let go of the pole and came flying at the Giant. He wrapped his squat little legs around the Giant's belly and got his arms around the Giant's neck. The Giant tried to reach back and get hold of the Gorilla Man, but he was too stiff and tight to manage it. Every time he moved, the Gorilla Man tightened his hold, like he was one of those big boa constrictors strangling an antelope or something. Even though the Giant had a big powerful neck, pretty soon you could see him starting to go red from the squeezing. He never tried to move. He just stood, with the Gorilla Man draped around him, squeezing the life out of him. I glanced at the man in black. He was standing off to one side, his hands clasped over each arm, his face expressionless. If he was worried about the Giant he didn't show it. The three Missing Links had managed to crawl off somewhere to nurse their wounds. The Rubber Man was nowhere in sight. I could see Lila and Lola peeking out from the side of the stage.

The Elephant Lady saved the Giant. She came rushing out from the side and ran right at the two of them. At the last moment, the Gorilla Man managed to twist himself around so that he didn't get the full force of the charge, but the poor Giant did. Unable to move, nearly out of air, he went down like a felled tree under her. The Gorilla Man flung himself off the Giant's back just before he crashed and so got away, but at least his hold was broken. The Giant lay buried under the Elephant Lady's fat. She had used up all her energy in the charge and so couldn't move. The two of them lay there, a great heap of flesh, mostly motionless. The Gorilla Man had recovered by then. He bounded over to the fallen Elephant Lady and, grabbing her with his massive arms, did a most amazing thing. He lifted her up—right off the Giant. Right up in the air. He got her about chest high and threw her. She didn't go far, of course, but it was enough. She landed with a terrible, sickening thud on the wooden floor, shook for a little while like a mound of jello settling, then became deathly still.

All this took only a couple of minutes. It sounds like a lot was happening, and I guess it was, but it was all happening in a flash, one thing right after another. I was off to the side still trying to clear my head from that first blow to my chin. Suddenly, the Gorilla Man whirled around and darted to the side of the stage, right past the man in black. I didn't know what he was doing at first, but then I heard a piercing scream and in a second he had emerged with the Snake Goddess under his arm. She had been hiding backstage, peering out, I guess, but the Gorilla Man had caught sight of her. He carried her down from the stage and to the middle of the tent area. It was like she weighed no more than a sack of flour. She was yelling and screaming and beating him with her fists but I think he never noticed. He got to the center pole and started climbing, the Snake Goddess under his arm. It was amazing, the strength he had—to climb up the pole with one arm and hold onto the Snake Goddess with the other. I didn't know what he was thinking or where he was going. Certainly there wasn't anything up at the top except some guide wires and bracing beams. But up he went and up went the Snake Goddess. This time when I looked over, the man in black's face had gone white.

"Stop him," he said to me.

The Gorilla Man was about a quarter of the way up. I had one good chance left. Otherwise he would be too high. I pulled myself together, charged and sprang. I gave it all I had, stretching my body as far as I could. I could feel the ligaments and tendons straining.

I got him just above the ankle with my teeth. They sank in and I locked my jaws. I knew it was cruel, but I was aiming for the Achilles tendon. He tried to shake me loose, but once I got that good and deep of a bite there was no hope for him. But he was so strong, so stubborn, that he still kept trying to climb. Imagine that: with the Snake Goddess under one arm and me hanging with my whole weight from his ankle. But finally that was too much, even for him. Slowly he began to weaken. He began to slip down the pole. Now I had to worry about the Snake Goddess. We were still quite a ways up. The man in black had managed to get the Rubber Man back out. He was waiting below, his arms out, his body bent backward, sort of like a trampoline. The Gorilla Man looked down a long moment. Then he looked at the Snake Goddess dangling in his arm. It was hard to read the expression in his face, but even despite the simian features, there was a look of tenderness. As I watched, the Snake Goddess slipped from his arm—or maybe it was only that he let her go. In any event, she fell through the air and landed in the arms of the Rubber Man. He nearly buckled under her weight, but held, finally, and though she bounced into the air a couple of times, she settled back down on him.

The Gorilla Man let out a bellowing roar and began to climb again. Even with me hanging on his leg, despite the loss of blood, he wasn't finished. Up the pole he went, higher and higher, toward the top of the tent. I tried digging my nails into the pole to slow him down, but still up we went.

Something happened. The Gorilla Man slowed. Then he stopped altogether. He looked at me, his eyes were closed. Sweat was pouring down. He seemed to sway back and forth, back and forth, like a tree before it falls. I, too, was swinging gently back and forth, my teeth clamped to his foot, bone-deep by then. I felt his fingers begin to lose hold, begin to slip from the pole. He had this wonderfully serene look on his face, like he was dreaming the best part of a beautiful dream. I knew that if I didn't break loose we would both go crashing to the ground. So with every bit of strength I had I jerked my head back as far as I could. My teeth broke free just as the Gorilla Man lost the last of his grip on the pole. We both went hurtling to the ground. I arched my back and twisted as I fell, aiming for the enormous bulk of the Elephant Lady. Even though I didn't hit her squarely, I struck enough fat to keep the fall from causing me any permanent damage. The Gorilla Man, though, landed on the ground, a battered, broken heap.

Slowly, we gathered around the dead Gorilla Man. He didn't seem so fierce or powerful. He seemed amazingly small, like when you cut the string of a marionette and the thing just collapses on itself. The Snake Goddess moved close to the body and touched it gently with her bare toe. Then she turned away, the Rubber Man and the Giant parting so that she could go.

We talked about it for a while, about what it all meant; about whether the Gorilla Man jumped or fell. Lila said that he fell, that his arm slipped from the pole. Lola said that he just let go, that he took a deep breath and smiled and let go.

For some time after, we would talk about why the Gorilla Man did what he did. What was he after? Some said he wanted to get to the top and untie all the lines and bring the whole tent down on us—sort of like Samson. Some said he wanted to get to the wires so that he could use them to swing down the far side and out the skylight. The man in black said simply, "Gorillas climb."

So who's to know? In the end he just lay dead in the deserted arena and was buried in a pauper's grave. The rest of us recovered, but nothing was ever quite the same. The Giant stayed for a while and then one day left. No one knows where or why. We replaced him with another, a little taller, who had a tattoo of the Empire State building on one leg and a tattoo of the Chrysler building on the other.

I had some peace for a while. Word leaked out. I had been the one to bring down the Gorilla Man.

The lull didn't last though. Pretty soon it got worse than ever. They kept coming and coming. It was as if the earth had parted and out poured all its half-finished forms. It was all we talked about. Every conversation turned to it, sooner or later.

"Did you hear?" someone would say. "Did you hear who's coming?"

Nothing was beyond belief. I remember once being told about the Shark Man. He had gills and rows of razor-sharp teeth. He could breathe underwater. He would come up out of the sea, or out of a sewer and drag his victim back in. He was coming for me, they said. How would I fight him—on land or in the water?

He never came, of course, but others did. Night and day, it seemed. A whole world of freaks. Bearded ladies. Dwarfs. Midgets. Giants. Men and women missing parts, or having extra parts. Or no parts at all. We never knew when. Or for whom they came. Or what the man in black would say.

We stayed up long into the night, whispering.

"Did you hear?" became our greeting, our salutation. The words hung in the air like the smell of decay.

"Did you hear?" the Snake Goddess would say. "A man is coming with his head where his navel should be."

"Did you hear?" the Rubber Man would say. "A woman is coming with the skin of a lizard."

And then we would debate, we eight human wonders of the world. Could such a thing be? And if so how would it behave? And how should we?

We learned to divide them all into the Possible and the Impossible. Our logic, of course, was curious. We decided a man with his head where his navel should be was a Possible. The head would be close to the stomach. It could feed. It could get blood like a fetus. Even the Siamese Twins agreed.

A woman with the skin of a lizard was an Impossible. She would have to be kept in water. Or in shade. How could she sweat? The heat would build up. She would die. And so on. We became biologists as well as philosophers. It was more than idle speculation. Our survival depended on it. We had to sort out the Possibles from the Impossibles. Otherwise how should we have the courage to go on? We were no match for our imaginations.

"Did you hear?" Lila would whisper. "A man is coming who only eats wood."

And then it would begin, the discussion, the debate. Could such a thing be? And if it could, whom would he replace?

A man came who did eat wood. He was an ordinary man, the kind you see walking down any street, of average height and weight, plain and nondescript, even a little shy.

"Show me what you got," said the man in black.

The Wood Man took out a stick and ate it, bit by bit. He had a set of short, flat teeth and he didn't seem at all disturbed by the splinters. The man in black gave him a small board to work on.

He began gnawing on one end of it, first with his incisors, then with his back teeth, his molars. Pretty soon he had the end of it gone. But it took him a very long time to do it, like someone who is eating a peanut butter sandwich with no jelly. It was amazing, but not very exciting.

"Thank you," said the man in black. "Keep the board." And he patted him on the back and sent him down the road.

It went like that—no one really special—for a good long time. But then someone did come, someone very special. He was there when we went backstage. Even the man in black seemed surprised. We all stood silent and motionless. Before us was this apparition. That's the only way I can describe that first impression of him. His face was pale, deathly pale, albino almost. And his hair was white without streaks of gray. He was very slender, even under the white silk cloth that was wrapped around him like a shroud.

Not one of us spoke. Not Lila. Not the Snake Goddess. Not even the man in black. It was as if we were afraid that the slightest movement would cause him to drift away or evaporate in the air like so much smoke.

I think all of us were frightened. What was it? For whom had it come? For its part, it just stood there, gaunt and shimmering, like an apparition. Its eyes seemed dark and veiled, even though it had no eyebrows or eyelashes. I quietly scented the air. I smelled the faintest presence of human flesh, as if it came from very far away, or as if the cells were spaced so far apart that only a light smell lingered.

And then the apparition moved, lightly, silently but for the rustle of the silk. A slender arm emerged, paler even than the garment, and began to unravel the bands of glistening fabric. It was a corpse being unwrapped, a living mummy being undone. The face seemed to take on form and substance: long and narrow, covered with nearly transparent skin that seemed to show the raw cells and blood vessels underneath it. But no expression on that face. A face neither man nor woman. Instead the face of some sexless thing, like a mannequin.

The arm continued to move and the neck emerged, white and slender as any swan's neck. As narrow as the head was, it seemed a wonder, still, that such a neck could support its weight. The silk unraveled further and our amazement grew. Bared were two slender breasts, small but fully formed, and tipped with nipples as white as the silk. We stared and still we did not speak or move.

The cloth unfolded and a childlike torso emerged, slim and without any curves, making the breasts even more remarkable, for there seemed nothing else female about the body. And then the arm moved again and the whole bottom part gave way and fell to the floor at the body's feet. We broke the silence then, but only to gasp. For beneath the waist and un-formed hips we could see, perfectly formed, a man's penis emerging out of a woman's vagina. Nothing childlike or sexless about them. The penis was long and thick and covered with curling black hair. The vulvae were wide and thick and covered with hair. Two thin, hairless, shapeless legs held the body up, ending in small, childlike feet.

Not one of us could take our eyes away from that groin, from the sight of those two sexual organs so intimately fused, so out of proportion to that wraithlike body. And then, as if all that were an insufficient miracle itself, something even more remarkable happened. Even as we watched, stunned, unable to look away, slowly, like an eel slipping back between some rocks, the penis began to slip back inside the vagina out of which it was growing. It was like intercourse in reverse, as if the man had some-how crawled within the woman's body and was withdrawing not back out into the world, but inside the body.

And then the penis was gone, the lips closing with a slapping sound. And except for a fine seam barely visible beneath the hair, the body seemed a sexless, lifeless, impenetrable thing. While we stood there, nearly lifeless ourselves, a pale arm reached down and drew the silken cloth up around the body till all but the shaded eyes were hidden away.

A voice spoke, then, but more the voice of a mourning dove mouthing human words than a human voice speaking.

"Now even you may wonder."

Then it was gone, the voice, the apparition. Only the world remained, and we in it, we Eight Human Wonders of the World. We had stared into a darkness no light could ever fully illuminate.

230

But life goes on. And all of us, even we freaks, have that human capacity to forget, or to pretend to understand. And if the hermaphrodite's visit changed us, who can say? As for me, I only knew that I had one more sin to atone for, the sin of insignificance.

27

The Long Road Home

EVERYTHING PASSES. HOURS MOVE ON AND WE ARE left behind with our accumulation of years. One by one we faltered. I roared on. The Leopard Man would not give way. I leaped at whoever held my chain. I rattled my own chains. I dreamed my leopard dreams.

"Unchain the Leopard Man. Unchain the Leopard Man."

But the world around me changed, faded, decayed. The old Fairs closed, the old meadows where we used to pitch our tents were paved over. Condominiums stood where the tall grass used to grow. Everything passes.

The people changed as well. The old stayed away in fear of the young. The young grew bored, then desperate, then bitter. Decay burns as brightly as life.

And one day, they came for me. The Wild Dog-Boy and his dogs. He, too, had changed, grown cunning and stronger.

"I took your advice, old man," he said grinning. Behind him, sitting rigidly in a half-circle, was a pack of dogs. They, too, looked cunning and formidable, mixtures of German shepherd, Doberman, and bulldog. "I went back. They took me in. I became their leader."

The man in black, the one unchanging, unaging constant, like the speed of light in Einstein's formula, said simply, "Show me what you got."

The Dog-Boy crouched low and bared his teeth. The canines were long and sharp, a little like a dog's. The rest of the pack stood erect, growling, their own teeth bared. They began to spread out so that they were in a circle, with me in the middle. I took a quick look around. I decided the Wild Dog-Boy would not be the first to attack. He would remember from before. He would hold back until he was sure I could be taken. To the right of me and ahead was a lean but powerful-looking shepherd. He bent low but would not look away when I stared. He would be the one, I decided. So I pretended to look behind me.

When I did, he sprang, hoping to get me from behind and knock me down. But I was ready. I let him get in the air and then I whirled and ducked under his body, raking him with my nails as he sailed by. He tried to cut short his bound, but he was too late. I dug into the soft underbelly.

I tried for the Wild Dog-Boy but he anticipated and leaped aside before I could get to him. Age exacted its certain toll. I had figured that if he was their leader and with the other dog wounded, maybe the rest would back off. But the Dog-Boy had figured that out as well.

The big dog I had ripped was far from beaten. He came at me again, head down, from the side. Instead of trying to bowl me over, he was going for one of my legs. At the same time two others began closing from the opposite side. I, meanwhile, hurled myself at the Dog-Boy.

None of us managed to do exactly what we had planned. The big dog missed my leg completely and the other dogs managed only to rip some skin on my thigh and arm. As for me, I did a little more effective biting, getting part of a tooth in the Dog-Boy's shoulder, but he was already bounding away and it tore loose, making only a fingerlike gash in the flesh. As soon as I hit the ground I leaped up, landing on all fours on the top of my cage. For the first time, I could feel myself weakening. I was conscious of myself, of my body, of my fatigue. It was not just in my bones. It was in my leopard heart. I looked to the man in black.

"I can beat them," I said.

The man in black only smiled. "That's easy to say," he said.

I turned to the Wild Dog-Boy.

"You can't win," I said.

"We'll see," he said, and reaching down he grabbed one of the smaller dogs and heaved it at me. That caught me by surprise and though I ducked, the dog's body knocked me back on one knee on the cage-top. I knew I had to get back up and spring, but the big dog who had circled round made a lunge for me, getting me by the forearm. I could feel the canines go in. I stood up, the dog dangling from my arm. In that single instant before I leaped, I saw before me the image of the Gorilla Man as he hung from the pole with me fastened to his leg. But a dog is no leopard and as I sprang down from the cage he fell from me. I landed on the Dog-Boy's back. I felt him go down beneath me, heard some bones crack.

Next, I got the big dog who had bitten me. He was getting to his feet but he slipped on something wet. It was my blood. And his. I got him in the belly again. His guts spilled out. That took the spirit out of the rest of the pack.

But I, too, was spent. Soul-tired. It was all I could do to growl.

Some of the others came out, then, some of the newer ones like the Chimp Men and the Strong Man. They started carting the Dog-Boy off.

"Take him to the hospital," said the man in black. "Tell them his dogs turned on him."

I waited till everyone had gone. Then I crawled into my cage to lick my wounds. I felt weak but not so much from the loss of blood. I felt old. More than that, I felt that I had lost my leopard-will.

I had no time to heal—not that it would have mattered. She was waiting for me the next night, after the show. I half-expected someone. The word gets out. It's the way of the jungle, the way of us all. But I had not really expected a woman.

She was waiting backstage, dressed in a tiger skin, her nails long and her teeth sharpened. She had painted black stripes on her tawny body to match a tiger's own. Her eyes were cold and deadly. There are things more fierce than a leopard.

She never said a word. She just came at me. She was very quick on her feet. But it didn't matter. I tried to get away but she got on my back, began raking me. All the time she was whispering.

"Take me, old man. Take me."

Her skin smelled of musk. An image flashed before me of the first time I saw Obaman's woman.

"Take me, old man. Take me."

I could feel the Tiger Woman on my back, but she was light as a child. I felt her fingers at my throat. As if she was caressing me. It seemed so peaceful, feeling her warmth, listening to her soft whisper.

"Take me, old man. Take me."

I wanted to lie down. I felt a tiredness come over me, a sweet tiredness. I wanted to rest. Slowly, I let myself to my knees. I didn't want to hurt her.

"Take me, old man. Take me."

I think I would have gone to sleep there, at the foot of the cage, on the dark floor. I think I would have just sunk down and closed my eyes and let her whisper until darkness filled every pore. But the leopard was still too much in me. My muscles willed themselves to move. Sinew and bone and blood readied themselves. I readied myself for one last spring.

But the weight was gone from me. So, too, the whispering and the warmth. I forced myself around to see. The Tiger Lady was standing across from me, hands were on her hips, her legs set apart. She was laughing.

"Take me, old man," she said. "Take me." No longer a whisper, it was a mocking chant. I took a deep breath to clear my head. I could feel the pain in my back. My throat. Blood dripped onto the floor. I tried to speak. I wanted to tell her something. I'm sure of that. I think I wanted to tell her that she reminded me of somebody, but no words came out.

The Tiger Lady stopped her laughing. Her face grew fierce. Her body tensed. She was getting ready to spring at me.

The man in black appeared. I hadn't seen him before. But there he was.

"It's over," he said. He was looking right at me.

It took her a long time to tear her gaze from me. I knew the look, knew what she was thinking, feeling. It was the look a predator gives its prey just before it springs—a look of hatred and of love. A look of absolute hunger.

"Tell him," the Tiger Lady said to me.

The man in black slowly came over. He reached into his pocket. He took out a wad of bills. He held them out to me.

I thought of a place far away and a long time ago, and the Lion Man walking off into the night. But there was no sadness in the thought. There is no way to regret what has to be. No road goes on forever.

I took the money and what little else was mine and walked out into the night. I didn't look back. I had nothing to look back to.

I knew where I had to go and what I had to do. I found a road going where I wanted it to go and I started walking on it. I walked a long way. A very long way. And at last I got there. Do you understand? In all the years I had stayed away. But it was time to return.

I went first to the zoo. There I stood, breathing in the air. The animals were restless. I could hear them stirring. Somewhere inside, a leopard. I hoped he was as fierce and black as the one I remembered. I would not try to see.

I went next to the cemetery beside the house where Obaman had lived. The house was gone, of course, but the cemetery was still there. It seems easier to sweep away the living than the dead. I went to the place where Mr. Smyth had buried his son, Simon. I had only gone there once. I had never wanted to go there again. It seemed such a lie and such a waste. You honor the dead by living. Simon still lived for me, in all I remember, in all my dreams, in all the times I was able to do something decent.

But on this night it seemed only right to go, to see the place where his road ended. It was quiet and still, only a light breeze stirring. Weeds had grown up all around. The grass was sparse. The stone had weathered, but I could see the name and the dates. And the single line Mr. Smyth had them carve for Simon.

"He died for his country."

He died for more than that. But yet there was truth in what it said. Everyone needs a home and a place to spring from. And a place to lie down in. And cemeteries are as much a part of what a country is as are mountains and meadows. And so it wasn't sadness I was feeling as I stood there so much as a quiet sense of something ending.

Last, I found my way back to the hardware store. It wasn't a hardware store anymore, of course. It wasn't anything. It was all boarded up. So were all the buildings. No one lived there but the rats. The whole place was going to be torn down, I guess, and rebuilt. All that was missing was the money.

I made my way up the stairs, past all the debris, to the top floor. Everything had been gutted; only the shell remained, like the bones when the meat is gone.

I went to the window where I had spent so much of my life sitting. I looked out at the city trying to sleep below me. It, too, was getting old. But even that truth can't be sad, not if cities are like men and live and die. What is important is that something take its place. Maybe something better.

I lay down on the floor beneath the window and slept. And dreamed. I dreamed that Obaman's woman was walking down a long narrow road toward a field of sunlight. I dreamed that Simon was walking beside her.

A Last Word

I HAVE STAYED IN THIS ROOM A LONG TIME NOW. I'VE managed the best I could. After all, I was not the Leopard Man for nothing.

And now I am almost done with this, this telling. It seemed to me something I had to do. A coming home. How else would it have mattered? Now it is up to you. If you remember any of it, then it will not have been in vain. And if you do, then remember it not for me, but for Simon, for Obaman, for his woman, and for the lion and the leopard and the lamb in all of us.

Sometimes I think to myself: what if it were all a lie? What if it only was that my mother, whoever she was, took one look at me and cast me away. What if everything else was something the others dreamed up for me and I believed in. What if I only dreamed it myself?

But then I remember the man in black saying he only gives names to what we are already. And does it matter? And do you have an answer?

I will try and find a way to get this to you. I give it freely. It's all I have to give.

The Leopard Man

. . .

There is one thing more. Almost every night I go back to the zoo. A woman also comes. I am certain she is the woman from many years before, the librarian, the one who had been raped and who wanted to teach the animals not to hurt each other. She has changed. She is old and bent and gray and small. She taps her way along the street with a cane. I stand guard, in the shadows, to see no harm comes to her. But once I decided I would speak to her, to see if she remembered.

She did not. But no matter. It was only a single night many years ago, and we both have changed. In the end, we forget many things. I remember Simon telling me once, long ago, in that remarkable way he had of looking past his own few days into the larger truth of things, that in the end it matters less what we forget than what we remember. He told me that people have a way of keeping what is most real to them.

Sometimes, when the night is gentle, the librarian and I talk. The long years have swept us past many things, and we say only what we feel we have need of saying. We stand by the same iron gates where once we stood those many years ago. Through all the years, through the many wounds that time inflicts on every living thing, she has remained gentle, hopeful. Last night, before a misted rain made her depart, she told me a story about the library, about a boy who came to her.

"He was skinny as an exclamation point," she said, "with great big searching eyes."

I think this memory was from a long time ago, but in the mind's last orientation, it had come to fill the present, as if it had happened only that morning.

The boy had come up to her and pulled gently at her sleeve.

"I want a book about Africa," he told her, looking up at her with those bright, penetrating eyes.

We have many, she told him.

"I want a book with pictures," he said.

Why? she asked him.

He lowered his head for a moment, then looked right back up at her.

"Because I can't read," he said.

She tried to find out why, if he went to school, what his life was like. But he wouldn't tell her anything more. So she let it go and took him to one of the shelves where the books on geography were kept. One book on Africa was filled with maps and pictures. She took it down and handed it to the boy. He went over to the corner, where he was mostly hidden, and he sat down on the floor and opened the book. He turned the pages slowly, as if each one were a magic play only he could see and hear. It seemed to take an hour to go through three or four pages. It was hard to believe that he couldn't read the words, because he let his fingers move over them, as if they were set in Braille and he was feeling for their meaning.

She drifted away to other things, and after a while she forgot about the boy. Until once again she felt a slight tug on her sleeve and looked down. The boy was looking up at her. He held the book in his arms. It was almost as big as he was. His eyes seemed filled with tears.

"Can I take it home?" he asked.

"I can't let you," she told him, and tried to explain that it was a reference book, a book for all the people to read, and that they didn't have a lot of money, and so on.

"I'll tell you what," she said. "I'll keep the book in a special place, just for you, so that when you come back you can read it again. Anytime you want."

The boy lifted his head and looked at her. His eyes were glistening.

"Just for me," he said, as if the words were too big for him to keep inside.

"Just for you," she told him again. "And I'll tell you what, when you come back I'll teach you how to read."

The boy didn't say anything for a while. She couldn't tell whether he heard the words, or understood them, or was just overwhelmed by them. Then, without saying anything more, he handed her the book.

"Whenever you come back," she told him, "you just ask for the book on Africa. I'll tell the other librarians."

The boy stood a moment more, then he turned and walked slowly out. He seemed so small, she said. So fragile.

She didn't say anything for a long time. I wanted to ask her. I wanted to know, but as I said, the years push you past many things, and one of them is impatience. If it was important to her she would tell me.

"I told the other librarians," she said, after a very long time. "We put the book in a special place."

She took a deep sigh, then, and looked up at me.

"But he never came back."

I wasn't surprised that he didn't come back or that she could not remember me. Every step takes you someplace, whether you know it or not, and a lot of times you can't go back, even if you want to.

"I should have given him the book," she said. She said it very softly, but very firmly, as if she had given it much thought.

I didn't say anything for a long time.

I had my own equations to work out, and I thought about a lot of things—the boy, the book, what the woman had said and what she had done. I thought about Simon, Obaman, and all the rest. And when I had done all that, it seemed to make sense.

"You gave him something more important," I told her, my own voice quietly certain.

She had begun to shuffle away, but when I said that, she stopped and turned back.

"What is that?" she asked, the silver rain settling on her stooped shoulders like a mantle.

"A dream," I said.

And then, old leopard that I was, I followed her home, keeping to the shadows.

BOSTON PUBLIC LIBRARY

3 9999 03203 313 4